Flour in the Attic

Books by Winnie Archer

Kneaded To Death

Crust No One

The Walking Bread

Flour in the Attic

Flour in the Attic

Winnie Archer

KENSINGTON BOOKS
www.kensingtonbooks.com

KENSINGTON BOOKS are published by

Kensington Publishing Corp.
119 West 40th Street
New York, NY 10018

All Kensington titles, imprints, and distributed lines are available at special quantity discounts for bulk purchases for sales
promotion, premiums, fund-raising, educational, or institu-
tional use.

Special book excerpts or customized printings can also be created to fit specific needs. For details, write or phone the office
of the Kensington Sales Manager: Attn.: Sales Department.
Kensington Publishing Corp., 119 West 40th Street, New York,
NY 10018. Phone: 1-800-221-2647.

Kensington and the K logo Reg. U.S. Pat. & TM Off.

First Printing: September 2019
ISBN-13: 978-1-4967-2439-7
ISBN-10: 1-4967-2439-9

ISBN-13: 978-1-4967-2440-3 (ebook)
ISBN-10: 1-4967-2440-2 (ebook)

10 9 8 7 6 5 4 3 2 1

Printed in the United States of America

Chapter 1

Emmaline Davis and I stood side by side, awed by the choices before us. "So, it's happening tonight?" I asked.

She nodded, her expression a becoming compilation of nervous excitement. "At the beach."

I cocked an eyebrow at Em, my best friend and sheriff of Santa Sofia, a small coastal destination spot in California, and my hometown. "He's pretty perceptive. He doesn't suspect?"

The twenty-something young woman helping Em had introduced herself as Kristiann. She was listening intently as we talked, all the while trying to look like she wasn't. Emmaline tapped her finger against the glass top of the display case. "Can I see that one?" she asked Kristiann. To me, she said, "Not a clue. I just said we should meet there to go for a walk. Beautiful day, and all, so it'll be an equally beautiful evening."

It would be indeed, I thought as Kristiann

stretched the coil keychain on her wrist out of the way so she could open the sliding door of the case. "This one?" she clarified. Em nodded, and Kristiann straightened back up and placed the silver band in a black velvet jewelry tray. "Nice choice."

It was. The polished outer rings shone like white gold, but a brushed gunmetal-gray strip ran around the ring. Kristiann launched into a spiel about the unusual wedding band. "It's made of tungsten carbide," she said, as if that were as common as silver and gold. "It's one of the strongest metals on Earth. It won't scratch. It won't get misshapen. It's practically indestructible."

"So, good for a man who works on cars and on construction sites?" I asked.

She looked at Em, a touch of envy on her face. "Is the what your guy does?" As Em nodded, Kristiann fake fanned herself with her hand, looking eerily similar to Lea Thompson in *Back to the Future.* "He sounds dreamy."

I did a double take. She sounded like Lea, too.

But Emmaline didn't register the sappiness of the moment. Her satisfied smile showed just how dreamy she thought her guy was. "He definitely is."

Em picked up the ring from the velvet tray. Slipped it on her finger. Looked at me. "What do you think, Ivy? Will he like it?"

The "he" she referred to was my brother, Billy. "I think it's perfect. He'll love it."

"Birthday or anniversary?" Kristiann asked.

"Proposal," Emmaline answered.

Kristiann's bright eyes popped open wide. "Wait, you're proposing to your boyfriend? Tonight at the beach?"

Em smiled sheepishly. She was the head of law enforcement—and tough as nails—but when it came to love, she was a romantic at heart. She and Billy had been ships passing in the night for so long, but had secretly (and not so secretly) loved each other since they were kids. They'd finally gotten together and now Emmaline Davis was ready to pop the question. Gender roles be damned.

"Wow," Kristiann said. "That's so cool. Usually couples come in together, or the guy comes in and doesn't know what kind of jewelry his girlfriend likes. Pretty nice for the tables to be turned."

"Equality. That's what we're all about," Em joked, but it was actually true. She had broken the glass ceiling in Santa Sofia by becoming the town's first female sheriff. Being a woman in that position was significant; being a black woman was even more so.

Emmaline Davis was a role model. She was powerful, independent, self-assured, and driven—all things I'd felt as if I'd lost for a while, but had been reestablishing since being back in Santa Sofia. She was my role model, too, come to think of it.

I'd done a reset with my life when my mother had unexpectedly died. I'd left Austin behind, along with my photography business, my exhusband, and the heavy Texas heat. Finding Yeast of Eden and Olaya Solis had been my first saving grace. Being back with my father and brother and Emmaline had been another.

Discovering Olaya's bread-making classes and the passion for baking that ensued had been a huge part of finding my place in Santa Sofia again. Getting back to photography had also helped. And meeting octogenarian Penelope Branford and becoming a de facto crime solver was the proverbial icing on the cake. Life was pretty good at the moment.

Em bought the ring, her expression giddy as she left with a little velvet jewelry box in hand. "Tonight Billy and I get engaged," she said, and then with a wink, she added, "You and Miguel are next."

"One happily-ever-after at a time, sister," I said. Reconnecting with Miguel Baptista, my boyfriend from high school, had been my final saving grace. We had a complicated history, but were giving each other a solid second chance, and it felt right. But marriage? We weren't anywhere near that life milestone. I'd done that once; infidelity on my first husband's part had ripped it apart. If and when I tied the knot again, it would be for keeps.

"Just saying, sister," she said, and then she laughed. "We really are going to be sisters! Officially."

I put my arm around her shoulders, and pulled her close. "We don't need a marriage for that, but I can't think of anyone I'd rather be family with, Em. Truly."

Chapter 2

My life seemed to revolve around baking bread and photography. Since I'd been back in Santa Sofia, I'd spent untold hours at Yeast of Eden, absorbing every bit of bread-making expertise I could from owner Olaya Solis. I'd stocked my own kitchen with every imaginable baking tool, from a heavy-duty stand mixer with a dough hook to proofing baskets in a variety of sizes to a Danish dough whisk. The process of mixing the flour, yeast, and water together, digging my hands into a mound of dough, and immersing myself in creating something life-sustaining from just a few ingredients fed my soul.

Photography did the same thing, only it fed my creative mind. Working with light and images let me freeze a moment in time. Finding something extraordinary in the ordinary was the greatest challenge. It was emotion . . . love . . . foreverness. When I wasn't baking, I was observing, trying to capture the humanity around me through the lens of my camera.

I'd been messing around with cameras since I was nine years old. My mother had given me my first one more as a means to keep me busy and out of her hair than for any other reason. Little did she know, she'd set me on an artistic path. I'd long since archived the photography blog I'd started back in high school, but had gone on to earn my bachelor's degree in design and photography. The business I'd had after college in Austin had collapsed when I moved back to my hometown, but now I was at it again, speaking not with words, as a writer did, or with clay, which a sculptor used, but with the images I captured from behind my lens.

Building a website was on my list of things to do now that I'd decided to rebuild my business. I had to start from scratch, given that I'd been in a different state for the last decade and a half, but I was up for a challenge. If I could spend every waking minute either baking bread with Olaya or exploring the world with my camera, I'd be utterly content.

After leaving Emmaline at the jewelry shop, I came home to work on my website, Ivy Culpepper Photography. Over the last several weeks, I'd been creating galleries—Business and Senior Portraits, Children, Maternity, Babies, Pets, Weddings, and Commercial—and loading images to complete the site, creating private Client Galleries so my future clients could view their portfolio of photographs from the comfort of their own homes.

At my feet, Agatha, my little fawn pug, stretched, squeaking contentedly. I leaned down to scratch her head. She looked up at me with her bulbous eyes, her lip caught on her teeth. "I'll be ready to launch next week," I told her. I'd been doing enough freelance, most recently photographing Baptista's Cantina and Grill for their new marketing material, to supplement what I made working for Olaya at Yeast of Eden. I'd saved enough over the years to buy my house on Maple Street, but I lived frugally. It was time to build my business again.

By eleven o'clock, I couldn't look at the computer for another second. My vision blurred, my eyes tired of staring at the screen. I'll continue tomorrow, I thought, shutting my system down for the night and putting my camera away.

By the time I'd gotten myself ready for bed, Agatha was already sprawled out on the comforter beside me. The phone call came just as I was slipping under my quilt, dead tired.

The screen showed Emmaline's name. I instantly perked up, answering with a blunt, "Tell me!"

"It didn't go quite as planned," she said.

Her voice carried a heavy note of forlorn exhaustion. I sat up, accidentally knocking Agatha with my knee. The dog gave a snort, looked up at me with her bulging eyes, and then settled back into slumber. "What do you mean? What happened?" I asked.

She sighed. "It started out just like I'd planned. I'd packed a little picnic. Cheese. Crackers. Strawberries. Wine. We parked over by Baptista's, walked to the shore, spread out a blanket."

"Sounds perfect," I said slowly. What could have happened?

"Right? I thought so, too. But—"

My heart dropped. "He didn't—you're not saying—oh my God, Em, did he turn you down?"

She gave a pregnant pause before she heaved another sigh. "He didn't have a chance to."

I started breathing again. "You didn't ask him?"

I sensed her shaking her head. "I didn't ask him."

My breath caught in my throat. "Why?" Surely she hadn't changed her mind.

"The thing about being the sheriff, I've discovered, is that it's a twenty-four-seven job."

I exhaled again, relieved. "So you didn't change your mind?"

"God, no," she said, "but I had no choice but to postpone. Duty called."

"What happened? Car crash? Beached whale? Cat stuck in a tree?"

"No, no, and I wish. There was a dead body, Ivy."

She couldn't be serious. "Come again?"

"A dead woman, to be precise, discovered floating just offshore. A fisherman called it in. Billy was sweet. Of course, he understood that a corpse means I go to work."

"God, that's horrible. She drowned?"

"Looks that way. Working theory is that she went out for a swim, got too far and either got a cramp, or was pulled out farther by the tide. As happens with drowning victims, the body resurfaced after being submerged. The ME thinks she was in the water a good twelve hours. Maybe more."

We were silent for a moment out of respect for the dead woman. "Any idea who it was?" I finally asked.

"We found a bag with clothes on the beach about half a mile from her location. No official ID, but there was a name tag clipped to it." I could hear the quiet rustle of pages turning as Emmaline flipped through a notebook. "Marisol Ruiz. I have an officer trying to confirm the ID—"

I stopped her cold. "Did you say Marisol Ruiz?"

"That's right. Mid, or maybe late fifties. You know her?" Em asked.

I ran my hand over my face, covering my mouth as I closed my eyes to process. "Yes," I said after a breath. "You do, too."

Em hesitated. "The bloating and the—like I said, the body wasn't recognizable—"

"Em, Marisol Ruiz has been a waitress at Baptista's since we were kids. Remember? She used to give us free guacamole if we helped her wipe down the tables?"

There was a brief pause before Em drew in a sharp breath. "Oh my God, *that* Marisol? I thought her name was Montoya or something like that."

"Morales. She got divorced, and then remarried. One of the chefs at the restaurant. Mmm, David, I think."

Tears pricked the insides of my eyelids. I only

knew Marisol from my memories, and from seeing her occasionally at Baptista's when I'd been recently. But Miguel had probably known her his entire life.

Em seemed to read my mind. "I'm going to confirm the identity before we tell Miguel."

I hoped the initial ID of the victim was wrong. Miguel had recently lost his longtime produce man, Mustache Hank. That had been hard. Losing Marisol, who had been a fixture at Baptista's for as long as I could remember, would be devastating. "Let me know," I said to Em before we said our goodbyes.

Every bit of sleepiness was wiped clear out of my body. I tossed and turned for a good hour before finally hauling myself out of bed and trudging down the hall to the little room I'd made into my office. I booted up my desktop computer, and then loaded up the Lightroom gallery I'd created for the Baptista's Cantina and Grill photo shoots. Miguel had chosen a total of seven photographs from the two hundred or so I'd taken, including a low-light shot of the outdoor patio with the streak of the boardwalk lights in the distant background. The night shot was one of my favorites; it captured the juxtaposition of the romantic ambience of the restaurant and the frenetic energy of the boardwalk.

But there were many more photos, including candids of the employees. When I took portraits, I tried to capture not just what people looked like, but rather who they were. I scrolled through the collection, lifting my finger from the arrow key when I came across one of Marisol and her husband, David. She had her arm threaded through his, and while he looked straight into the camera, she had her head turned and tilted back, looking up at him. She wasn't exactly smiling, but if I had to pick a word to describe her in that frozen moment, it would be *content*.

She was trim and fit. She had a vibrant olive complexion, although the sun-kissed color didn't hide the wrinkles around her eyes and skin damage that living on the coast had caused.

David was older than Marisol and stood several inches taller. While his gaze was directed at the camera, the tilt of his head toward his wife, the slight lift of one side of his mouth in the faintest smile, and the softness in his eyes told the story. He loved the woman next to him. My heart instantly ached for him. Once he got a call from Emmaline, assuming they confirmed the identity of the dead body, the ease in his expression would be gone forever.

I'd finally been able to fall asleep, but the fitful night had left me groggy and unrested. I kept envisioning the animated and always cheerful Marisol I'd known as a child, washed up on the beach. I hoped against hope that Emmaline would call me to say it was some other poor soul she'd found. Instead I got an early morning call from Miguel. "I have some bad news," he said, launching right into it.

"I talked to Emmaline last night," I said, hoping he wouldn't wonder why I hadn't called him with the news.

"So you know." His voice sounded weighted with disbelief.

"I'm so sorry."

"I can't think of a time when she wasn't"—he broke off, swallowing the sadness that was on the surface—"when she wasn't in my life," he finished hoarsely.

I pressed the speaker button on my phone, laid it down beside me, and hugged my arms around my knees, burying my face into them.

"It's a tragic irony, you know?" he said after he swallowed his emotions.

"What do you mean?"

"Mari was a swimmer. She did triathlons, for chrissakes. She swam in the Pacific all the time. To drown in the ocean . . . it doesn't seem right."

I hadn't remembered that about her. Or maybe I'd never known. No wonder she was so healthy and fit-looking. "It doesn't," I agreed.

"I remember her telling me about the first time she competed," Miguel continued. "It was in Northern California somewhere. The swimming portion of the race was in a lake. It was only a half mile or so, compared to nine miles on a bike and three miles running, but she said she didn't make it past the first leg. Fighting the current and constant waves did her in. That's when she started training in the ocean. She said she would conquer that lake if it was the last thing she did."

"Did she?" I asked.

"The next year. Went back and competed like a boss." I heard the smile in his voice, but it vanished as quickly as it had materialized. "How could she have died out there?"

"Maybe she got a cramp. Or maybe the tide took her too far out."

Miguel let out a sorrowful sigh. "Her father just died, you know. She was having a really hard time dealing with that. She couldn't have—"

He stopped, but I knew right away what he'd been thinking. I'd lost my mother not long ago, and only recently had I begun to find a new normal. Death wasn't something you just got over. No, you learned to cope and eventually, like yeast proofing in water, you realize that you've changed, but that you're alive.

Only sometimes people didn't overcome. Sometimes depression set in and the dark hole became too deep to climb out of. "Didn't she have kids? And grandkids?" I asked, because even if she was wrought with grief over losing her father, children or grandchildren of her own might have given her perspective and purpose.

"Yeah. Sergio, Laura's husband," he said, referring to his sister.

Laura and I had recently made amends. She'd been less than happy that I'd come back to Santa Sofia—and into her brother's life—because she'd spent years blaming me for the fact that Miguel had left his hometown to join the military. We were on good terms now, and I was besotted with her children. Eighteen-month-old Mateo, and Andrea, his two-and-a-half-year-old sister, were adorable. To think that the dead woman was their grandmother felt like a sucker punch to the gut.

And Sergio Morales. I'd met him briefly not that long ago, but I hadn't made the connection between him and Marisol. I put my hand over my mouth.

Miguel continued. "Then there's Ruben, the oldest, and Lisette. She's the baby. Christ." I could picture Miguel running a ragged hand over his face. This was all too close to home for him, and the people around him—his people— were hurting.

"I'm so sorry, Miguel. Can I do anything?"

"They're all coming to the restaurant at five," he said. "Lisette, Ruben, Sergio, Laura. If you want . . ."

He trailed off. We'd found our way back to each other after what felt like a lifetime apart, but at the same time, we were still new. Did he think he was asking too much of me to come be a shoulder for him?

"I'll be there," I said, and I would. Always.

Chapter 3

Baptista's Cantina and Grill was Santa Sofia's answer to high-end Mexican seafood. It sat on the pier overlooking a rocky inlet, had the best brisket queso this side of—anywhere, and was owned and operated by Miguel. He'd recently renovated, a project he'd sunk his heart and soul into. The restaurant had been his father's brainchild, and Miguel and Laura had spent their youth learning every aspect of it. Miguel's mother still worked there, mostly manning the hostess station from her perch atop a cushioned stool, and Laura filled in when she was needed, but since Miguel's father had passed and Miguel had come back to Santa Sofia, the restaurant had, for all intents and purposes, become his.

He'd started by shutting off the back room, starting the remodel there. It had gone more quickly than he'd planned, and with my brother

Billy on board as the contractor, the entire restaurant had gotten an interior facelift in no time. Gone were the Naugahyde booths and ancient tables. Now the look of the restaurant fit the menu. Aztec-patterned tile graced the floors. An open fireplace with bold and graphic—but not folksy—tile stretched up to the tall ceiling. The walls were wood planked, huge windows overlooked the pier and ocean, and blown glass fixtures illuminated the space. I'd chronicled the renovation for him, and had taken pictures of the finished spaces for new promotions he'd put in place, and I'd done extensive food photography (and tasting) for the menu.

A long, sleek bar stretched along one side of the restaurant, to the left of the entrance and waiting room. "We've got a hundred tequilas and mezcals," he'd told me, "and Jorge is our new mezcal concierge. He knows all there is to know about our list."

The classic menu that Miguel's father created remained, in essence, but Miguel had upped the ante. Now he featured things like chicharrón quesadillas; tortas filled with roasted turkey, chorizo, avocado, and onion; prawns and lobster in a cast-iron skillet; and tuna carnitas. And, of course, tacos diablos and brisket queso. Taking these two things off the menu was a deal-breaker for me.

It was an incredible transformation, and one that the people—and tourists—of Santa Sofia were embracing. I arrived a few minutes before five and the place was already packed, the people waiting spilling outside. I found Miguel's mother taking names for the waitlist, and, in her broken English, directing the hosts and hostesses in their tasks. "Ivy, *mija*," she said when she saw me. "*¿Cómo estás?* You are well?"

I smiled, nodding. "Very well." It was true, I realized. Marisol's death notwithstanding, I was finally feeling settled in Santa Sofia, my freelance photography business was on track, and I could make an outstanding loaf of sourdough. I was in a good place.

"Miguel, he is with the Morales children," she said to me. The puffiness around her eyes and her sallow skin revealed that she was grieving Marisol's death. Still, she'd pulled herself together and let work distract her. She directed one of the hosts to take me to the family. I thanked her, and then I was led through the dining room, past the blazing fireplace, and into a small private room at the back of the restaurant. The young man leading me opened the French doors, closing them again after I'd passed through. I spotted Laura first, standing next to her husband, her eyes red-rimmed, a wad of tissue clutched in one hand. She was about five-foot-five, a couple of inches shorter than me, but her grief seemed to make her body collapse in on itself. She still carried baby weight, yet her cheeks appeared hollow, her nose red and raw, and her olive complexion had turned pale. She looked more grief-stricken than Sergio, whose face was stoic. It was as if he was actively refusing to give in to his emotions in this public setting. He caught Laura's eye, giving her an affirming, almost imperceptible nod. I'd sensed his love for her the first time I'd met him; his attentiveness to his wife now, despite his own loss, reinforced it.

I wasn't familiar with the other people in the room, but I knew they were Marisol's other children and their spouses. The man I presumed to be Ruben could have been Sergio's twin. Each stood about five-ten, had a stocky build with wide shoulders and thick limbs, and had thick hair shorn close to the scalp. Ruben carried a few more pounds on his bones, but both men were fit. Like his brother, Ruben was stoic. I imagined they'd both shed tears earlier, and would again later, in the privacy of their own homes. Ruben stood next to a petite woman who, based on the wedding band on her ring finger, I took to be his wife. She had dirty-blond hair pulled into a low ponytail, and unlike her husband, her grief was palpable. Mascara-stained tears ran in rivulets down her cheeks and her mouth pulled down on either side as she struggled to control her crying.

Another woman stood next to Miguel. She looked to be about my age, with chestnut hair, a dark complexion, and unusually piercing green eyes. This had to be Lisette. Like her brothers, she seemed to be in command of her emotions, although as I watched, she drew in a deep breath, closed her eyes, and pushed her lips together as she exhaled. Clearly the control she was exercising wasn't coming easily.

A man in his early sixties, gray peppering his hair, stood on the other side of Lisette. One trembling hand cupped his forehead, his head angled downward, and the other hand held a wad of tissue to his nose. I recognized him right away from the photos I'd taken during the remodel, although he looked ten years older now than he had just a few short weeks ago. David Ruiz, Marisol's husband, didn't have the stoicism of his stepchildren.

Miguel had had his back to the French doors, but now, as if he sensed a change in the air, he turned toward me. He met my gaze and gave a wan smile, the deep dimples, like parentheses on either side of his mouth, present, but lacking mirth. His hair and complexion both seemed darker in the dim light of the room, and his goatee, neatly trimmed, gave him a hard edge. His emotions were in check, but I could see the strain Marisol's death was taking on him. He broke away from Lisette and David, skirting around the dining table in the center of the room to meet me. "Thanks for coming," he said as he brushed my cheek with a light kiss, stepping back when the French doors opened again and three of the waitstaff came in, their arms loaded down with family-style dishes of traditional enchiladas, platters of street tacos, Spanish rice, and frijoles de la olla. Refried beans were always an option at the restaurant, but the standard was beans in the pot simmered with bell peppers, onions, garlic, and cumin.

The table had been set with plates and silverware, water goblets already filled with ice water. Miguel cleared his throat, gesturing to the table. One by one, Marisol's family took their seats. Platters and bowls were passed around and plates were filled with food, but no one spoke. Laura picked at an enchilada, finally putting down her fork and running the backs of her fingers under her eyes. Lisette took a few bites, but then pushed her plate away. Ruben's wife didn't eat at all. Ruben and Sergio managed to choke down more than their wives and sister, but not by much. Conversely, David's head was bent down over his plate. He brought his fork from his food to his mouth in a steady rhythm, not pausing enough to breathe in between bites.

I sat next to Miguel, feeling the grief pressing down the air in the room, but the silence grew and grew, becoming uncomfortably awkward. No one seemed to know how to talk about Marisol. Finally, when none of the family did, Miguel stood. "It's impossible to understand that Marisol"—he looked at Sergio, then Ruben, and finally at Lisette—"that your mom is gone. I have always felt like part of your family. I can't actually remember a time when she hasn't been here. I know what you're experiencing right now and I can't take your pain away, but if there is anything I can do, I'm here for you."

The sincerity in his voice and the empathy in his eyes seemed to open the floodgates in the room. Laura's tears flowed again. Sergio laid his hand on the back of her neck, giving a gentle bolstering squeeze. He spoke, looking at the center of the table rather than at any of us. "She was a good swimmer, you know? I know the ocean is unpredictable, but still, it's hard to understand how she could have drowned."

"She shouldn't have been swimming in the

ocean," David said, his voice tinged with something close to anger. "I told her over and over again to practice at the Y, but she said it wasn't the same."

"Because the races aren't always in tame pools," Ruben said. "It's not the same. Remember when she did the Rancho Seco race? The swimming nearly did her in."

"She wanted to tackle that one again. That's what her training was all about," Sergio said.

David scoffed. "You mean that's what killed her."

Lisette spoke up. "She was stubborn—"

"She was distracted."

Lisette spun to face her stepfather. "You're acting like it was her fault. She's dead! Don't you get that?"

He came right back at her, his voice raw. "Don't you think I know that? I'm angry, okay? She buried herself in her training to get away from—"

He stopped, but everyone was staring at him now. "Get away from what?" Ruben asked.

But David shrugged helplessly. "I don't know. From whatever was bothering her. Losing her father mostly, I think."

They all fell silent at that. Had Marisol's grief made her careless? Had that carelessness led to her death? Whatever the cause, she wasn't going to walk through the door, ready for her shift, as she always had. She wasn't going to be there to cuddle with her grandkids. She wasn't going to kiss her husband goodnight.

Obviously David got that his wife was dead.

He'd skipped right over the first stage of denial and was solidly into stage two: anger. I wondered how long before he jumped to depression, bargaining, and finally true acceptance. Everyone was different, but I knew enough to understand that it was a lengthy process and that David needed to allow himself time to grieve.

"You're probably right," Lisette said, "but you can't blame her, David."

He'd been clenching the handle of his fork in a fist, but now his muscles seemed to give out all at once, the utensil falling to the table with a clatter, his chin dropping, his chest heaving. He let out a wail, like a wounded animal, shoved back from the table, and stumbled toward the French doors leading from the private room to the restaurant. "Something's not right about this," he said through a sob. "I wish she'd listened to me. She shouldn't have been out there. She shouldn't have drowned." He flicked away the tears on his cheeks with a violent, jerky movement, then wagged his finger at us all. "She shouldn't have drowned," he repeated.

He opened the door, gripping the handle with one hand. His eyes scanned the room, stopping briefly on each of his stepchildren, the spouses, then at Miguel and me. His finger twitched as he directed it at us. At me. "You."

I startled. My hand flew to my chest. "Me?"

"You've done this before."

Miguel's arm had been draped along the back of my chair, but now he laid his hand on my shoulder, his protective instinct kicking in. "She's done what before?"

David's Adam's apple slipped up and down in his throat. My earlier assessment was wrong, I realized. He hadn't skipped over denial; he was experiencing it simultaneously with anger. His conglomeration of emotions were warring against each other—grief battling with anger battling with disbelief. "Solved a murder."

The reaction in the room seemed to happen in slow motion. Laura gasped at the word. Sergio muttered something unintelligible under his breath.

Ruben leaned over the table, staring at his stepfather and said, "What the hell are you talking about?"

Lisette jumped to her feet. "Murder?"

David's gaze, however, had not wavered. It remained steady on me, eyes narrow and intense. "Can you do it again?"

"Do what again?" I asked.

"Solve a crime. Bring someone to justice."

"What are you talking about?" Ruben demanded. "You're saying it wasn't an accident? That someone killed our mother?"

David jabbed his finger in the air toward me, then at Miguel, too. "You find out. Both of you. Find out what really happened to Marisol."

Chapter 4

After the dinner at Baptista's, I went home to Agatha and my thoughts. Freed from her crate, the little pug spun in circles, her tail curved into a tight curlicue. She looked up at me with her giant bulbous eyes. "Outside," I said, opening up my own set of French doors and releasing her to the wide-open space of the backyard with its flowerbeds, patio, and Adirondack chairs.

I sat at the outdoor dining table, chin on my fist, doing my best to ignore David's implication that something sinister had happened to Marisol. No matter how hard I tried, I couldn't shake the intensity of his plea. Finally, I called Emmaline. "Still no proposal," she said when I asked for an update on her personal life. "After this case is wrapped up I can think about it again."

"You have to be able to balance work and play," I said. I'd lost so much of myself during my previous marriage, and then after losing my mother, sometimes I didn't know how to relax anymore. I hadn't known what I wanted to do, or how to spend my time. And then I'd discovered Yeast of Eden, Olaya Solis, and bread. The lengthy process of baking long-rise bread had taught me how to let my emotions unfurl and float away, allowing me to focus on other things. Allowing me to remember that there is more to life than just work or chores or grief.

I'd been singing this tune to Emmaline since she'd taken over as interim sheriff, but she was still challenged by the concept of work-life balance. "Don't I know it," she said. "I'm working on it."

With Billy's help, I knew she'd get there, so I cut to the chase. "Is there any evidence that Marisol didn't, um, die a natural death?"

"Drowning is not natural," she said.

"You know what I mean." I rubbed the grit from my eyes as I told her what David had said.

There was a distinct pause, she blew out a weighty breath, and said, "He thinks his wife was murdered?"

"He didn't come out and say that, but it was definitely implied."

She paused again, and from across town and via pinging cell towers, I heard the tapping of Em's fingers on a computer keyboard. "The ME's report just came in," she said a moment later. "They expedited."

"So an autopsy was done?" I asked.

"Absolutely. In the case of a drowning, and with no witnesses, we can't assume anything.

And when a body is waterlogged, there's no time to waste. Deterioration happens too quickly."

"What did he find?" I asked, expecting her to denounce David's wild supposition and to confirm the obvious: that Marisol had accidentally drowned in the Pacific Ocean.

"It wasn't a drowning," Emmaline said instead.

I held the phone away from my ear for a second, processing her statement. "But you said the body resurfaced and that the ME said she'd been in the water for at least twelve hours."

"Here's the deal, in a nutshell. Drowning is a silent but violent death. The victim is literally fighting for her life . . . fighting for air. Eventually—usually after just two or three minutes—and with no other choice, she gulps in water. It goes to her lungs and stomach, then throughout the body."

I closed my eyes, trying not to imagine Marisol going through this horror, but I couldn't block the images of her coughing, convulsing, losing consciousness, and then finally succumbing to death.

"Unfortunately, we live on the coast. I've seen a few drownings during my time with the sheriff's department," Em continued, "and I've learned that, without exception, if a body isn't taken immediately from the water, then it drifts downward before putrefaction gases cause it to rise again. And—this is key—no matter what, the body ends up in a semi-fetal position."

"Okaaayy," I said, not sure where she was going with this. "And Marisol—?"

"Was *not* in a fetal position."

"But you just got done saying it would end up in a fetal position, no matter what."

"The body tells a story, Ivy. If it isn't in a fetal position, or if the head is tilted to one side or the other, it's telling us that it wasn't drowning."

I gulped, replaying David's parting words from earlier. *Something's not right about this*, he'd said. *She shouldn't have drowned.* "Cut to the chase, Em. What does it mean?" I asked, but I already knew the answer.

"Marisol Ruiz was put in the water post–rigor mortis to make it look like a drowning, but Ivy, the woman died on land. The ME says strangulation."

Which meant David was right. Marisol Ruiz was murdered.

Chapter 5

Olaya Solis, and Penelope Branford, my eighty-something sidekick, weren't the family I'd been born with, but they had become the family I'd chosen to have in my life. We were an unlikely trio, to be sure, especially given the former love triangle they'd been part of. Olaya had been in love with Penelope's husband, and although nothing ever came of it, theirs was a complicated friendship. After years and years of harbored animosity, they'd reached a peaceful coexistence with each other, for which I was grateful, because they'd become my female inspirations. I was thirty-six years old, and while my mother would always be a huge part of who I was and was like a guardian angel, her spirit always with me, Olaya Solis and Penelope Branford were in my daily life. They were women I wanted to emulate. They both embraced life fully, were positive and impactful, and knew what it meant to be a friend.

Now, the morning after the sleepless night I'd had, I parked in the back lot and entered the Yeast of Eden kitchen. The stainless-steel counter-tops, a large demonstration mirror, racks of cool-ing baked goods, and commercial-grade ovens were a welcome reprieve from my whirling thoughts. I wanted nothing more than to dig my hands into a bowl of soft and pliable bread dough, turn it onto the counter, and knead it till the cows came home.

Which is just what I did. I pulled out the or-ganic flour Olaya sourced from a local mill, sugar, yeast, salt, olive oil, sesame seeds, and filled a measuring cup with warm water. The end result would be a loaf of crusty rustic Italian bread bak-ing in the oven.

The process of baking bread, I'd discovered, was therapeutic. I let myself get lost in the expe-rience, letting the yeast proof with the sugar and a quarter cup of warm water. It took about ten minutes to bubble and foam, and once it did, I was ready to add the rest of the warm water, combine it with the flour and salt, and mix until the dough formed a ball. With floured hands, I did a soft knead of the dough, formed it into a smooth, firm ball, placed it in an oiled proofing bowl, covered it, and placed it in the commer-cial refrigerator for a long rise. I'd come back to-morrow to actually bake the bread.

Just as I closed the refrigerator door, Olaya came into the kitchen from the front of the store. She wore a vibrant blue maxi dress with an abstract design artfully patterned across the fabric, and beige suede Birkenstocks. Her short, loose, iron-gray curls bounced playfully as she glided into the room. "I thought I heard a little mouse here in my kitchen," she said with a slight Spanish accent. She spoke nearly perfect English, but her native Spanish was part of her speech. Her gaze traveled from me to the workstation I'd used to mix the bread. "What is wrong, *mija*?"

Olaya had come to the United States from Mexico when she was a young woman. She'd brought her country's tradition of long-rise bread with her, something many people didn't automatically associate with Mexican cuisine. She'd learned from her mother and grandmother, and had continued the tradition, infusing her love into her work—and many people believed infusing magic into her bread, as well. She baked with lavender and anise and myriad other herbs, all of which were associated with love or healing or contentment or some other universal human emotion.

She also had a sixth sense for understanding what *I* was feeling, and today was no exception.

"Did you hear about the body down by the pier?" I asked.

"*Pobrecita*," she said. "Martina knows Marisol Ruiz very well. Running, always running together."

I told her what the autopsy had revealed. "Emmaline is going to talk to the family. She may have already. I can't help but feel for them. I've been through it—losing my mother to a violent death was the worst thing that ever happened to me. I wouldn't wish that pain on anyone."

Olaya nodded sagely. "And yet you cannot make it better. The pain is theirs to experience. You can only be there to support them."

I'd had ample support throughout the grieving process, most importantly from Olaya and Mrs. Branford. Without them, I'm not sure how I would have coped. I also may never have gotten to the truth of what had happened to my mother.

"*Entonces*, what will you do?" Olaya asked.

She was right a moment ago. I couldn't take away the pain Marisol's family was experiencing, but I could do what David asked of me. I could help Emmaline get to the bottom of what had happened to her. "The family is meeting at the funeral home. Miguel is going for moral support. He asked if I'd come."

Olaya nodded her approval. "*Bueno.* Then that is exactly what you should do."

Santa Sofia had two options when it came to funeral homes: the Lutz Family and Vista Ridge. My mother's final arrangements had been handled through the former. Marisol Ruiz's family had opted for the latter.

I didn't make a habit of visiting funeral homes, so although I'd driven by Vista Ridge probably hundreds of times, I'd never really registered the details of the place. The marquis for the funeral home was a large backlit rectangle on a post at the front edge of the property. The back-

ground was stark white, Vista Ridge Funeral Home
in bold navy letters, a single line drawing of a
cross with a closed loop at the top—a symbol
for eternal life—artfully displayed behind the
business name. Beneath and running along the
bottom of the sign were the funeral home's services:

BURIAL * DONOR * PRE-NEED * MONUMENTS *
CREMATION

Miguel and I joined Marisol's kids in the front
lobby. Sergio, Ruben, and Lisette were all there,
but Laura and Ruben's wife, Natalie, were absent, but none more conspicuously than Marisol's husband. "Where's David?" I asked. My own
father had been so distraught after my mother's
death that Billy and I had stepped in, but I didn't
equate David's absence to his distress over losing
this wife. All the emotions associated with loss
were bubbling under the surface, but for the
time being, his anger was front and center. So
where was he?

"No idea," Miguel said with a shrug.

I'd spoken quietly, but Lisette had heard and
now she answered. "We asked him not to come—"

"No, *you* asked him," Ruben corrected. "Whatever you think of him, Lis, he was still our
mother's husband. You shouldn't have excluded
him."

"He basically said our mother was murdered!"
she screeched. "He's causing drama in an already stressful situation. Maybe *you* don't mind,

but *I* do. I don't want to listen to his stupid theories about"—she made air quotes—"*something not being right.*"

I inhaled sharply, realizing that Emmaline hadn't told the family what the autopsy had revealed and her theory about when Marisol actually died.

"Are you all right?" Miguel asked me. He was so tuned to me that he'd picked up on my change of breath and the slight step backwards I'd taken.

I took him by the sleeve and dragged him toward the door. "Be right back," he managed to say to his childhood friends before I'd hauled him all the way outside.

The second the door closed behind us, I dropped his arm and spun around, my back to him, my fingers splaying through my hair.

"What the hell is wrong, Ivy?"

I turned back to face him. "What David said last night? It bothered me, so I called Emmaline. Marisol was murdered, Miguel. David's right."

He stood there, motionless. Stunned. Then, at last he said, "Holy shit. Is Em sure?"

"She seemed one hundred percent positive. The ME did a report of his findings. Strangled."

"Jesus," he muttered, still struggling to process what I'd told him.

"And then, only after she was already dead was she thrown in the water."

David's absence suddenly felt wrong. Even if Lisette had told him not to come, Marisol was his wife. My mind conjured up the photograph I'd taken of the two of them. He'd looked like a man in love. Happy. Content. And last night, he'd been overwrought at the idea that Marisol had been killed. Could he be at the sheriff's station talking to someone about his theory? Could he have transitioned from anger to distress? Whatever he was feeling, and regardless of what Lisette had told him, he should have been here.

Chapter 6

Miguel and I came back into the funeral home to find the siblings had moved to the director's office to go over burial details. "Sorry," Miguel said. "We should go."

Sergio shook his head. "Stay. You're part of this family. You loved her."

That was true. She'd been with Baptista's forever. Miguel nodded, ushering me just in the doorway.

The siblings were seated in a semicircle around Benjamin Alcott's desk, the director himself in a high-backed black office chair, clasped hands resting on the blotter pad in front of him. I wondered if there was a special etiquette class morticians attended to get the body language, expressions, and mannerisms exactly right.

A series of brochures were neatly displayed on a side cabinet. I scanned them, noting the different facets of the business. It was almost identical to the funeral home we'd used for my mother. There were brochures for "green" burials, cremation options, casket sales, organ donation, planning a funeral for a loved one, and pre-planning services. It was a lot to take in.

"I'm very sorry for your loss," Mr. Alcott said. "And on the heels of your grandfather's death, it makes it that much more difficult." He made a sorrowful *tsk tsk tsk* sound. "My sister and I knew your mother from school. Hers was a life taken far too soon."

His voice was low, with a measured cadence that all on-screen funeral home personnel exhibited. The woman we'd dealt with at Lutz Family Funeral Home, Susan Hollister, had spoken with the same slow and empathetic tone. Another learned behavior, I thought. "Again," he said, "I am so sorry for your loss. It's a difficult time, but we do need to make the, er, arrangements."

My thoughts drifted back to my mother's death. Billy and I had been in charge of organizing her funeral. Cremation had been an option, but in the end, we'd wanted a physical grave site. What I'd realized since then was that the entire funeral process and the rituals of death were not for the deceased at all; they were for the people left behind who were grieving and needed to hold on to something tangible. *Closure* was such a cliché word, and yet a funeral provided just that. It was the final step in letting go of the person you'd lost. I wasn't sure cremation could offer the same closure—I liked to visit my mother's grave, to sit and talk to her, to bring her a blue-bell and tiger lily bouquet—but ultimately, it was a very personal decision.

"She wasn't particularly religious. We'd like to hold the wake or the service here," Sergio said. "She chose cremation for Abuelo. I think we should do the same for her, then scatter her ashes in the ocean."

Lisette crushed a balled-up tissue against her eyes to absorb her falling tears. "If we do that, there's no place to visit."

Ruben made a sound. "Hmmm. But I think Sergio's right. If she didn't see the ocean every day, she felt like something was off."

Lisette scoffed as she looked from one brother to the other. "So what I want doesn't matter?"

"It's not about you, Lisette," Sergio said in a placating voice. He sounded remarkably calm, though his face was tense. "It's what she would have wanted. You know that."

It made sense to me. From what I understood, Marisol had spent a good portion of her life in the water. What better way to honor her than by returning her to the place she loved so much?

Lisette threw up her hands and turned her back on us. Sergio and Ruben ignored her.

"We spent a lot of time with your mother, making arrangements for your grandfather," Benjamin Alcott said after giving the grieving family a moment to gather themselves.

"She didn't talk that much about it," Ruben said. "Would you take us through it?"

"Of course. Let me start, though, by thanking you for coming to us during this difficult time. We know you have a choice, and we appreciate the confidence you're placing in us as we lay your mother to rest. My sister and I worked with her on her father's cremation. From our many conversations, I believe I have an understanding of her perspective on her eternal rest."

Lisette had calmed down enough to listen, but now her chin fell, quivering, and her tears flowed. Her hunched shoulders heaved as she sobbed.

Mr. Alcott was unfazed. He had seen it all before. He gently slid a box of tissues closer to the edge of his desk and within her reach and continued. "Vista Ridge Cemetery is incredibly picturesque," he continued. "It combines the natural beauty of the area with complete tranquility." He looked pointedly at Lisette. "Now, this is most definitely an option. We also have donor services for those who wish to donate their bodies to science. However, based on my conversations with your mother as we planned for your grandfather, I do believe that she would have opted for cremation."

"Why did she choose that?" Ruben asked.

Mr. Alcott didn't seem surprised by the question, but he did tilt his head to the side slightly, as if he were wondering why Ruben didn't already know the answer to his question. "She felt strongly that he return to the earth."

"But his ashes are sitting in an urn in her house," Lisette said. "She couldn't do it. She couldn't just scatter him to blow away in the wind because she wouldn't have a place or anything to visit. Which is my point. Don't we want that?"

"She wasn't ready, that's all," Ruben said. He looked at Sergio, eyebrows lifted. "What did she tell us the other day? Something about needing to know where he was."

Sergio nodded. "She was still grieving, but you know Abuelo. He spent his life camping and fishing. She wanted him to have that forever after."

Mr. Alcott cleared his throat softly, bringing the attention in the room back to him. "Let me tell you about our services. There is a growing request for cremation, and of course we take every consideration possible to ensure the purity and authenticity of the remains. We have a state-of-the-art crematory and offer a viewing room for your family to view your mother prior to cremation."

I recognized the silence that ensued. The three siblings wanted to remember their mother however they'd seen her last, not bloated and waterlogged.

Mr. Alcott continued. "We also have a lovely memorial garden where we offer in-ground burial with a separate scattering area where you may spread the ashes. You are always welcome to take your mother's ashes, of course, as she did with your grandfather, or, finally, we have an above-ground inurnment in our lovely columbarium."

"A place to come visit would be nice," Sergio

said. "I know she loved the ocean, but maybe we could spread some of the ashes here in the garden? I like the idea of her being in one place."

They discussed the pros and cons of each scenario, their voices—even Lisette's—amazingly calm and composed. It was as if the reality of what had happened had been filed away, allowing them to deal with the nitty-gritty details that had to be sorted through. "But she chose cremation for Abuelo," Ruben said again. "She liked the idea of him going back to the earth."

"Cremation," Sergio said, making up his mind.

"Cremation," Ruben agreed.

Lisette looked ready to combust, but she closed her eyes for a moment and calmed herself down, finally nodding. It wasn't her choice, but she acquiesced. "Fine."

"Excellent. It's a fine choice and I do believe it's what your mother would have wanted." Mr. Alcott talked through the basic contract for funeral services, including the burial-versus-cremation options, the memorial garden, donor services, headstones for the cemetery, plaques for the garden, and reception services. When he'd finished with his talk, he slid the contract across the table toward the siblings. Ruben reached for it, but Lisette stepped up, taking the pen from the mortician and placing her hand on the paper to hold it in place.

It was interesting that, in an era when so many contracts were electronic and iPads and other devices were used to acknowledge and sign, the funeral home business was still pen and paper. Or maybe it was just Santa Sofia. The contract for my mother's burial had been more extensive and had been done in triplicate, but it was still paper, nonetheless. They'd catch up with technology at some point, I imagined.

"We just need your initials, please." He pointed to the lines as he ran through them, one by one. Lisette scribbled LM on each of them so quickly that I wondered how much attention she was paying.

"And signature here," Mr. Alcott said, pointing with his index finger.

After she scratched in her name, he turned to the next page. "Here you acknowledge additional services offered," he said. "Initial in the spaces."

"If we want to add or change something with the wake, we can do that?" Ruben asked as Lisette went down the list adding LM to each space. From where I stood, they hardly looked like letters at all. Anyone who didn't know the letters stood for Lisette Morales would be hard-pressed to figure them out.

"Most assuredly. We'll meet to discuss all the details. I'll need to get your stepfather's approval, as well, as next of kin."

Lisette finished initialing, signed in the final spot Mr. Alcott indicated, and slid the contract back to him. He rose, coming out from behind his desk and extending his hand to Ruben, Sergio, and finally, to Lisette. "Again, I am so sorry for your loss."

"Thanks. We appreciate it," Ruben said.

"Of course. I understand from the authorities that we will be in possession of your mother's remains shortly. We can plan the service for Thursday. I can phone you later this afternoon to confirm."

"Call me," Lisette said.

Ruben looked at his sister with an expression I couldn't quite decipher. Was he irritated at her inserting herself as the go-to person? Or was he grateful that she was willing to take on that role? Or was he just happy that she was calm?

Miguel and I had been standing by the door. We scooted out without handshakes, and I wondered if Mr. Alcott's hand was cold or warm, clammy or sweaty, dry or soft. Lisette's ringing cell phone wiped the questions away. She answered as Mr. Alcott saw us all out. He'd just gone back inside, leaving us to ponder Marisol's eternal rest, when Lisette cried out. "What are you saying?" Her voice was panic-stricken. She dropped her hand, the phone dangling from her loose grip.

Sergio grabbed it before it fell, holding it to his ear and talking with whoever was on the other end. We all stared, but I had a pretty good idea about what had upset Lisette.

Sergio confirmed it thirty seconds later. "That was the sheriff." He raked his hands through his short hair, his fingers curving, pressing into his scalp like a metal claw. "She needs to meet with us. About Mom's death."

A mournful silence fell over them. It was as if they knew that Em was going to tell them the unthinkable—that their mother hadn't drowned, she'd been murdered.

Chapter 7

The Morales children scattered and Miguel and I drove down Pacific Coast Highway. A breeze blew in from the ocean, but the day was warm and sunny. Tufts of white, cottony clouds dotted the bright periwinkle sky. Bristol State Beach had public access and was brimming with sunbathers. Kids built sand castles, small groups played volleyball in the sand pits, and a few surfers paddled out to the breaking waves. I sometimes walked along the pathway parallel to the sand, people-watched, and took photographs, but generally, I preferred the secluded areas near the pier at Baptista's and in the rocky inlets hidden away from the tourists.

When we were kids, Billy, Emmaline, and I had spent countless hours burying each other in the sand, building castles with moats that the tide would fill, and running back and forth, chasing the waves at the shoreline as they ebbed and flowed. Billy was two years younger than we were, but at that point, the difference in age didn't matter.

As we got older, though, we moved from sand toys to boogie boards and body surfing, and once we all became teenagers, everything changed. Miguel entered the picture. We flirted endlessly until finally, when I was sixteen and a junior, and he was a senior, we started dating for real. Em and Billy had always crushed on each other, but the age difference back then had been too much. As they'd gotten older, even through their twenties, they'd tried to get together, but when one was single, the other wasn't. They were always at different places at different times.

Their friendship had started with our time at the beach as kids. Emmaline had intended to bring it full circle with her marriage proposal . . . until Marisol's body had washed up.

"We should check on David," I said suddenly, knowing that no one else was going to. Whatever suspicions he'd had about his wife's death were now confirmed and I worried about his state of mind.

Miguel called the restaurant and spoke briefly to his mother to check on things, then turned the truck in the direction of the house Marisol and David had shared. The neighborhood was farther north along PCH and was a mixture of old and new, of houses and apartments. It was reminiscent of Venice Beach with its hip, grungy vibe featuring homes with million-dollar-plus price tags.

"This is where Marisol lived?" I asked, shocked.

Any home that came on the market was snapped up by the highest bid from multiple offers. No matter what the California economy did, this part of Santa Sofia would always be a seller's market.

"Marisol's parents bought their place as a fixer-upper way back before it was the place to live," Miguel said. "Right place, right time. Her father quick-deeded it to her when his health started failing."

He edged his truck into the narrow alley driveway next to a turquoise and lavender bungalow. Anywhere else, the vibrant colors of the home would have been gaudy, but two blocks from the beach in this trendy, gentrified neighborhood, it fit right in. The house was quaint and charming—and had to be worth a couple million.

"Marisol moved back in to take care of her dad when he couldn't manage on his own anymore."

"David too?"

"Yeah, after they got married. She always said he was really helpful to her. Took her dad to doctor's appointments, chased him down when he'd skipped off in the middle of the night—"

"Skipped off?"

"Alzheimer's. He didn't know her in the end. It was rough. There were a lot of days she came to work looking like she hadn't slept at all. I don't think she would have gotten through it in one piece without David."

Poor Marisol. She had not just seen her father die, she'd seen him deteriorate to a shell of his former self.

There were no sidewalks on the block, and very little yard to go with the small houses. It didn't matter, though. It was a trade-off for the palm trees dotting the landscape and the sound of crashing waves carrying on the breeze. We made our way across what yard there was and up to the front stoop. The door was open, a flimsy screen door the only thing separating the inside of the house from the outside. I rang the door-bell as Miguel peered through the dark screen and called, "David, you in there?"

We stood back and waited, but David did not appear. We looked at each other, contemplating what do. "That's his car," Miguel said, pointing to a black sedan, "and the door is open. He's gotta be here."

"Maybe he went for a walk," I suggested. Strolling along the water's edge was one of my favorite things to do, and it always cleared my head. Given what David was going through, it wouldn't surprise me if he needed a change of scenery.

But Miguel shook his head. "Santa Sofia is a nice small town, but that doesn't mean you leave your house wide open if you're not there."

He knocked again, calling David's name louder this time.

Finally, we heard stirrings inside. First a grumble. Then heavy footsteps lumbering down a back hallway. At last, we caught sight of David heading toward us. I'd only met him a few times, but he looked like a different man from the one I'd photographed. His gunmetal-gray hair looked oily and uncombed. He looked unkempt. Rumpled. Unshaven. My gaze traveled down his arm to the longneck bottle of beer dangling from his loose fingers. He hadn't been in good shape the night before at Baptista's, but now it looked to me as if David Ruiz had come undone.

He took one look at us through the screen door, shook his head, and turned back around. He held up his free hand as he started back in the direction from which he'd come. "I can't talk," he said, his words mashing together. I'd say the bottle of beer he currently held was not his first.

"Have you talked to the sheriff?" Miguel asked. No pleasantries. No beating around the bush. There was no point. Anything else would have been forced, and, frankly, disrespectful to David.

He stopped in his tracks, slowly turning around to face us again. "I did."

Which explained the drastic change in his demeanor.

"I didn't wanna be right." He tilted his head back as if he were suddenly considering something on the ceiling, but I knew he wasn't actually focusing on anything. He jerked, and his left arm shot out, his fist smashing against the wall, leaving a crumpled hole behind. "She shouldn'ta been out there swimming—"

Miguel flung the screen door open and rushed inside, grabbing hold of David's arm before he was able to punch the wall again. "She wasn't. She didn't drown, man," Miguel said, trying to assuage the man's guilt. "That's not how she died. It's not your fault."

David turned his head to look at Miguel before his knees gave out. His shoulders slumped and he collapsed like a rag doll in Miguel's arms. I surged forward, catching the base of the beer bottle before it crashed to the ground.

"She was such a good person," he said, his words slurring. "Such a good person. Why would anyone hurt her?"

My eyes pooled with tears. David's grief was so palpable. So raw. "The police are going to find out," I said. "I know Sheriff Davis, and she won't rest until Marisol's killer is brought to justice."

Miguel half carried, half dragged David to the small living area of the house, depositing him on a sofa covered with an off-white slipcover, thin piping rimming the cushions. I went to the kitchen, emptied the remaining beer into the sink, and came back with a glass of water. He managed to sit up, but I held the cup to his lips to help him. The liquid dribbled down his chin despite my best effort.

He pushed the glass away. His head wobbled as he tried to focus on me. "You."

I placed my open palm on my chest. "Ivy."

"You're still going to help me," he said, his words slurring. It was a statement, not a question. He turned his glazed eyes to Miguel. "Mari loved you like one of her own children. You have to find out what happened to her. You owe her that."

Miguel met my gaze. The police were on it. I'd meant it when I'd said that Emmaline wouldn't rest until she found out who had killed Marisol Ruiz and dumped her body in the ocean. But despite that, I nodded at Miguel, he dipped his chin back at me, and told David that we would get to the truth behind his wife's death.

Talking to David in his heavily inebriated state was like chasing a rabbit through a field. We started with some basic questions, he'd start to answer, but then he'd slip away, following some jumbled thread of logic in his mind that wasn't, in fact, logical at all. He was far too drunk to make much sense.

I made a pot of coffee to try to help sober him up as Miguel pressed on, trying to get any little bit of information to help us. "David," he said, circling around to the same question he'd already asked three times. "You must have some idea. Who would have wanted to hurt Marisol?"

David spoke more clearly this time, but his head still lolled against the back of the couch and he still talked in circles, not answering the question, but going off on another rabbit trail. "The triathlon she was training for is coming up. Lisette thought she was too old to be competing. Ridiculous. She was the youngest fifty-seven-year-old in the world." He pointed a crooked finger at Miguel, then trained it on me. "In the whole world. She ran circles around her training buddies. They didn't have a chance of winning against her in their age group. She was good. Real good."

"David." Miguel's voice was sharp. "Come on, man. Was someone upset with her? Did she have any enemies?"

"Pft. Enemies? She was a waitress, for chris-sakes. What kind of enemies could she have? Everybody loved her."

I sat down next to him, taking his hand in mine. "You're right. But David, someone killed her. That means there's somebody who didn't love her. It means there is somebody out there who wanted her dead. Do you have *any* ideas? We just need a place to start."

He tried to focus on me. "She wasn't the same after her dad died, you know. She missed him, of course. Didn't want to believe that he was gone. But it was more than that. She was afraid she'd get old-timer's. She would forget where she'd put her keys and freak out like her mind was going. Or she'd completely blank on where her dad was. She'd actually say to me, *He's not here.* And I'd say, *He is. He's with you,* and I'd show her the urn. It's right there." He dragged his finger through the air, as if he were pulling it through a vat of pea soup. He stopped when he was pointing to a turquoise container accented with a gold band with embossed repeating leaves. The lid was trimmed in gold. It sat on a small oc-casional table against the wall, surrounded by family photos. "It's like she didn't remember that he'd died, or she thought we'd buried him instead."

"Stress can affect your memory," I told him. I'd gone through bouts of forgetfulness after my divorce and after my mother's death. My theory was that the mind ignored the trivial in order to devote itself to healing or coping.

"I guess that was it." He shook his head, angst-ridden. "Finally, she just shut down. Stopped talking to me about it altogether, like she was afraid."

"Afraid of what?"

He shrugged helplessly. "That I'd judge her? That I'd leave her if she was losing her mind? I don't know. I tried. I really tried to be there for her, but she shut me out. And now she's gone and I just want her back." His eyes drifted closed. I thought he'd fallen asleep, but then they jerked open. "Could she have done it to herself? Ended things before she got to the state her father did?"

From the way he described her state of mind, it sounded possible, if not for the ME's report. She couldn't have strangled herself and then thrown herself into the water. Still, everyone needed someone to talk to. If David had stopped being that person for Marisol, who had she turned to? I paused for a moment to give Miguel time to explain why Marisol hadn't killed herself, and to give David time to get his emotions in check, then I asked, "Do you think she might have confided in someone else? A best friend? Her daughter?"

He looked up suddenly. "Martina Solis."

I felt my eyebrows rise in surprise. I knew from Olaya that Martina and Marisol had been friends and running partners, but it had left my brain somehow.

"They ran a couple times per week," he continued. "If she talked to anyone about anything, it would be Martina. They've been friends a long time."

We had a place to start.

David didn't have much more to offer, but Miguel had one more important question for him. "Did Marisol have an advance directive? A will? Anything that could tell us what she wanted, um, after she died?" Clearly the discussion about burial versus cremation was still weighing on his mind, even though Marisol's children had made the decision.

David nodded. "After her father died, we saw an attorney and set up wills. But we didn't make, you know, any other plans."

"The funeral director thinks Marisol would have wanted to be cremated like her dad."

"I don't know if it's what he would have wanted. Before his mind started to go, he still went to church. I think he would have wanted a Mass and burial, but it made sense to go with cremation. Mari agreed with it, so I think she would want the same."

It was hard second-guessing yourself on something as big as this, but it seemed that Marisol's kids had made the right decision. I hadn't realized that had been weighing on my mind. David's blessing lifted the weight.

After a few more minutes, we left David to sleep off his lingering alcohol haze and drove back to town. Miguel planned to drop me at Yeast of Eden before heading back to the restaurant. "I'll let Lisette know what David thinks about"—he paused, closing his eyes for a few seconds, thinking—"about laying Marisol to rest. I think it'll make her feel better about it."

"I'm not sure Emmaline will actually want our help, but I'll reach out to Martina. Maybe she can tell us something."

He pulled into a curbside parking space just past the bread shop, rolled down the windows, and cut the engine. He stretched his arm across the space between our seats, his fingers playing with the spiral curls of my hair.

"Are you okay?" I asked, although I knew there wasn't a simple answer to the question.

Miguel and I had history, but we'd spent so many years apart, leading separate lives. Despite the passage of time, I knew him, and I knew he was struggling to deal with losing Marisol. Just as he had been like a son to her, she had been like a second mother to him. I met his gaze as he leaned toward me. I met him halfway, our lips brushing, and then his hand splayed through my hair, pulling me closer as he kissed me more deeply. After a moment, he broke the kiss and leaned his forehead against mine. "I will be," he said. Then again, "Yeah, I will be."

Chapter 8

Olaya, Consuelo, and Martina Solis were as opposite as three sisters could be. Olaya was the oldest and somewhere in her early sixties, although she never spoke her age aloud. Her almond-shaped green eyes were flecked with gold and her hollow cheeks defined her face with elegance, but she was a free spirit through and through. Consuelo stood a few inches taller than Olaya and had a booming voice and much more boisterous personality than both her sisters. Although she and Olaya resembled one another, the middle Solis sister tended to wear jeans and blouses rather than the caftans, maxi dresses, shawls, and clogs Olaya favored.

Martina was the youngest of the three by a good ten years. Unlike her fairer sisters, she had a darker complexion. Like her sisters, she had flecks of gold in her big, round eyes, but her base color was brown rather than green. And

while Olaya had embraced her hair's natural
iron-gray shade and Consuelo dyed hers a deep
brown, Martina kept hers almost jet black.

The biggest difference between the three of
them, though, was how Martina presented herself to the world. She was quiet. Shy, even. Even
though she was probably in her late fifties, she
looked much younger than that. Hair and on-
trend clothing could shave ten years off a person's age, and it definitely did that for Martina.
If I had to pick one, I'd classify her as the edgiest
of the three sisters.

The Solis sisters had each followed their own
distinct paths. Consuelo was a real estate agent
in Santa Sofia and Martina did administrative
work in a doctor's office, but they all knew the
art of artisan bread-making and were pinch hit-
ters for Olaya whenever she needed their help.

I walked into the bread shop hoping I'd find
Martina behind the counter helping out, but no
such luck. Instead, Maggie, the high school girl
who worked part-time, was behind the counter.
It looked to me like she'd dyed her hair darker
than it had been, which made her alabaster skin
look even paler. She listened as the customer
she was attending to rattled off what she wanted.
One by one, Maggie gathered the different breads,
ending by putting two baguettes into thin brown-
paper sleeves. She rang her up on the old cash
register, and collected the money.

Three of the scattered bistro-style tables had
customers sipping tea and eating almond or choc-
olate croissants or savory scones, which, aside
from her sugar skull cookies, were the closest

things to traditional bakery items Olaya carried. Once in a while, she'd bake Mexican wedding cookies or, if she had a hankering for something sweet, she might make palmiers. Otherwise it was bread, bread, and more bread—which was fine with me.

Maggie moved on to the next customer while I perused the display cases. One of Olaya's traditional decorated skull cookies lay tucked behind a rye batard—a dark rye bread that Olaya made with a sourdough starter to add dimension and depth to the flavor. It had become one of my favorites lately, especially on a chilly evening, and was one I was trying to recreate in my home kitchen.

The sugar skull cookies were her special treat for the kids of Santa Sofia, the tourists who came through town, and everyone in between. She made the cookies, decorated them, and hid them amidst the rest of the bread-shop fare, like Easter eggs to be hunted for. If I was lucky and encountered Olaya mid-decorating, I was able to sneak one for myself, but once they were hidden in with the other breads, they were strictly for Yeast of Eden's youngest patrons.

After Maggie finished with her customer, I approached the counter. She spoke before I had a chance to. "Olaya's not here," she said, "but Mrs. Branford was in looking for you."

"How long ago?" I asked. I hadn't seen my elderly neighbor since before Marisol's body had been discovered. I knew she was itching to get the lowdown on everything that had happened.

Maggie glanced at the clock hanging on the

wall behind the counter. It was three o'clock now. "About an hour?"

"How about Martina?" I asked. "Has she been in?"

"Actually, yes. She picked up Olaya. They went to talk to someone about the woman who just died."

This caught me by surprise. "Talk to who?"

Maggie looked toward the ceiling for a second, trying to remember, but she shook her head. "Not sure."

I felt a frown tug my lips down. I was like Curious George; I wanted to know where they'd gone. But all I had to do, of course, was call one of them and I'd probably get my answer.

Maggie snapped her fingers. "But I know they were going to the funeral home. We're going to help cater the . . . what do you call it? Wake? Service? Funeral?"

Good question. A funeral, I believed, usually included a burial, so I didn't think it would be called that. A wake was typically a Catholic tradition stemming from the belief that the family and friends stayed awake all night to protect the recently passed from evil spirits until he or she could be properly buried. In my experience, a wake and a viewing were more or less the same thing now. The bottom line was that they all offered a chance for the grieving to pay respects to the family of the deceased, and to celebrate the life that had been lost. Whatever it was called, there would be memorial photographs celebrating Marisol's life, and the cremation urn. And, apparently, baked goods courtesy of Yeast of Eden.

"Probably a wake or a viewing," I said, venturing a guess as to what they'd actually call it.

The bell on the door dinged as two men and a woman came in. They chatted happily, their voices light and airy. They did not have death on their minds. I left Maggie to man the bread shop and headed back to Vista Ridge Funeral Home for the second time that day.

The Yeast of Eden logo was a simple oval with the name of the bread shop in a classic typed font with "Artisan Bread Shop" written in cursive just beneath it. There it was in the funeral home parking lot, emblazoned on the side of the bread shop's white delivery van. Olaya was an active member of the Santa Sofia community, participating in festivals and events. She also catered. The van was put to good use.

The lobby inside was empty, but voices drifted from the director's office. The door was cracked open. The director, Mr. Alcott, wasn't there this time, but Olaya, Martina, and Lisette were seated in the available chairs, turned so they faced each other. Olaya held a notepad on her lap, a pen in her hand, and as Lisette spoke, she took down notes. "I want it to be things my mother loved," Lisette was saying when I scooted into the room. They all acknowledged me in their own ways: Olaya nodded, almost imperceptibly; Martina raised her hand and fluttered her fingertips; and Lisette lifted her chin.

They spoke for a few minutes, with Olaya throwing out suggestions, Lisette countering with other ideas, and Olaya making notes she could come back to when she had time to sit and think about it. The one thing they agreed on at the moment was that Baptista's would make carnitas, which would be served as sliders in small buns Olaya provided. Yeast of Eden would also make bite-sized scones, as well as mini pan dulce, lemon curd, strawberry butter, and whipped butter.

"Will there be a viewing or a wake here, or at Marisol's church?" I asked when they'd wrapped up the menu.

"She didn't go to church much," Lisette said, "so no Mass. We're doing a 'memorial service.'" She made air quotes around the words.

"But then we'll take her ashes to the pier," Martina said, confirming what Sergio and Ruben had wanted.

It wasn't quite a poetic full circle offering because the ocean hadn't actually taken Marisol, but it was symbolic: The power and cleansing, almost baptismal element of the ocean had always spoken to Marisol, and her family knew it was where she needed to return to.

Mr. Alcott returned a few minutes later. "Good to see you again so soon," he said to me. "Are you a family friend?"

I realized we hadn't actually been introduced. "Yes, and I work in the bread shop," I said.

He clasped his hands in front of him in that mortician manner. "Excellent. We will take care of everything on our end, rest assured. We have the okay from the authorities to proceed. The memorial service will be Thursday."

Two days from now. It seemed so fast, and yet I knew those hours would creep by at the same time. Mr. Alcott led the four of us back through the main hallway to a room on one side. It was neutral and nondescript, with peach-tinged beige walls, several tall, cylindrical off-white ceramic pots with tame leafy plants in them dotting the room, and a sideboard with candles and flower arrangements as the centerpiece in the front of the room. There was also a small oak freestanding podium, microphone attached, and several wooden stands holding additional flower arrangements. In lieu of church pews, the room had six rows of attached wood-framed black upholstered chairs. As in a church, an aisle ran down the center of the room, dividing the rows of chairs into two sections.

"Since there will not be a Mass or church service, we have two options," Mr. Alcott said. "The first is to have the final ceremony here, as we did with your grandfather," he said, specifically looking at Lisette. He swept his arm wide. "This is a lovely room, as you can see. With a cremation, of course, we don't have a traditional viewing. The urn will be showcased, as will any memorial photos you'd like to feature. We will help you plan the ceremony, of course—who will speak, how to best celebrate the life of your mother, things of that nature. The reception would also be here— all the food must be brought in from the outside. We do not have any kitchen facilities. Or you can welcome the bereaved back to your home for a more personal setting."

"Oh, I hadn't thought of that," Lisette said. "We had the entire thing here for my grandfather. I didn't think about doing it at the house." She looked to Martina. "What do you think?"

Martina's eyes welled with tears, but somehow they didn't spill over. She simply nodded. "If you think David would be up for it."

Lisette scoffed, dismissing any say David might have. "It's not his house."

My ears perked up, first at the open disdain Lisette seemed to have for David—he and Marisol had been together plenty of time for Marisol's grown children to accept their marriage, so why did Lisette resent him?—and second at her belief that David hadn't inherited the house, which directly contradicted what David had said about he and Marisol having written wills. If they'd been happily married, and had made each other the beneficiaries, then it stood to reason that the house would go to David.

But . . . maybe not. It was quite possible that Marisol had bequeathed her family home to her children, and not her husband. "It's not David's house?" I asked.

"No way. It goes to me and my brothers," she said without a moment's hesitation.

I'd caught a glimpse of Martina's puzzled expression as Lisette spoke. She tried to tamp down her confusion, but she couldn't erase it from her face. "I thought when they had their wills done—"

Lisette cut her off. "When they had their what done?"

Martina swallowed, her left eye twitching nervously. "Their wills."

Mr. Alcott melted into a corner. Smart man. I stayed still, listening. Watching. I'd learned that when you questioned people directly, they usually told you what you wanted to hear, but when you stood back and observed, they showed you things they didn't intend. Marisol clearly didn't want to be the bearer of bad news for Lisette; and Lisette, for her part, wagged one finger toward Martina, as if she were scolding a young child. "No, no, no. She would have told me if she changed her will. The house is supposed to come to the three of us. To me and Sergio and Ruben. It is not supposed to go to David," she said, her voice dripping with contempt when she uttered her stepfather's name.

I wondered where the animosity came from. Miguel thought highly of the man, and I thought he was a pretty good judge of character. So why didn't Lisette like him? That question flickered in and out of my mind, replaced by a better one: Why wouldn't Marisol have told her daughter about her new will, if she'd indeed changed it? A couple of scenarios came to mind: One, Lisette and her mother—and her other children, presumably—had been at odds, enough for Marisol to change her will, which could be a motive for murder; two, David had manipulated his wife by forcing a change in the will, which could be a motive for David if Marisol had started to have second thoughts and/or if he hadn't really loved his wife; and three, maybe Lisette was an Oscar-caliber actress and knew about the will, which still gave her a motive for murder.

I looked at Lisette with a new perspective. Could Lisette or David have had anything to do with Marisol's death? For that matter, Sergio and Ruben needed to be considered if they were no longer going to inherit their mother's house. That cottage by the beach was worth a mint. People had killed for a lot less.

"She could not have cut us out," Lisette said again. "No way."

Martina was wide-eyed. A deer in the headlights. I knew she was wishing she hadn't uttered a word.

"Martina," Lisette implored, her voice desperate. "Did she?"

Martina threw up her hands helplessly. "They talked about it, and I thought they did because of your fath—" She stopped. Regrouped. "I do not know for certain." Her Spanish accent was usually hardly detectable. She, like Olaya and Consuelo, didn't use many contractions, and once in a while, their sentence structure followed the Spanish language rules instead of English. But, like her sisters, stress pushed the English to the back, the Spanish rising like yeast proofing. "I am sorry, *mija*. I do not know more."

"You were going to say she did it because of my father," Lisette said. "What does he have to do with anything?" A flurry of emotions crossed her face: anger, hurt, disappointment, puzzlement. She cupped her hand over her mouth and closed her eyes, drawing in several deep breaths.

I watched her, still questioning the veracity of her feelings and reaction to Martina's bombshell. I hated the idea that Marisol's own children or husband could have had something to do with her death, but Emmaline's voice sounded in my head. *Motive. Follow the motive.*

Olaya, Martina, and I stood outside the funeral home and watched Lisette drive away. "Do you think she will be all right?" Martina asked.

There wasn't an easy answer to that. If she was guilty of killing her mother and I was able to prove it, then, no, she wouldn't be all right. If her grief and distress were real, then who knew? People healed in their own time, and in their own way. I kept my thoughts to myself. Tossing around ideas in my head was one thing. Saying them aloud was another. I wasn't ready to go there.

"The shock of her mother dying followed by the news she just got . . ." Olaya stroked her chin thoughtfully. "It is a lot to take in. She needs time."

"I talked with David a while ago," I said. "He's kind of a mess."

"¿*Que?*"

"He's drinking."

"Too much pain," Martina said. She turned to me, her voice quivering. "Ivy, is it true what the news is saying? Mari was killed?"

I repeated the story I'd already told Olaya, ending with the fact that Marisol's recovered body didn't have the characteristics of a drowning, and the ME's report on cause of death.

Martina grew pale. She blinked heavily, as if she were trying to erase the image of what I'd described. "But why?" she asked, more to herself than to either of us specifically. "Who would want to kill her?"

Instinctively, I looked over my shoulder in the direction Lisette had just driven off in. When I turned back, I took the opportunity to probe Martina a little bit. "You were Marisol's running partner?"

"For, mmm, two or three years now, yes. I run to be able to eat Olaya's bread," she said with a small smile, "but Mari, she liked to compete. There was something inside of her. What is that expression? Like a dog with a bone? She set her mind to something and she never let go."

Just then, the door to the funeral home opened and a woman emerged. She wore jeans and a long sleeve T-shirt. Her short, dyed red hair was brassy and harsh against her pale skin. She looked to be in her fifties, but the angled cut of her hair and the dark makeup around her eyes told me that she was fighting against the idea of growing older. She strode down the walkway, holding something to her lips and puffing, intercepting us a moment later. "Afternoon. How are you ladies doing?" she said, taking another puff and smiling in that subdued way Mr. Alcott had.

Olaya and Martina nodded their greeting. I bounced an "Afternoon" back to her. "Do you work here?" I asked, realizing she held a vape pen.

She held it to her mouth again and took a drag as she nodded. "Suzanne Alcott," she said, extending her hand.

Ah, the sister Benjamin Alcott had mentioned.

"We know you have a choice in Santa Sofia," she continued, "so we appreciate your business. You're with the Ruiz party, is that right?"

Her words were almost verbatim what her brother had said to Marisol's children. There had to be a playbook of standard phrases to use with the bereaved.

Olaya spoke up. "We are helping to cater the memorial service."

"Oh, I'm sorry. I thought you were with the family."

"We are," I said. "Olaya owns Yeast of Eden. She and Baptista's Cantina and Grill are catering the food. But we were all close friends of Marisol's, too."

Suzanne Alcott nodded. "Death is so hard to cope with, especially when someone was so full of life. When you add in foul play, well . . . It's hard to make sense of any of it."

"How do you know there was foul play?" I asked. I didn't think the circumstances of Marisol's death were public knowledge yet and I wondered how much Emmaline and her people shared in a situation like this.

She took another unhurried pull from her vape pen before responding. "We work with the local authorities on the timeline so we can prepare the deceased for the service and work with the family so they understand what's happening. I spoke with someone from the sheriff's office this morning who shared the preliminary findings. Poor woman. It can be so difficult to wrap your head around the idea that someone who was so alive, who you just spoke to, is now gone."

She'd put into words precisely what we all felt. "Did you just speak to her?" I asked.

"Pretty regularly since her father passed. She came to sit in the memorial garden to mourn him. She felt connected to him there."

I remembered the urn David had shown us. "But didn't she have his ashes?"

Suzanne Alcott took a puff of her vape pen, giving a long blink. "I believe so," she said, "but that's not really the point. People process through their grief in different ways. They bring blankets to a gravesite, and lie down alongside the deceased; they sprinkle ashes in a favorite location; they cry; or they may not shed a single tear; they pray in church to feel closer to their lost loved one. Marisol seemed to find solace in the memorial garden."

"I worried if she would ever get over losing her father," Martina confirmed. "She did all of those things. She cried, then she didn't cry anymore. She was angry, then she wasn't. I stopped her from throwing her father's urn in the garbage can. She said none of it meant anything, but then she went to church to pray even though she was not religious."

Suzanne Alcott held her hand up as if her take on the deceased had just been validated by Martina. "We see it all here."

"That must be hard," I said. I couldn't fathom the idea of being surrounded by death every single day.

She took another drag of her liquid nicotine. "I imagine it's kind of like being a homicide detective or a medical examiner. You learn to turn if off at the end of the day. If you don't, it can be like a poison."

I'd stick with my baking and photography, thank you very much. "And the grieving families. Seeing all that sadness has to be hard, too."

"Oh, yeah, absolutely," she said, "but you'd be surprised. One thing I've learned over the years in this business is that everyone has secrets. The things that come out after a person dies!"

"What kind of secrets?" I asked, immediately intrigued, although I could certainly imagine the types of things people would work hard in life to keep hidden.

Suzanne glanced back at the front door of the funeral home as if to make sure she wasn't overheard. Turning back to us, she puffed on her smoking device, then said, "Affairs. Debt. Secret children. Second families. Hidden money. You name it." Suzanne shook her head at the memories.

Martina drew back, as if she'd been personally affronted. "Secret money. Second families. Marisol did not have secrets like these," she said indignantly. "She was a good person."

Suzanne Alcott finished smoking her pressurized nicotine and tucked the vape device into her coat pocket. "You can be a good person and still have secrets," she said, "and I'm not saying that Marisol had any. All I'm saying is that a lot of people have something to hide."

I tended to agree with the woman, but Martina vehemently did not. "Marisol was killed. There is a violent murderer out there and he needs to be stopped. Whatever secrets Mari had or did not have were not things to be killed over."

"There is nothing a person should be killed over," I said, although I also knew that *shouldn't* didn't really mean a thing. The fact was, people *were* killed over ridiculously stupid things all the time. I'd seen that firsthand. Whatever had happened to Marisol had certainly not been warranted, but it had happened nonetheless.

Suzanne Alcott offered her condolences, excused herself, and disappeared back inside, leaving Olaya, Martina, and me to wonder about Marisol's secrets.

Chapter 9

Olaya Solis was a savant when it came to bread-making. I'd learned everything I knew from her, and I didn't even begin to touch the depth of her knowledge. She could tell you anything you wanted to know about the myriad flours used in baking, including the specialty flours used in gluten-free baking; she understood the challenges that came with high altitude baking versus baking at sea level; long rise versus short rise was something she had strong opinions on; but one of the things that truly set her apart was her gift for understanding people and how her bread affected them. Folks came from far and away because of the mystique of Olaya and her bread. "It's magical," people said. "It can heal you," others claimed.

If you were experiencing heartache, the fig and almond loaf was a go-to selection. Feeling anxious? Her rosemary brioche was instantly

calming. Whatever ailed you, Olaya had something that could make it better. Her breads were
bewitching. Her breads were gifts that she shared
with the community, but no one understood
how it worked. They just knew that anything from
Yeast of Eden put a skip in their step, or lessened
their pain, or filled them with a warm glow from
the inside out.

When I stepped into the kitchen at Yeast of
Eden that afternoon and saw Olaya in a half
apron, hand-kneading a round of dough, I knew
she was up to something specific. The day's baking was long finished, and the bread shop was
closed. She wasn't holding any classes tonight,
and aside from the funeral, she didn't have any
immediate special orders or events.

There was something about the way she looked
right now—peaceful, yet focused—that made
me dig my cell phone from my purse, swipe to
the camera, and take a few pictures of her. I
stood back, taking a full body shot from the side,
then came closer and zeroed in on the flour dust-
ing the stainless-steel countertop and the strength
of her hands as they kneaded the dough.

I snapped another picture as she looked up at
me, capturing the mischievous look in her gold-
flecked eyes. "What are the pictures for?" she
asked.

"For myself," I said. I pointed to the dough.
"Who is that for?"

"The widower," she answered. "To ease his
pain."

I looked more closely at the dough, wondering if I could guess the type of bread she was

making. I recognized the container that held her sourdough starter, the stone-ground whole-grain wheat flour she'd chosen, and saw the canister of wheat malt. Jars of cinnamon and cardamom were pushed to the back of the counter-top, as well as salt and olive oil. I breathed in, detecting a faint floral scent. "Wheat bread, but what's that?" I asked, pointing to the jar of an orangey-brown substance I didn't recognize.

"Ah, that is rosehip powder."

I knew that rose petals were edible, and that hips were the fruits or seed pods found at the base of the petals, but that was the extent of my knowledge. I'd certainly never cooked with either the berries or the powder, let alone put them in bread. "Why rose hips?"

She formed the dough into a round, patted it down with her fingertips until she had a rectangle, then folded it in in thirds, gently laying it in a loaf pan she had at the ready. "The rugosa rose produces the best rose hips," she said. "High in vitamin C and flavorful like their cousin the crab apple. Tart. But the powder, ah, the powder has healing elements. It cannot make sadness disappear, of course, *pero* it can help to make it more bearable. For David, I hope it will help him to be strong."

There was a knock at the back door as the door itself opened. Penelope Branford strode into the bread shop's kitchen, her cane swinging alongside her. She was a fan of the velour sweat suit; she owned one in every color of the rainbow, and every color in between. Today, she had on a vibrant teal set, pristine white leather sneakers, and a matching teal and white bandana as a headband that pulled the tight snowy curls away from her forehead. Her sprightly step, the pink of her cheeks, and her colorful outfit made her look not a day over seventy. I wanted to be her in my old age.

After the bread shop, I'd planned to head straight home to get Agatha, then head across the street to Mrs. Branford's house. Apparently she hadn't wanted to wait for me to come to her, so like Muhammad and the mountain in the Turkish proverb, she'd come to me. "I knew I'd find you here, Ivy Culpepper," she said.

Mrs. Branford had been an English teacher for the better part of her life. She used my first and last name to address me now, as I imagined she had during her decades in the classroom when she had been displeased with a student. Although I didn't know what I'd done to vex her.

Instead of getting rankled, I smiled—because Mrs. Branford always made me smile—and bent to kiss her on the cheek. "I was on my way home, but stopped when I saw the lights on in here," I said.

"Well, I'm sure sweet Agatha is in desperate need of a walk," she said, mirth lacing her voice. She loved my little pug nearly as much as I did. "Since I'm here, however, you can fill me in."

Olaya and I stole a glance at one another. I knew Mrs. Branford was talking about Marisol Ruiz, although I didn't know how she knew I was involved in any way, shape, or form. At the same time, I wasn't surprised. She had her proverbial ear to the ground.

I told her everything I knew so far about Marisol, not expecting her to have any specific insight, but she surprised me. "I taught school in Santa Sofia for more decades than you've been alive," she said. "Three generations of families in some cases have passed through my classroom. I taught Marisol and her children, you know, although she was Betancourt back then. I also taught Johnny Morales. They were high school sweethearts, those two. I never did think they'd get married, but they did. Invited me to the wedding, in fact. Their divorce was disappointing, to say the least. I thought they'd make it. Amicable, for the kids, which is unusual, but heartbreaking just the same. There are too many divorces," she said. "Far too many divorces."

Mrs. Branford wasn't judging me, but her words made me think of the shambles that had been my marriage. It had nearly crushed me. After my high school love affair with Miguel had ended, I'd run far away from Santa Sofia, ending in Austin, Texas. Luke Holden, who I'd always described as a swashbuckling cowboy, had thrown a lasso and caught me when I'd been at my most vulnerable. I met his Louisiana family, spent long weekends with him in the Texas Hill Country, and had buried my heartbreak over Miguel. For all his faults, he'd helped me move on. Which didn't mean I should have married him, but I had. In the Rhinestone Chapel in Nashville, no less, married by an Elvis look-alike.

My family hadn't been there. I hadn't had the white dress, the walk down the aisle on my dad's arm, the something blue, along with words of wisdom from my mom. I'd sacrificed those things in order to get over the love of my life.

I'd made a choice. A bad choice, as it turned out, which I'd discovered after spending countless hours sleuthing, confirming what I had already known: My husband was a lying cheat. In retrospect, I realized that I'd naïvely chosen to ignore the clues. I'd wanted so much for the marriage to be real. For it to last. I hadn't wanted to be a statistic, or a woman who'd fallen for the wrong sort of man. But in the end, I couldn't deny the truth of the matter: Luke Holden had not been the man I'd thought he was.

So I, like Marisol and so many others, had ended up divorced. It certainly had not been in my life plan, but ending my marriage had given me a chance for a new beginning—or a reboot of an old one—with Miguel Baptista. Mrs. Branford had said he was my soul mate, and Olaya had had no doubt that Miguel and I would end up together again. I, however, hadn't been so sure. We'd had baggage in the form of a hugely overblown misunderstanding, but turns out that those two women—the women I valued most of all in the world—had been right. Miguel and I did belong together and we were figuring that out. He'd told me that he was "all in," and I believed him. I'd been fortunate enough to find love again, just like Marisol had with David.

"Penelope, how you do love the *chisme*," Olaya said with a tsk, but then she urged Mrs. Branford on. "I believe it is you who need to, how did you say, fill us in? You tell us what you know about Marisol and Johnny."

Mrs. Branford looked around, spotted a stool in front of the baking station next to Olaya, and scooted over to it. She perched, propping her cane on the floor in front of her, looking like she might break into a rendition of "All That Jazz." She was only missing the top hat. Well, and a black halter burlesque outfit with black stockings and garters, à la Liza Minnelli, but still.

I found my own stool opposite Mrs. Branford while Olaya set aside the loaf pan with the rose-hip wheat bread and started to clean the area.

"Can you listen and work at the same time?" Mrs. Branford asked. Her expression was innocent, but there was a mocking undercurrent to the question. She and Olaya had forged an unlikely friendship after years of steadfastly avoiding one another. They were still navigating the shift in their relationship and it wasn't always smooth sailing.

Olaya flashed an indulgent smile. "I know that must be challenging for you, Penelope, but remember, you do have a few years on me. You tell your story. I will manage just fine, *gracias*."

Mrs. Branford ran her gnarled fingers along the edge of her bandana, tucking a stray silver curl back under the teal fabric. "To teenagers, a tragic Romeo and Juliet or Maria and Tony love story fraught with discord and forbidden love is what it is all about. Something stable and normal is, quite sadly, not exciting enough to so many. But Marisol and Johnny, they were different, as I recall. They genuinely liked each other. Their families approved. They were friends before they were anything else. It happened quite naturally for them."

"Your memory of them, it is quite strong. How many years ago was this?" Olaya asked, one eyebrow raised skeptically.

Mrs. Branford tapped her temple with the pad of her index finger. "My mind is a steel trap."

I did a little mental math. If Marisol was in her fifties and Mrs. Branford taught her when she was sixteen or seventeen, that had been up to forty years ago, back when Mrs. Branford herself would have been in her forties. Her mind really did have to be a steel trap for her to remember the ins and outs of two students' relationship that long ago.

"So you're saying they were really in love?" I asked.

"As much as two teenagers can be," she said. "And then their relationship developed into something more mature. More adult. And they married and had three very smart, very lovely children."

By this time, Olaya had finished wiping down the stainless steel countertop where she'd been kneading bread. She turned her full attention to Mrs. Branford. "What went wrong?"

"Now that, I'm afraid, I was not privy to. Of course I ran into Marisol once in a while at Baptista's, but the failure of one's marriage isn't typical lighthearted conversation during one's meal. And although I do sometimes see Johnny, as well, he isn't one to make small talk."

I'd wondered about Marisol's ex-husband. There was always the possibility of a motive there. And Martina had started to say something about the change in the will being about Lisette's father. From what I'd gathered, they'd been divorced a good many years, but had the dissolution of their union been mutual, or could he harbor disgruntled feelings about it? About her? About her second marriage to David? About the house? "Where do you see Johnny?" I asked.

"He's a loan officer at my bank. Of course, I don't have much occasion to speak with him, given that I have no need to borrow money. Still, he's of the generation that values the elderly and he is always quick to show respect in that way, even if he's reserved. He asks about my health, as so many are wont to do when speaking to someone as old as I am. I ask after his children. That is about the extent of it."

She fell silent just long enough for me to meet her gaze. "Did you say you were thinking of fixing up your backyard?" she asked randomly.

I had, but not with any real intent, but I nodded. "You need money for that."

She tilted her head. "Money in the form of a loan, perhaps?"

"I don't want it that badly," I said slowly, my mind trying to catch up with whatever she was suggesting.

"You could come to my bank."

"I could," I agreed, finally catching her drift. "And I could speak to Johnny Morales about it—"

"Among other things—" she suggested.

"Like his ex-wife's death," I finished.

Olaya looked from Mrs. Branford to me, her brows tugged together like two thin caterpillars crawling toward one another. "You are changing your backyard?"

"No, no," I said, hiding a smile. Something had been lost in translation during my quick exchange with Mrs. Branford. "I mean, maybe, but no. I just want to talk to Marisol's ex-husband to see, mmm, you know, if he might have any ideas on Marisol's death."

Olaya's face cleared of confusion. "Ah, *entiendo*. A loan is simply an excuse to talk to him."

"Exactly," I said. "Because maybe he knows something."

Mrs. Branford stood, using her cane to steady herself. I was never sure if she really needed the walking stick or not. Half the time she had it with her, she swung it around more like a prop. But then there were times, like now, that made me doubt my skepticism. "If we leave now," she said, "we will just make it before closing."

Chapter 10

Mrs. Branford and I made it to the Golden State Credit Union thirty minutes before closing. We sat side by side in the lobby of the credit union she'd been a member of throughout her teaching career. The building was smaller than some of the national bank branches. It was more utilitarian than luxe, with countertops of neutral quartz, equally neutral walls, and dark wood accents. A pneumatic tube system was prominent behind the main counter, where one teller manned the three drive-up stations. I watched as car after car after car drove into the bay. The drivers called the cylindrical carrier to them, filled it with deposit slips, and sent it back through the tube line to the bank. The teller's voice was loud in the quiet bank. "I'll have this deposited for you right away," or "Can I help you with anything else?" echoed though the building, as well as through the intercom system that traveled to the car station and customer he was actually speaking with.

I'd put my name on the sign-in sheet to speak to a loan officer. From what I could tell, only one was on duty at the moment. Mrs. Branford confirmed that the man was, indeed, Johnny Morales. He worked intently with the customer seated across the desk from him, taking notes, typing on his keyboard while looking at his monitor, and relaying information back to the customer.

Mrs. Branford had pulled out her smartphone and opened a card game app. "Bridge," she told me.

I came from a generation of Bunco players, but Mrs. Branford was of a different era. She had learned, like so many of her contemporaries, to play the complicated card game. It required concentration, understanding of the vocabulary, and skill in betting and playing the cards. "It is not a game of chance," she told me once when I'd watched her play.

"Do you play in a bridge group?" I asked. I'd met her little posse of friends, but she'd never mentioned playing cards with anyone.

"Jimmy and I used to play duplicate bridge in a group," she said. "Now I just play on this"—she held up her phone—"to keep my brain young, you know."

It certainly did the trick. Mrs. Branford was one clever woman, and age hadn't slowed her down any.

The man who'd been sitting with Johnny Morales stood. They shook hands, and he left. Johnny straightened up the papers on his desk before coming to the waiting area, checking the list, and calling my name. He was all business from his button-down shirt and tie to his serious demeanor. I wondered if he'd be difficult to talk to, or if he'd open up about anything other than loans.

As I stood, holding on to Mrs. Branford's elbow to help her rise more easily, recognition dawned on Johnny's face. "Mrs. Branford," he said with a subdued smile. "Good to see you."

"You too, Johnny. You too." She wasn't much of a hugger, but she handed her cane off to me, stepped closer, and wrapped him up in a warm embrace. It was what they both needed, I realized. Mrs. Branford had been one of those extraordinary teachers who realized that kids learned, not because they were fascinated with the curriculum, but because they felt safe and loved and often because they'd made a real connection with a teacher who cared. More than anything, Mrs. Branford had worked at building those relationships with her students. It didn't matter how many years ago she'd taught a student, that relationship would always remain.

He stood back, masked the glint of emotion that had shown briefly on his face, and pointed his finger back and forth between us. "You're together?"

"That's right. This is Ivy Culpepper," Mrs. Branford said with a single nod in my direction.

"Okay. Great. This way." He led us to his open office space, holding out one of the chairs for her while she sat. It was only after Mrs. Branford was settled that he looked at me, held out his hand, and formally introduced himself. "Johnny Morales, Ms. Culpepper. Nice to meet you."

"You too." I sat in the other free chair while he took his place back behind his desk. The collar of his shirt bunched slightly at his neck when he clasped his hands in front of him. The stark white made his olive skin take on a darker hue, and given it was getting on toward the end of the day, a five o'clock shadow had started to form along the sides of his face and chin. Bits of gray intermixed with the darker color of his hair gave him a weathered and wiser look than he might have had otherwise.

"What can I do for you?" he asked. Even after the hug he and Mrs. Branford had shared, I could see that he was a no-nonsense kind of man. For an instant he'd let his feelings rise to the surface, but just as quickly, he pushed them back down to a place where he could manage them.

"I'm thinking about doing some work around my house," I said. I didn't want to mislead him, so I quickly added, "But this is very preliminary. I'm not sure if I need to borrow to do it, or even if it's financially feasible. I just bought the house recently, so taking on another loan may not be the smartest thing to do."

He nodded, his eyes pinching slightly at the outer edges as he thought. "I can't say anything for sure until we look at your specific situation, but overextending yourself is generally not a good idea. You have steady income, I assume?"

"Yeesss," I said with a tinge of hesitation, but I didn't elaborate. My wage from Yeast of Eden was nominal. I worked at the bread shop mostly because I wanted to, not for the money. Photography was where I drew most of my income, although it was still slow going at the moment. I earned steadily as a contributor to a stock photography website, my assets bringing in a decent monthly amount. My freelance work was irregular, at best, but it would be growing.

I'd put nearly my entire savings into the house, and I dipped into what was left now and then to make ends meet. The bottom line was that Johnny Morales was right: I didn't want to overextend myself.

I shared a little bit about what I'd like to do to the house—add to the backyard landscape, remodel the master bathroom, and upgrade some of the other bathroom fixtures. It wasn't a lot, but it was enough that I had to carefully consider my options.

He didn't even need to think before responding to me. "You haven't been there very long. I suggest you live there for a while before deciding on changes. It takes a while to adjust to a new house and to appreciate things the way they are. Give yourself time to do that before you start making changes. That's my advice. Then, if you decide to make some changes, a second against your principal through the credit union is definitely an option." He darted a quick glance around the credit union before continuing, more quietly. "There are other ways to go about it, too. When you're ready, if that's what you decide, we can talk the different options."

I had no idea what he meant, so I just nodded and smiled. "Mrs. Branford said you'd be able to give me sound advice. I appreciate that, Mr. Morales."

"Ivy is dating Miguel, Laura's brother," Mrs. Branford said, changing the subject.

He nodded, but his face was expressionless. Was he always this serious, or were his feelings about his ex-wife's death leaving him numb? "Laura's a good girl. A good mother. She makes my son very happy. Can't ask for more than that from a daughter-in-law."

"She seems like she is," I said. Laura hadn't always been my fan, nor I hers, but we'd hashed out our differences recently and were at a good place. I'd seen her with her children. Being a mom was a role she seemed made for. "I knew Marisol," I said, transitioning the conversation to the reason we'd come to talk to Johnny in the first place. I didn't know what their relationship had been like, but they'd shared three children so I went with a safe sentiment. "I used to go into Baptista's all the time as a kid. She meant a lot to Miguel. I'm so sorry for your loss."

The tendons of Johnny's neck tightened like vertical ropes bulging from under his skin and he slowly closed his eyes. "I—we're all having a hard time wrapping our brains around what happened. I can't—We just—It doesn't seem possible."

The very idea of death was impossible to comprehend at times. One minute, a person is alive and well and you're talking to them. And then they're simply gone. It was what Suzanne Alcott had said to us, and she was right. I took his bafflement as an opening. "Do you have a theory, Mr. Morales?"

He stared blankly at me. "A theory?"

"As to who could have killed Marisol? Or why?"

He looked over our shoulders to the open space of the credit union. The place was practically deserted by this point. No one paid us any heed. "So many people get divorced and hate each other," he said. "Me and Mari, we decided we weren't going to be like that. We had kids together. We loved each other. We spent more than half of our lives together."

"High school sweethearts," Mrs. Branford commented.

"She was the one. Our marriage didn't work out, but we still cared about each other."

Mrs. Branford shifted in her chair, propping her cane in front of her, clasping the top with both hands. "I thought you two would make it," she said.

He didn't say anything for a minute, then spoke sadly. "So did I."

I could hear the regret in his voice and it made me wonder where things went astray. I hesitated, not sure how much to push, but I wouldn't find out anything that could help get to the truth if I didn't pry. "Do you mind . . . can

I ask what happened between the two of you? It sounds like you still loved her."

His right hand found his left and, although he wasn't wearing a wedding ring, he rubbed his ring finger. A wedding ring was a touchstone for a lot of people. For Johnny, it was an old habit. "I never stopped loving her. It was stupid. I met some—I just—" He hung his head. "I made a mistake."

I read between the lines. A mistake in marriage, as I knew from my own experience, usually meant unfaithfulness. Sometimes it was the wife who strayed, and that happened more and more frequently, but men still took the top spot with infidelity. From what Johnny said, I took it to mean that he'd let someone else in.

That was a betrayal I'd never been able to forgive, and based on their divorce, it looked like Marisol hadn't been able to, either.

I felt bad for the guy; he was obviously remorseful. But on the other hand, he'd made a choice, albeit a bad one, and he'd paid the price for it. I didn't have words of sympathy for him about that. Mrs. Branford, though, came to the rescue. "Johnny, these things happen more than they should, but what's done is done. No good is going to come from continued guilt. You and Marisol were amicable, did the best you could for your kids, and that, in and of itself, is admirable."

I thought about my own situation. I didn't blame myself for my ex-husband's infidelity. I'd done the best I could in my marriage. The fact

that he'd strayed had been his failing, not mine.
I also didn't hate him, although my friends back
in Texas, as well as Emmaline and Billy, couldn't
understand that. "How can you not want to go
postal on him?" Em had asked when I told her.

I'd felt the anger and frustration and betrayal,
but I also knew that hanging on to those feelings
wouldn't change what had happened, wouldn't
change Luke, and I'd be the one suffering from
my own emotions. I, like Marisol, had moved on.
Marisol had married David, and they'd seemed
happy. Johnny, on the other hand, still seemed to
be beating himself up over what had happened
years ago.

As Mrs. Branford continued to ease Johnny's
mind, I looked at the situation through a different lens. What if Johnny wasn't as adjusted to
the divorce itself as he projected? Maybe the fact
that Marisol hadn't been able to get over his
cheating and had divorced him over it had an-
gered him. Or maybe the fact that she'd moved
on with David had pushed him over the edge.
People who were guilty often placed that culpa-
bility onto someone else. What if he blamed
Marisol for whatever had made him stray, enough
that when they divorced, he still harbored that
resentment and blame?

They'd known each other for so long that he
certainly had to know her habits. He could have
followed her to the beach, killed her, and then
dumped her body in the sea. I came back to the
question I'd asked Johnny earlier. "Mr. Morales,
do you have any ideas about who could have
killed your ex-wife?"

He rested his forearms on the desk, looking at us intently. "I'll tell you what I think."

Mrs. Branford and I both leaned forward. This man probably knew Marisol better than anyone, so his suspicions were well worth listening to.

"David."

My mind quickly processed David as a murder suspect. He and Marisol had been married for several years, but what if things in their marriage weren't all that great? No one knew what went on behind closed doors; their marriage could have been in a shambles for all anyone knew. Could Marisol have regretted leaving Johnny? Or could she have done to David what Johnny had done to her? David would have known her habits, too. Whatever the scenario, could David have been pushed to murder over it?

"You think David killed Marisol?" I asked.

He tapped one of his hands against the other. It seemed like a nervous action. Was he unsure about throwing David under the bus as a suspect? Was it a real belief, or was he trying to divert attention away from himself? "No question. I've never trusted that guy. He told Mari about—"

He stopped short, swallowing hard.

"Told Marisol . . . ?" I prompted.

"She turned to him after our divorce. I tried to make things right. I wanted to get back together with her, but by then it was too late."

I watched him, taking in his demeanor. He'd buried whatever misery and guilt he'd been feeling and now was squarely blaming David for the end of his relationship with Marisol. If David hadn't swooped in, Johnny thought he and Marisol might have mended things.

I didn't understand what he was saying, though. "If David was there for Marisol after . . . whatever happened between you two, why would he kill her?"

His chin quivered slightly and his nostrils flared as he breathed in. "She called me the other day. She wanted to get together to talk about something. I think things were going south for her and David."

"What did she tell you?"

His eyes turned glassy. "She didn't show. Now I know why."

"Wait." My head snapped up. "Are you saying she was going to meet you the day she died? That's why she didn't show—because she was dead?"

He drew his lips together and shrugged. "It's the only thing that makes sense. The timing's right. She left me a message to meet her."

My head felt fuzzy. "Where?"

He scrubbed his face with a trembling hand. "The pier."

I jumped up, feeling antsy. "Okay, wait. So you're saying that she wanted to meet you—on the day she died—at the pier?"

"That's what I'm saying. She said she needed to talk. That she didn't know what to do. We were best friends since the beginning of high school. Our divorce didn't change that. She needed to talk and I was there for her."

"But she didn't show, so you don't know what

it was about?" I asked, trying to clarify and understand his leap to David as a killer.

"Not for sure, but if it was about one of the kids, she would have told me over the phone. She couldn't have kept that from me. We were good together, she and I. And we were good parents."

"All right, let's say it wasn't about your kids, then," I said.

He agreed. "Which leaves David."

So many thoughts circled in my head: Did he tell this to the authorities? Did he still have the message from Marisol? If what he said was true, what did she need to talk about specifically? Were she and David having problems? Had he done something? Was the grief we'd witnessed all fake? Did she regret leaving Johnny?

I went with the question that rose to the top of the heap. "Do you still have the message?"

He nodded, pulling his phone from his jacket pocket. He swiped and tapped until the voicemail screen came up, tapped one final time, and then he laid it on the desk between us. Marisol's voice drifted to us from the little black device. *"Hey. Um, sorry to bother you. Something's happened and, um, I don't know what to do. I need to talk. Can you meet me at the pier tomorrow? Let me know."*

Hearing her voice was like seeing her ghost. It made it that much harder to comprehend the fact that she was gone. She didn't sound scared in the message, but she did sound worried. Or maybe agitated. "Johnny," I said, trying to control the urgency in my voice, because this felt like it was really important. "Have you shared this with the police?"

He put his phone off to the side of his desk. "Not yet."

Mrs. Branford nearly jumped out of her chair. "Johnny Morales, what are you thinking? This is important. The police need to hear that message!"

His gaze darted around the credit union before settling back on us. He lowered his voice. "What if they think—" He stopped. Lowered his voice. "What if they think I killed her?"

"Did you?" Mrs. Branford asked, quick as a whip.

Johnny reared back. "God, no! I told you, I loved her."

"Then you have to share the message with the police," I said, perching on the edge of the chair I'd vacated a minute ago. "It could help them."

He was motionless for a moment, and then, abruptly, he stood, his gaze darting over my shoulder. I heard the low thud of footsteps against the floor. A man's voice came from behind me. "Everything good here, Mr. Morales?"

Johnny came out from behind his desk. "Yes, sir. Everything's good. I was just showing these ladies out." He sent us a pointed look with a clear message. He wanted us to leave.

I held Mrs. Branford's elbow as she stood, and I tried to catch Johnny's eye, but he avoided my gaze. He ushered us to the main floor, skirting past the man who'd come to check on him. "Let me know what you decide about the loan," Johnny said, although from the way he just threw the words out there, it wasn't clear if he was talking to me, Mrs. Branford, or the credit union manager.

"I will," I answered, but a loan was the last thing on my mind. The second I got outside, I was calling Emmaline to tell her about the message from Marisol.

Chapter 11

Maple Street, one of just a few blocks in the historic district of Santa Sofia, was tree-lined and canopied, giving it a fairy-tale quality. Modern amenities and vehicles notwithstanding, driving down Maple felt like a gateway to a different time. Each home was unique, from the ladylike Queen Anne Victorian to the Craftsman-style to the old farmhouse on the corner, they each had character and a distinctive identity.

I still had to pinch myself sometimes when I drove up to my quaint redbrick Tudor. It had a traditional half-timber exterior, old brick, a steep gable, and the roofline had a high-pitched slope. The deep red wavy edge of the siding at the gable peaks made it feel like a gingerbread house, and the enormous trees shading it softened the harder edges.

Colorful flowerbeds lined the cobbled walkway leading to the arched front door. I slowed as I passed the house, noticing a car parked right in front. I wasn't expecting anyone and it wasn't a vehicle I recognized. I craned my neck before turning into the driveway, but the car was empty. It was only after I parked in the garage and doubled back to the front yard that I realized someone was leaning against the brick archway near the door.

I stopped short, registering the broad shoulders. The artfully spiked dirty-blond hair. The cowboy boots that were more fashion than function. What the hell? Had his ears been burning? "Luke?"

My ex-husband smiled, his eyes genuinely lighting up when he saw me. He pushed himself off the wall and strode toward me, arms outstretched. "God, you're a sight for sore eyes," he said, wrapping me up in a hug.

My body went stiff, his very presence, let alone his touch, like a shock to my system. "Um, yeah, you too," I managed. Although Luke Holden had lied and cheated and had not been a good husband, I'd known we weren't meant to be together and I didn't harbor ill-will toward him. He didn't often leave Texas, and when he did, it was usually to go home to Louisiana. The California coast was certainly not part of his stomping grounds. "What are you doing here?"

Instead of answering my question, he asked one of his own. "How's Aggie?"

Luke was the only person who called Agatha Aggie. Given that we'd both gone to the University of Texas in Austin, and the A&M Aggies were rivals, it always surprised me that he'd glommed on to that as a nickname, but he had, and even after years apart, it was still how he knew her. "She's great. She loves it here," I said as I slipped past him and unlocked the front door.

I dropped my keys and purse on the vintage sideboard next to a Galileo thermometer. Luke let his fingers trail over the glass. "Nice," he said.

It was. It had been handblown in a local glass shop on the pier and was a housewarming gift from Miguel. I moved into the long living area, heading toward Agatha's crate. She greeted me with three quick barks, then just looked up at me expectantly, her little tail curled up happily.

I opened the crate's door and out she popped, instantly spinning in joyful circles at my feet. She scrabbled toward the French doors, her paws struggling to make purchase against the hardwood floor, ready to be released to the backyard, but she stopped short when she heard footsteps followed by Luke's voice. "Aggie!"

She turned, saw him, and immediately backed up, spun in a new circle, threw her black and tan head back, and yelped ferociously.

Luke laughed, crouching down in front of her. "Same old Aggie," he said, scratching her head.

"She's so much better now," I said. She'd been the last dog surrendered by a backyard breeder and had been petrified of people when I'd first gotten her. That first year had been rough. It had taken a lot of patience and love, but she'd finally come around. After she'd accepted me, she'd become my little shadow.

Agatha plopped her backside down, her lip caught on her teeth in a little Elvis grimace, and let Luke scratch her head. She'd only ever tolerated him, which had worked out just fine given that she'd come with me after the divorce.

I opened the French door and called to her. "Come on, outside, Agatha." She hopped up, spun in another circle, and trotted outside.

Luke had always been one to operate at his own pace and under his own terms. I could ask him why he was here, but he wouldn't tell me until he was ready. So instead I offered him something to drink.

"I'll take a beer," he said, following me into the rustic kitchen.

My shoulders rose in a shrug. I'd been thinking iced tea or water. "Sorry, no beer."

He spotted a piece of furniture that I'd turned into a makeshift liquor cabinet. It was from Mexico, was made from reclaimed unfinished wood, and had slats on the lower cupboards with blue and red and white paint. "Wine," he said, striding over to it and taking a bottle and two stemless wineglasses from behind the glass doors on top.

I sighed, torn between the idea of having a glass of wine with my former husband, which was not how I wanted to spend the early evening, and curiosity as to why, exactly, he was here.

"Your hair's longer."

I absently touched my ginger curls. They'd grown from shoulder length when I'd seen him last to midway down my back. What could I say? "Yeah."

"You look good," he said appreciatively. "California seems to suit you."

I'd pulled the front strands of my hair back and clipped them at the back of my head, allowing my silver hoop earrings to be more visible. With my peasant blouse and jeans, I looked a bit more free-spirit than I had when I'd been with Luke. I felt more like me. "It does."

He found a corkscrew in the cabinet and opened the bottle. "Aggie seems to like it, too."

I leaned back against the island, giving him time to work up to his reason for being here. "She does. She loves my dad, too."

Luke splashed wine into one of the glasses, swirled it, sniffed it, then took a sip. "How is your dad?" he asked after he filled the glasses and handed one to me.

I took a sip of the Malbec he'd chosen, before answering. "He's doing pretty well. Keeping busy with work."

"And your brother?"

I sighed. Next we'd be talking about his family. "Yeah, Billy's good, too."

"Good. Glad to hear it," Luke said.

We continued with small talk for another few minutes, but just as I was about to ask him what he was doing here, the doorbell rang. "You get that," he said. "I'll wait here."

I rubbed my eyes as I left him to answer the door. What in the world did Luke Holden want? I made it partway down the hall, stopping short at the sight of Mrs. Branford already standing in the entryway. I'd given her a key for emergencies. Apparently a strange car parked out front qualified in her book. "I just saw you at the credit union and you didn't mention company, so, of course, I had to be sure you were quite all right."

"It's my ex-husband," I whispered as we walked back into the kitchen, my eyebrows raised to communicate my surprise at his presence.

Our two glasses of wine sat on the counter next to the open bottle of red, but Luke was nowhere to be seen. Mrs. Branford marched around the center island before turning to face me, arms spread, hands gripping the butcher block. "Well, where is he?"

That was a very good question. "I don't know." He hadn't passed us in the hallway, so he hadn't gone out the front door. Which left the entire rest of the house, or the backyard. I peered through the window, but other than Agatha, who lay casually on a strip of sunlit grass, the yard was unoccupied.

"He's gone exploring," Mrs. Branford said knowingly.

"Or just to the bathroom," I said, but I suspected she was more on the money than I was. "I'll be right back," I told her, and then given the fact that he'd seen the living room when he'd arrived, I headed left out of the kitchen and down the back hallway toward the bedrooms.

"Luke?" I called. "Where are you?"

Silence.

"Luke?" I checked the two small bedrooms as

I passed. My office was sparse, with only a desk with my desktop computer, and an external hard drive that I used to store my photographs. I'd had a few of my photos blown up and framed so I could hang them in the house, but it was something I hadn't gotten to yet and they leaned against the wall.

The other room was for guests, complete with a queen-size bed, a night stand, and a lamp. Luke was not there.

Next was the bathroom. The door was wide open and vacant.

I called his name again, and this time I got a response. "In here," he said, his voice coming from the last room at the end of the hall. The master bedroom. I'd shared a room with Luke for far too many years, but when it was over, it was over, and I didn't relish the idea of him in my bedroom—in any capacity—again.

I stopped in the doorway, ready to grab him by the scruff of his neck and drag him back to the kitchen, but then I saw him sitting on the side of my bed, his back hunched, his head in his hands, and I couldn't berate him for invading my private space. Instead, I went into the room and sat next to him, placing my hand on his back in a comforting gesture. "Is everything okay?"

He didn't say anything for a few seconds. His shoulders and back lifted, then fell as he breathed heavily. "Luke? Are you okay?" I asked again.

"I messed us up, Ivy," he finally said, his gaze directed to the floor. "We were good together, and I messed it up."

I hadn't even spoken to Luke in years, so I couldn't fathom where this was coming from. Before I could say as much, he looked up at me. "I think it was a mistake, us splitting up."

I stared at him, trying not to look as flabbergasted as I felt. I shook my head. "It wasn't a mistake."

"What if we were meant to be together—you know, soul mates—and we blew it?"

"Luke, we weren't soul mates," I said slowly, taking my hand from his back and scooting away from him to create more space between us. I could start ticking off all the reasons it wasn't a mistake that we split up, but I didn't. Instead, I simply asked, "Do you really want to rehash all of this?"

He turned his body to face me, taking one of my hands in his. "I want you back, Ivy. I'm just—things aren't—I miss you," he finally said.

Mrs. Branford's voice from the kitchen reminded me that she was here. She must be talking to Agatha. Looking for a treat to feed her, no doubt.

"Luke, I don't know what's going on, but us splitting up was not a mistake. Remember Heather?"

Heather was the woman Luke had cheated on me with. I'd sleuthed, discovering a contact on his computer under the name Mike, and that, as they say, was all she wrote. Like Marisol Ruiz, I was not the type of woman to give a cheating husband a second chance.

"She's a psycho," he said. "Like seriously Glenn Close crazy. If I had a rabbit, I'd be scared for it."

Now we were getting to the nitty-gritty. Luke and Heather had gotten married after my divorce from him was final. As far as I'd known, they'd turned their affair into something that had lasted. But now, apparently, things had gone off the rails "Did you cheat on her?" I asked, resisting adding the word *too* at the end of the question.

"I guess it depends on how you define cheating." He leaned toward me, still holding my hand. "I miss *you*, Ivy. I still love *you*."

Oh God, I thought as I registered a sound—the *thump thump thump* of Mrs. Branford's cane—from the hallway. It drew my attention and I turned, but it wasn't Mrs. Branford standing in the doorframe. It was Miguel. It took all of one second to read his body language with his arms by his sides, his hands fisted, his jaw tight, and I wondered how long he'd been standing there. What he'd heard Luke say. He looked at me, at Luke, and then his gaze dropped to our clasped hands.

His voice, when he spoke, was strained with barely controlled anger. "What the hell is this?"

Instinctively, I jerked my hand free and stood. The irony of my last thoughts—that I would never tolerate a cheating partner, were not lost on me. Miguel had spent the better part of his adult life believing I'd cheated on him back in high school. It had been a mistake. A misunderstanding. And finally, he'd accepted that fact. I'd come to terms with what I'd believed had been his abandonment of me, and I didn't want even one iota of doubt to creep into his mind.

We were at a good place together, and I wanted it to stay that way.

Except the look in his eyes, dark and molten from whatever he thought was happening here, didn't reflect that good place. "Miguel, this is Luke," I said, and then added, "my ex-husband. Luke, this is . . ." I hesitated, unsure of how to introduce Miguel. Was he my boyfriend? My partner? We were more than friends, and he'd told me he was *all in*, but how did we define our relationship at this point?

"Miguel Baptista," he said tightly, finishing the sentence for me.

Luke stood, facing Miguel and sizing him up. Miguel had a few inches on Luke and was broader. Fitter. He'd spent ten years in the military, which had raised his level of fitness beyond what Luke's had ever been—or would ever be. Standing in the doorway, with Mrs. Branford's much smaller body beside him, he looked intimidating.

Luke had always been a charmer. He'd been distraught a moment ago, but now he threw on an affable smile and surged forward with his arm outstretched. "Wait, *the* Miguel? The one that broke her—" He stopped abruptly, then looked at me, notching his thumb back toward Miguel. "This is the guy who broke your heart back in high school?"

I nodded. "One and the same."

Just like that, Luke's demeanor shifted from charmer to defender. He turned back to face Miguel, puffing his chest out and throwing his shoulders back. "You," he said, jabbing his finger in the air, "should not be here."

Miguel let out a wry laugh. "*I* shouldn't be here? Last time I checked, you and Ivy were divorced. To my mind, that means *you're* the one with no right to be here."

Luke was impulsive and his statement that us splitting up had been a mistake showed me that he wasn't thinking clearly. His nostrils flared, like a bull ready to charge a matador. In this case, the matador was Miguel.

"Luke," I said, intervening before he could say something he'd regret, "why *are* you here? What do you want?"

"For us to be together again," he said, taking my hands again and spinning me slightly so that my back was to Miguel. "I want you, Ivy."

Not being able to see Miguel didn't mean I couldn't sense his anger. His jealousy. "Too bad you can't always get what you want," he said through gritted teeth.

"So Mick Jagger says, but I don't agree," Luke said. "Ivy and me, we were good together. We made mistakes, but we gave up too soon."

My hackles went up at that. "*We* made mistakes? *I'm* not the one who had a little something on the side, so I have to disagree with you there, Luke. *We* didn't make mistakes. *You* made the mistakes."

"Maybe you didn't have an affair, but you never forgot about this guy," he said, pointing over my shoulder at Miguel. "He was in our relationship as much as Heather was."

I cupped my hand over my forehead. He was right. I'd never gotten over Miguel, and Luke had been one long, unsuccessful rebound, but the idea that we'd been good together, or that we somehow belonged together just made me wonder what alternate reality my ex-husband was living in.

"You should go," Miguel said to him.

"I have just as much right to be here as you," Luke retorted, looking again like he was ready to face off with Miguel in a WWF match, right here, right now.

"Actually, you don't," I said, and I gestured toward the doorway. "Miguel and I are together now, and you need to go."

I could see Luke's mind working as he processed through what my words meant. He shook his head, looking at me like I'd lost my mind. "This guy messed with you, Ivy. You're really with him now?"

"It's *really* none of your business," I said. I moved past Miguel, who followed me to the kitchen, Mrs. Branford on his heels. She wasn't relying on her cane, and her step had a definite zip to it. She was the Gladys Kravitz of the neighborhood: She liked to know everything that was going on, and she owned up to her curiosity. This encounter with my ex-husband would fuel her gossip circle for a good while to come.

Luke hemmed and hawed, but finally he seemed to understand that whatever he'd wanted when he'd shown up on my doorstep was not going to turn out the way he'd hoped. "We still need to talk," he said to me when I ushered him out. "I need you—"

But I chose to ignore him, turning the lock once he was outside and I'd shut the door. I returned to the kitchen, taking my wineglass from the counter before sinking down on a chair at the table. Mrs. Branford had already drunk half of Luke's wine.

Miguel leaned back against the island, arms folded over his chest. The bottom of a tattoo peeked out from under the sleeve of his shirt. I'd yet to see it in its entirety. He revealed himself to me a little at a time, and the tattoo was something he didn't talk about, and didn't flaunt. One day soon, I thought.

"What the hell was that about?" he asked, his voice still tense.

I propped my elbow on the table and rested my head on my hand. "Best guess? I think his current wife is freaking out over something he did and he's running away."

"So he ran here? From Texas? To you?" Miguel shook his head. "Why?"

I didn't have the answer to that, but Mrs. Branford ventured a guess. "People rewrite their history," she said. "What actually happened is reworked and reworked and reworked in their mind until the new version becomes the truth. It's revisionist. If things are bad with his current wife, he's compared that to how he remembers them being with Ivy, and of course the grass is always greener. He has let his mind focus on the good things in their marriage, burying the bad things. The truth of his affair and their incompatibility is all pushed aside. Instead, he remembers a fairy-tale version, which allows him to villainize his wife, and gives him the courage to come here and want to rekindle what he thinks was a better relationship."

We stared at her. How had she come up with such a thoughtful psychoanalytic response on the fly? I was just about to ask her, but she offered us a sly smile and her eyes twinkled. "Before you ask, no, I didn't take psychology classes, and no, I didn't miss my calling. I've just read enough literature, and seen enough relationships over the years, that I understand human nature. And your former spouse, Luke Holden, is rather an open book, I might add."

I couldn't argue with that. At the time I'd discovered it, I'd wondered how in the world he'd managed to hide his infidelity for so long.

"Is he staying in Santa Sofia?" Miguel asked, still worked up over the encounter.

This time I shrugged. "He didn't say, so I don't know." I looked at him, wondering what had brought him here. "Is everything okay?"

His shoulders relaxed, but just slightly, because even if Luke was gone—at least for the moment—Marisol had still been murdered. "I went to see Emmaline," he said. "I was there when you called her—after meeting with Johnny."

That was rather shocking. Emmaline had orchestrated quite a few "chance" meetings between Miguel and me since we'd both returned to Santa Sofia. She was among the cadre of women, including Mrs. Branford and Olaya, who were certain that Miguel and I belonged together. She had to have been utterly focused on Marisol's case to neglect mentioning that he'd been standing right next to her when we'd talked on the phone, which was to her credit. Crime-solving before matchmaking. As far as I knew, she still hadn't gotten down on one knee to pro-pose to Billy. She was single-minded and couldn't think about her own love life when a murderer prowled the streets of Santa Sofia.

Before I could ask him why he'd been at the sheriff's office, he offered up the information. "I had lockers installed in the staff break room when we remodeled. Everyone has their own. Some people use them, some don't. Marisol did."

"Did you find something?"

"Marisol kept it locked, so no, not yet."

"Lisette is meeting us back there in"—he flipped his wrist to look at his watch—"half an hour."

"And you came by here in case I wanted to come with you?" I asked, a small smile playing on my lips. He could have simply told me what they found after the fact, but Miguel knew that I'd want to be there. We were in this investiga-tion together.

"Do you want to?" he asked. He still hadn't smiled, but his hands had unclenched.

"Do I want to?" I repeated. "Uh, do fish swim in the sea?"

"I'll take that as a yes," he said.

"Yes." I called Agatha in from the yard. Ten minutes later, Mrs. Branford was back across the street safely tucked into her Craftsman-style house dog-sitting the pug, and I was next to Miguel in his truck, heading for Beach Street, which would take us to the pier and Baptista's Cantina and

Grill. Luke's presence in my house was a pink elephant sitting squarely on the seat between us. We ignored it for a few minutes before Miguel stopped at a traffic light. He closed his eyes for a few seconds, drawing in a deep breath as if he were calming himself. He turned to me. "Do you need to tell me something?"

I could have pretended I didn't know what he was talking about, but we were no longer twenty-somethings who were still figuring things out; we'd been around our respective blocks, and I knew full well what he was talking about.

Luke Holden.

"No, Miguel," I said. "He just showed up. I was as surprised as you."

"If he wants you back—"

"Whether he does or doesn't isn't important. *I* don't want *him* back," I interrupted.

The light turned green and he stepped on the gas, propelling the truck forward and giving him a moment to process what I'd said. "You sure about that?" he asked at last.

I turned in my seat, angling my body toward him. He'd told me, in no uncertain terms, that a relationship with me was what he wanted, and that he was in it to stay. After two major misunderstandings, and the resulting years apart, I didn't want any miscommunication or ambiguity. "I am one thousand percent sure about that. My marriage to Luke helped me move on. But he never was you, and you're the only one I've ever wanted or needed."

The Pacific was on our left as we drove along the ocean road. He kept one hand on the wheel, taking my hand in his other. The palm trees lining the road zipped past. "You're sure about that?"

"Mmm-hmm," I said, squeezing his hand. I was never more sure about anything in my life, in fact. If his truck had had a bench seat, I would have scooted over, butting my thigh against his. As it was, safely apart in our bucket seats, I leaned over and kissed his cheek. "Never more sure about anything in my life."

Chapter 12

Lisette and Emmaline were already waiting in the lobby of Baptista's when we walked in. I met Em's eyes, hoping she'd give me a sign about Johnny Morales and whether or not she'd contacted him and heard Marisol's message to him. She wasn't giving anything away, though.

"The break room is upstairs," Miguel said, leading the way through the bustling dining room and into the kitchen. Lisette followed him, with Em and me bringing up the rear.

"What do you have there?" I asked her.

"Bolt cutter," she said, holding up a tool she carried at her side so I could get a better look. The red steel handles had black grips at the ends and the steel jaws looked sharp enough to cut through more than a simple drugstore lock.

Miguel's kitchen hosted a small but skilled kitchen brigade to execute the complex and varied dishes on the menu. During the remodel, he'd established stations for streamlined meal preparation. We passed the sauce station, where the most experienced chef worked in front of a multiple-burner gas range. He held tongs, scraped a sauté pan on the black iron grate, and made sauces, sautés, and pan-fried entrées.

There was a grill station with a char broiler, which I knew David usually manned. He'd been off since Marisol's death. An older man whom I recognized as Miguel's uncle, Tío Tomas, was filling in for him. The fryer was next to the flat-top grill, which Tío Tomas was also handling. We passed the salad and dessert stations last, which were side by side. There one person created salads, cold appetizers, and plated the desserts. Between the cooking stations and the kitchen line, where the plates were readied for delivery to the tables, was a stainless steel counter that held the garnishes, extra plates, a spindle for the orders, and heat lamps to keep the food warm. Miguel worked the line, if he was needed, but normally he left the cooking to the chefs while he acted as floor manager and the expediter—making sure every dish met his expectations before it left the kitchen.

I could see him taking it all in as we passed, not missing a single detail of the well-oiled machine he'd created. Looking satisfied, he gave an approving wave and kept walking, leading us up the staircase. "What's in there?" Emmaline asked, pointing to a closed door.

"My office," he said. "Unless I'm in there working, it's locked."

Miguel's and my rekindled relationship was still new. I hadn't yet been to his house, and while he'd cooked for me in a private section of the kitchen, this was my first time upstairs. I'd never really seen the businessman side of him. He had the lean, strong physique that came from his time in the marines—something he'd yet to share details about with me. He had the attention to detail needed to run a successful business, and he knew his way around a kitchen. I wondered if there was anything the man couldn't do.

"This is the break room," he said, turning the handle of the door, swinging it open, then stepping back to let us pass through. I was last and he put his hand on the small of my back as I entered. His touch, light as it was, sent a wave of warmth through me. We were connected and it felt good. It felt right.

Emmaline was in her head, observing what was around her, but keeping her thoughts to herself. One wall contained a row of lockers. A small round table with five chairs sat in the middle of the room. On another wall was a kitchenette area with cabinets, a sink, and a coffeemaker. Against the back wall was a dark brown couch. I couldn't tell from here if it was real or faux leather, but either way, it looked like a comfortable place to sit and take a break.

"Everyone uses this space?" she asked.

"A few people keep their stuff downstairs, but most people come up here."

"But Marisol?"

"Oh yeah. Probably more than anyone. She

liked to come up here, make a cup of hot tea, and have a little time to herself before her shift started. Sometimes she'd just stop by."

I took my gaze back to the lockers. There were ten of them lined up like soldiers. They were about six feet tall, had laminate natural wood-grain doors and sides, and had metal hasps that allowed for padlocks. Only two of them actually had locks. Both were the inexpensive drugstore variety. One was silver metal with a blue combination dial, while the other was gold colored, the combination mechanism at the base of the lock.

Em waited for Miguel to show them which locker had been Marisol's. After he pointed to the one with the blue dial, Emmaline withdrew a pair of protective goggles from the small black backpack she had slung over one shoulder and slid them on. She dropped the backpack, then lifted the cutters to the lock. Miguel gave her a look that said he'd do it if she wanted him to, but she ignored him and held up the cutters. In her head, I knew she was telling Miguel that she didn't need a man to do her work for her. "Step back," she said. "In case any part of it goes flying."

She positioned the jaws of the short blade on one side of the lock's shackle, braced herself, and forced the handles together.

Nothing happened.

She regrouped, positioned the cutter blades against the shackle again, and, spreading her legs to brace herself, she tried again, her neck muscles straining with the effort.

There was a grating sound of metal against metal, but the lock didn't break.

Emmaline was not one to give up. She planted her feet again, held the blades of the bolt cutter to the lock's shackle, and forced the handles together. On the third try, the long handles and short blade with the hinge mechanism gave her the leverage she needed. The cutters snapped right through one side of the shackle.

She nodded, affirming the success, then positioned the cutters on the other side of the shackle. This time it took just two tries to break through the metal. She set the cutters down, took a pair of latex gloves and several evidence bags from her backpack, and in one bag she placed the parts of the lock.

Up until now, Lisette had been silent, but now she spoke up. "What are you doing?"

"Another officer will be here any minute to dust the locker and what's inside. We have your mother's fingerprints. We're looking to see if there are others."

Lisette scoffed. "Why, you think whoever killed my mother brought her here first, then to the pier? That doesn't make any sense."

Emmaline turned to her. "We don't know what happened to your mother, so we have to look at all possibilities. We don't know what or whom she may have been involved with, Lisette."

Miguel's phone pinged with an incoming text. He glanced at it, excused himself, left the room while Emmaline carefully opened the locker she'd just freed of a lock. A hanger with a change of clothes hung on the rail spanning the top of the space. On the shelf above was a small box and a cluster of things I couldn't identify from where I stood. On the floor of the locker were two pairs of shoes, both black flats, and a pair of flimsy gray flip-flops. Finally, hanging from another hook was a blue and black backpack.

"I was wondering where that was," Lisette said, pointing to the swim bag. "I got it for her for Christmas a few years ago." She started toward the locker, reaching for it, but Emmaline stopped her. "Please don't touch anything."

Lisette's hand froze in midair and her face paled. Emmaline had let us all be here as a courtesy; she wanted Lisette's input on whatever she found. But there was no doubt about the seriousness of every step of the investigation and she certainly wasn't going to let it be compromised.

Emmaline moved in front of Lisette. She took the bag from the hook and set it on the table in the middle of the room. It looked like a normal backpack, but upon closer examination, I saw that a good portion of it was mesh, and the solid material was waterproof. It had shoulder straps, two side pockets for water bottles, one of which held a disposable plastic bottle, and a small mesh zipper pouch in front.

Lisette and I stood back, watching, as Emmaline activated a micro voice recorder. She stated the date, time, and location before setting it on the table and beginning her sorting of the bag's contents. She started with the main section. "Two swimsuits, both blue, both one piece," she said as she removed them, setting them off to the side. "One beach towel." She shook it out, then set it aside. "One pair of black workout shorts." She felt the fabric, looking for anything in the hidden interior pocket, then set it with the other items. She withdrew a navy sweatshirt, then dug out a bottle of energy chews from the interior pocket.

Satisfied that the inside of the bag was empty, she moved on to the small front pocket, removing two pairs of goggles, a small yellow digital device that looked like a timer, two silicon swim caps—one white, one blue—and an inhaler.

"Did your mom have asthma?" I asked Lisette.

Lisette nodded, but she was distracted, her attention on the things Emmaline had taken from the bag. "That's her tempo trainer," she said, pointing to what I'd thought was a timer. "She wouldn't train without it."

"Okay, but we know she was killed first, then put into the water," Emmaline said, stating what we'd already been told.

"I know, but she was . . . she was in her swimsuit, right?"

"Right," Em confirmed.

"But her swimsuits are here."

"The one she was wearing when she was found was red," Emmaline said.

Lisette gave a little shake of her head. "She doesn't have a red one."

Emmaline considered this. "Surely she had more than these two. Is it possible she had one you didn't know about?"

Once again, and without a bit of hesitation, Lisette shook her head. "No. No way. My mom

Winnie Archer

was superstitious. Blue was her color. She's been wearing it since she was on the high school swim team." She indicated the things on the table. "Blue bag. Blue cap. Blue goggles. Blue towel. Blue swimsuit. She wouldn't have worn red."

Interesting. We knew Marisol had been killed, because of the autopsy findings. I was sure Em had entertained the idea that the murder was a killing of happenstance. That she'd been in the wrong place at the wrong time. But the fact that Marisol had been killed on land but found in the water meant that whoever killed her had known enough about her habits to try to make it look like a drowning. It also meant that whoever killed her hadn't known about the physiological response from drowning and had tried to make it look as if she'd been out there training, thinking or hoping that evidence of strangulation would not show up after the fact.

"She also never swam without her tempo trainer."

Emmaline studied the little digital device, looking up at Lisette for explanation.

"You set the tempo to keep your pace. She wore it hooked to her goggles. She swore by it."

So, more proof that she hadn't actually been out training, but that someone had wanted it to look that way. None of this, however, helped us get any closer to answering why.

Emmaline replaced the items in the bag, putting the entire thing into a large clear plastic bag she pulled from her own backpack. "Someone wanted us to believe that she drowned while she was training, which we know didn't happen.

It was clearly premeditated if she was put into a swimsuit to add to that narrative." She turned to Lisette. "Anyone close to your mother, would they have known about her superstition about blue?"

Lisette's eyes rolled toward the ceiling as she thought. "No," she said slowly. "I don't think so. Maybe they'd think she really liked blue because those were her swimming colors, but I don't think she talked about why that was. I mean, my dad knows, of course. And my brothers. Probably her training buddies."

"David?" I asked, noting how she'd left his name off her list.

"Well, yeah. I mean, probably."

If her killer had known her well, he or she wouldn't have put Marisol in a red swimsuit, that was the takeaway. Unless, of course, it was a diversion technique.

Miguel returned, standing aside to let a man carrying a black attaché case enter before him. "Great. Glad you're here," Emmaline said, and I got the impression she'd called in an expert from a neighboring municipality. She didn't bother to introduce him to us, instead giving him directions to examine the locker for evidence and fingerprints.

"Already took prints of the employees for cross-reference," he told her as he set his case down.

Emmaline nodded in acknowledgment, then asked us to step out to the hallway while he worked. Miguel was lost in thought. I imagined the myriad conflicts going through his mind:

His employee was not only dead, but had been killed; not only that, but the victim was his sister's mother-in-law; the police were in the break room of his restaurant searching for evidence; the people who worked for him—and whom he trusted—had been fingerprinted.

Oh, and his girlfriend's ex-husband had shown up unexpectedly.

I felt for him. I put my hand on his arm. There wasn't anything else to be done here. "Shall we go?" I suggested.

"Yeah. I have to get back to work," Miguel said.

The sounds of a busy kitchen traveled up the stairs to us: pots clanging against stove burners, chefs and waitstaff talking to one another, a timer going off. I knew he planned to drive me home, but the dinner shift was in full swing and he was needed.

I turned to Lisette. "Would you mind giving me a ride back to my house?"

She nodded absently. "Sure."

Miguel threw me a grateful smile. He led us back downstairs and out to the bustling dining room. "I'll call you later," he said, giving me a quick kiss before disappearing back into the depths of the kitchen.

A few minutes later, I sat in the passenger seat of Lisette's silver sedan as she wound through Santa Sofia, following my directions to the historic area of town and Maple Street. It was a short drive, but I took her the long way to give me a few extra minutes alone with her. "You were telling me about your mom and David," I said.

She glanced at me. "Was I?"

"You said he would have known about your mom's superstition about the color blue. Do you think they had a good marriage?"

Even from where I sat next to her, I could see her eyes roll up. "I guess. I don't know."

"Don't you like him?" I asked, wanting to get to the bottom of her feelings about her step-father.

She shrugged noncommittally. "He's fine, I guess. I didn't have to be married to him."

That hadn't really answered the question. "Were they happy together?" I asked, my mind returning to the fact that Marisol had called Johnny, requesting to see him. Why had she needed to talk to her ex-husband? Why not talk to David about whatever was bothering her? I would never call Luke over Miguel. It just wouldn't happen. Then again, Miguel was my Johnny. He was the one I'd known forever.

"Is anyone?" she retorted, pulling up to a stoplight.

So she was a cynic. "I think so," I said. My parents had been. My brother and Emmaline, when-ever they tied the knot, would be. Mrs. Branford and her husband, despite a few bumps in the road, had been. It was true that marriage could be challenging and wasn't always easy. There were ups and downs in every single one of them. It was also true that sometimes, despite one's best efforts and intentions, it didn't work.

Lisette gave a small sigh before clarifying her words. "I guess you never really know about other people's relationships. We—me and my brothers—we always thought our parents had a good marriage. I know the idea that they might get divorced never crossed my mind. But then you learn about something and it's like finding out Santa Claus isn't real. I've read plenty of articles that talk about intimacy, you know, but I never thought about my parents like that—as sexual people, you know? But my dad . . . and then my mom and David . . ." A shudder wove visibly through her body. The light turned green and we lurched forward as she stepped on the gas. "My parents, they were supposed to grow old together, you know?"

I did know. Exactly. I'd had the very same thoughts about my own parents. My dad was still adjusting to not having my mother there by his side. It took time to find a new normal and move forward when the life you'd planned suddenly and inexplicably changed. Johnny and Marisol may not still have been married, but the history they'd shared meant that her death had permanently changed his world, just as my mother's had changed my father's.

Lisette hadn't answered my question about whether or not her mother had been happy with David. I circled back to it. "Do you think she was happy with your stepdad?"

She sighed again, this time with resignation. She couldn't keep dodging the question. "I told you we weren't really talking much."

"You and your mom?"

She nodded.

She had mentioned it. "What happened?"

She didn't speak for a minute, focusing on

driving. Then she abruptly pulled the car alongside the curb, threw it into park, and turned her body to face me. "I'm going to be honest with you, okay?"

"Okaaay," I said, drawing out the word. Had she been dishonest before this?

"My dad, he made mistakes." She cupped her hand over her forehead, her head angled down. Her chest heaved, rising and falling with her heavy breaths. It was obvious that she was still having a hard time dealing with her father's betrayal and the fallout from it. "She couldn't forgive him."

"Do you blame her?" I asked. I hadn't been able to forgive Luke for his infidelity, although I'd done enough reflection to know that I had probably been looking for a way out and had seized the opportunity.

She shrugged helplessly. "I don't know if I do or not. I wonder if things would be different right now, though, if they'd stayed together."

I curled one leg onto the seat of the car, turning to face her. "What do you mean, Lisette? Why would they be different?"

"After my *abuelo* died, she started losing it. If they hadn't gotten divorced, I'd have been there. My dad would have been. We could have talked her off the ledge."

It felt like she was talking in puzzles. I struggled to understand what she was getting at. "What ledge, Lisette?"

"She was turning delusional. Nightmares. Boogiemen. Seeing blood and bones everywhere. She had horrible dreams about my grandfather.

Heaven versus hell. She was obsessed. And she was worried about her mind."

"What do you mean?"

"She was becoming forgetful. She'd lose her keys. Forget where she parked her car. She thought we'd buried my grandfather, then we'd show her the ashes, and she'd freak out."

My mind went back to what David had told us about his wife. Lisette's words now echoed his. Did Marisol really believe she was developing early Alzheimer's or dementia? No one could answer that question except Marisol. "Did she confide in you?"

"She told my brother. Ruben," she clarified when I raised my eyebrows. "He told Sergio and me, but we couldn't do anything to help her. She wouldn't answer when *I* called. What could any of us do? She was off the deep end with it all. Conspiracy theories and crazy talk." Her chest heaved again, and she let out an anguished sob. "I was so angry at her for giving up on my dad. I didn't go to her and David's wedding. How could I do that to her? How selfish do you have to be to not go to your own mother's wedding? To begrudge her happiness?"

She looked at me, imploringly, as if I had some magical answer that could absolve her of her guilt. Unfortunately I didn't. That was something she would have to figure out how to deal with on her own. "Do you know if she shared all of this with David?" I asked. Although he'd told us about her forgetfulness, he hadn't said anything about his wife's nightmares or obsession.

Lisette turned to stare out the front windshield, her face blank. "She told Ruben no one would understand, so . . ." She hung her head. "I don't know."

I played that over in my head. Marisol thought no one would understand her nightmares, but she'd contacted Johnny. She'd known him since they were kids. A relationship that had lasted that long could have meant that she trusted him not to judge her and to just listen, or it could easily have meant the opposite—that he'd seen this sort of behavior from her before and knew how to, as Lisette had said, talk her off the ledge. Maybe that is exactly what Marisol had needed.

Or—I came up with a more sinister idea—whatever she was obsessing about *involved* Johnny. I couldn't pursue that line of thinking with Lisette, though. She'd lost her mother; I couldn't in good conscience introduce the idea to her that her father could be involved. Not to mention that I had no concrete idea how he could be.

Her voice grew quieter and I had to lean forward to hear her. "I could have just let her be happy, you know? Why didn't I just let her be happy?"

"I'm sure she forgave you."

She wrung her hands, nodding, her expression a mix of shame and regret. "It's my fault."

The poor woman was falling apart before my eyes. "What's your fault, Lisette?"

"If I hadn't shut her out . . . If I'd been there for her, maybe . . ."

"Lisette," I said, gently placing one of my hands on hers. "None of this is your fault. You'll drive yourself crazy, and you can't change what happened. We all make choices. Your father made his. Your mother made hers. Those choices had nothing to do with you."

"But if I'd accepted her and David, maybe she'd have come to me. Told me what she was feeling. I could have helped her."

"Maybe, but maybe not," I said. "You can second-guess what's already happened, but you certainly can't change it."

Her eyes welled and she squeezed them shut, pressing her fingers into the corners to keep her emotions in check. After a valiant try, however, she gave in to them, breaking down. The tears flowed.

After a few minutes and my litany of encouraging words to her, she pulled back into traffic and drove the remaining distance to Maple Street. As she pulled up to Mrs. Branford's house, where I'd directed her so I could collect Agatha, I thought about Marisol and the turmoil she'd been in before she died. The loss of her father had sent her over the proverbial edge. She'd been grief-stricken, had felt alone, and her mind had been playing tricks on her. What had Lisette said? Her mother had been dreaming of blood and bones.

But as I stood on the sidewalk and watched the piercing red of her taillights disappear into the waning light, a new thought formed in my mind. So far, we had no motive for Marisol's death. What if she hadn't been delusional? What if she hadn't been having nightmares in her sleep, but had actually witnessed something that had spooked her? What if her conspiracy theory, whatever it might have been, was not conspiracy at all, but real?

She'd wanted to talk about it. She'd reached out to her son, Ruben. And then she'd called Johnny. She'd called him, I thought, and then she'd died.

New questions came to mind. Why did he wait to share the message with the police? He'd said he was afraid it would incriminate him by placing him at the scene, but what if he *was* there? What if he'd been seen? Had he decided to share the message in order to cover his tracks to make himself look like an innocent, when actually, he was anything but?

A shiver wound down my spine. Did the blood and bones Marisol had talked about have something to do with him?

Chapter 13

There's something about the idea of a man killing his wife—or in this case, his ex-wife—that I have a hard time understanding. I turned it over and over in my mind, trying to make sense of the theory that Johnny could have killed Marisol. I spent the night tossing and turning, thinking about it, moonlight filtering through the louvered blinds covering the window. Agatha had curled up in a tight little spiral beside me, oblivious to the turmoil that had prevented me from falling asleep. She slept like a log, moving only when I readjusted her head to stop her light snore.

No murder is justified. I know that. But a man killing his wife seemed particularly heinous. The fact that Marisol was Johnny's former wife added distance to their connection. Except, of course, they weren't distant, because Marisol had reached out to Johnny and had wanted to meet him.

On the day she died.

At the location of her death.

When I thought about perception, I knew Johnny was right to be scared of sharing this information with the police. The message from Marisol made him an obvious suspect. I didn't want to believe that he could be behind her death. In my mind, it always came down to the children. They'd raised a family together. They had grandchildren. Marisol's death had taken a toll on her children. It didn't matter that they were adults. What mattered was that someone they each loved with all their heart was dead. I couldn't fathom a father choosing to put his children and grandchildren through that pain.

But, I reminded myself again, Marisol had wanted to meet with him. At the pier. And then she'd died. It could have had to do with David, for all I knew, but somehow I didn't think so. If I went with my gut, all roads at the moment seemed to point to Johnny.

At some point, I finally drifted off. I didn't sleep long before I woke with a start at the clanking sound of a truck somewhere outside. I sat bolt upright, realization hitting. Garbage day! I'd completely forgotten! I jumped from the bed, not taking the time to pull on socks or slippers, and raced to the garage. I pressed the garage door button and headed straight to the corner where the green recycle and blue trash cans sat. I grabbed the first one, using my bare foot to lever it onto its two back wheels, then I spun it around and hauled it down the driveway and onto the street just in front of the curb.

The hulking city waste-management truck, with its massive pronged lift system, was in front of my neighbor's house after having made its way down Maple Street. The driver maneuvered the forks of the lift to grip the blue can next door, lifting it up and over, letting the contents spill into the hopper. He did the same for the green can after he pulled the truck forward, dumping the recyclables into a different compartment in the truck's hopper.

I ran back into the garage, dragging my second can to the street just as the massive truck lurched forward, stopping in front of my house. I'd gotten the cans out in the nick of time. The driver emptied the cans, gave me a wave and a smile, threw the truck into gear, and it jerked toward the next house on the street.

Now that my adrenaline had receded to normal, I felt the chill of the cement of the sidewalk against my feet and the cold breeze against my body. I folded my arms across my chest and hurried back inside. Part of me wanted to crawl back into bed and snuggle up next to Agatha, but reason kicked in. I had places to go. People to see. A murder to solve.

The bottom line was that I knew I had to get out of the house to clear my head. I decided to start by taking Agatha for a short walk at the shore before heading to Yeast of Eden. Olaya was short-handed today, so I'd offered to help for a few hours. It would also give me a chance to fill her in.

I bundled up in a heavy UT Austin sweatshirt, snapped Agatha into her green and black harness, and drove to the little parking lot near one of Santa Sofia's state beaches. We headed down the pathway running alongside the cement retaining wall. Beyond the expanse of sand, violent whitecaps topped dark, tumultuous waters.

The ocean water seemed to reflect my thoughts last night as I'd tried to fathom what Johnny could be involved in that would have caused Marisol to have nightmares about blood and bones. I drew a blank. The guy worked in a credit union. Unless he was involved in the unsavory underbelly of the loan industry, which involved loan sharks and other disreputable people—and did that even exist in Santa Sofia?—then I couldn't make a connection.

I tried to move on with my thinking, but then circled back around. Johnny had given me good advice about living in my house for a while before making changes, but then he'd said something odd. A second against my home mortgage was possible, but then he'd said there were other ways to get the money I might need. What had he meant by that? Ways of borrowing money off the books? Separate from the banking system? Could he be involved in something less than aboveboard? Maybe it wasn't so farfetched.

I played devil's advocate. If I assumed that Johnny was, indeed, involved in some sort of illegal enterprise—gambling . . . money laundering . . . prostitution . . . loansharking, then I was also assuming that whatever it was, Marisol found out. Would Marisol have protected him if he was doing something illegal? Would that make her an accomplice after the fact? Or a coconspirator? I didn't know the legalities in such a situation, but it seemed to me that Marisol would be putting herself in a sticky situation if she'd known something incriminating and was keeping that secret.

That begged another question, though. What if she wasn't keeping it secret? Could she have intended to blackmail Johnny? Was that why she wanted to meet with him on the pier?

Agatha had been obediently trotting along beside me, picking up speed when I did or slowing down when I got bogged down with my thinking and my pace lagged. "If Marisol knew something about Johnny, I don't think she told David," I said to Agatha. The guy was genuinely distraught and might be drinking himself into oblivion at this very moment. If he thought Johnny was involved in some way, I couldn't see him keeping it to himself.

"But the color of the swimsuit was wrong," I muttered, remembering what Lisette had said about her mom's superstition. Agatha looked up at me. Her ears were back, her tail curled happily. "If Lisette is right, wouldn't Johnny have known about her affinity for the color blue? Could he have just forgotten?"

Agatha barked in response.

"Yeah, he might have," I said, reasoning that they'd been divorced, and who knows what their relationship had really been like prior to them splitting up. He very well may have forgotten about Marisol's superstition. Or, more likely, he was agitated over whatever it was that she knew and hadn't been thinking clearly.

I did an about-face and headed back to the car, anxious to get to the bread shop to talk through this theory with Olaya, because what I didn't know how to do at the moment was find out what Johnny Morales might be involved in.

More than an hour passed at the bread shop before it slowed down enough for me to help Olaya in the kitchen rather than in the front of the store. The table she used as a desk took up a good portion of her little office, but she'd managed to get a small chair in the room, opposite the desk, which is where I sat. She turned her computer to the side so I could see the screen. "This is the menu for the funeral," she said as she closed the notebook she'd had with her when she'd met with Lisette at the funeral home.

I read through the list of baked goods, both savory and sweet, my stomach rumbling. I hadn't eaten since the banana I'd had during my walk with Agatha. I hadn't been hungry then, but now I was starving. "I'll be right back," I said, leaving Olaya to stare after me while I foraged for something to eat. I returned to the office a few minutes later carrying a plate laden with a stem of red grapes and several slices of a peppery cheese, both of which I'd found in the fridge, and a small baguette from one of the bakery racks.

"Ivy, *mija*," she said, gesturing first to my plate then to the clock on the wall. "You take things too much to heart if you are not taking care of yourself. You must eat."

"I know," I said as I tore off a piece of the bread, added a bit of the cheese, finishing the bite off by popping a grape into my mouth. Olaya was right. I'd been so wrapped up in my head during my walk with Agatha, and then had been in a rush to get to the bread shop, that I'd simply forgotten. That didn't happen often.

We both turned back to the menu for the funeral and I read the list.

> *Carnitas sliders*
> *Air-fried shrimp with lemon and chili*
> *Albóndigas with bread*
> *Black bean and corn mini tostadas*
> *Cheese and chili quesadillas*
> *Asparagus mini quiches*
> *Baked brie en croûte with spicy fig compote*
> *Butternut squash and bacon tarts*
> *Bite-sized scones*
> *Mini pan dulce*
> *Lemon curd and strawberry butter*

Olaya was pulling out all the stops for one of her sister's closest friends. The celebration of Marisol's life was going to be a feast for the palate. "Baptista's is doing the carnitas, but the rest? Is that you?" I asked.

"Miguel and I, we have divided the items. He is making the spicy fig compote, but I will make the puff pastry for the baked brie. I will make the pastry for the tarts, but he will do the filling. He will do the tostadas and the quesadillas, the *albóndigas,* and the shrimp, and I will make the breads to accompany them. I will make the scones and the pan dulce, of course. The timing of it all will be important. Your Miguel will be busy today."

The tune to the Beatles song "Michelle" suddenly played in my head. My Miguel. It had a nice ring to it. "So will we," I said.

She smiled. "*Exactamente.*"

My cell phone rang. I dug it out of my back pocket, swallowing the bite of bread and cheese I'd just taken before answering. Emmaline's voice greeted me. "We're releasing the body to Vista Ridge," she said.

"Funeral's tomorrow afternoon," I said. "Any new information?" With the body having been underwater, I didn't know what other forensic evidence might surface, but I suspected there wouldn't be much.

Em confirmed that with a succinct no, then followed it up with a single question that was full of hope. "You?"

I hesitated. All I had were suppositions and theories, none with evidence to back them up at this point. Until I had more, I didn't relish throwing anyone under the bus. I did, however, recognize that my best friend had resources that I did not. "Not really, but did you find a will?" I asked, still wondering about the house and the beneficiaries.

"She had one. Redone after she and David Ruiz married."

"Does he inherit the house?" I asked. The theory that Johnny was involved in something illegal was thin. Marisol's property, however, was incredibly valuable. I hated thinking it could be a reason for murder, but there it was. Money and greed topped the list of motives for killing.

"It goes to her husband, with a provision that he does not sell it for ten years. At that point, it is to be sold to her three children for a price of—get this—one dollar."

I stuck my finger in my ear and wiggled it, wondering if I'd heard correctly. "Let me get this straight. David inherits the house, which is worth a pretty penny—"

"In excess of a million and a half, I'd say. At least."

"—but he can't sell it for ten years. And whenever he does sell it, assuming he does—"

"No, the way it reads, he has to sell it at ten years—"

"But only the Ruiz kids can buy it?"

"That's right," she said.

"Is that enforceable?" I asked. "I mean, can you make that kind of a stipulation in a will?"

"We're looking into that, believe me. Whether or not it's enforceable, though, the three kids have something big to gain. They also had a possible grudge. Ten years is a long time to wait if you want something now."

"But that would be a motive to get David out of the way."

"True."

What was Marisol's state of mind? Her kids might have grounds to contest her will if they thought she'd not been of sound mind. If she'd been worried about her mental health or her brain function, that might be enough for them to stop David from inheriting. They might not want to wait ten years. They could easily say that he'd coerced her, or that she'd been mentally incapable of looking out for her own best interest, although he would gain only an awesome house to live in rather than a million-plus dollars.

But then there was the issue of the swimsuit. Her children would have known about her superstition.

I could hear the *tap tap tap* of Emmaline's fingers as she typed something on her computer keyboard. She was a multitasker, and since she'd become the sheriff, she was rarely able to devote even five undivided minutes to someone on the other end of a phone call. When we were together in person, she was present, but across cellular waves, she was always thinking about something else at the same time she was talking or listening to me. I knew she was thinking about the motive for Marisol's murder.

"Gotta go," Emmaline said abruptly, severing the connection. I tucked my phone away, uneasy. Why would Marisol have cut all of her kids out of inheriting the house immediately upon her death?

"What is happening with the investigation?" Olaya asked, closing up the computer and heading into the kitchen.

I told her what Emmaline had said about the will and the house. Olaya tsked. "How well does Miguel know this man, David Ruiz?"

"That is a good question," I said. Miguel and I had made plans for dinner with his sister and her husband. Sergio might be able to shed some light on his and his siblings' relationship with their mother. In the meantime, I decided to track down Ruben.

"Take them bread," Olaya said after I told her where I was headed. She thought for a moment, then nodded. "Crusty sourdough, I think."

"David's not the only suspect in my mind," I told her as I pulled two loaves of sourdough from a bakery rack and slid them into paper bread bags.

"Who else?" she asked. She had pulled out containers of flour and salt and had set to work creating a dough out of just those ingredients. She measured, mixed, and then turned the mixture onto her work surface, creating a trough in the center of the pile. She added water and deftly fluffed the mixture, repeating until it started to clump together.

Puff pastry, I realized as she pressed it all into a ball, rolled it up in plastic wrap, and placed it in the refrigerator to chill. Later, she'd roll it out with her French rolling pin, lay a slab of butter in the center, and fold the dough in on itself before rolling it out again and repeating. The process of rolling the butter into the dough created the flaky layers of puff pastry.

As she set to work making another batch, I summed up my wonderings about Johnny Morales, ending with, "He's obviously not going to tell me if he's involved in anything shady, so I've been thinking about how to find out."

Her hands had continued to work the dough while she'd listened. Now she looked up at me, her fingertips resting lightly on the countertop. "When I was a girl in Mexico, my sisters and I, we did not have many toys or books. There was not much to do in our little village. We had to entertain ourselves. Games of the imagination. I remember there was a time when our uncle, he acted very strange. Suspicious, as if he had something to hide. We were obsessed about it, my sisters and me. For days and days, we followed him, sometimes on foot, sometimes on our rickety bicycles, but always with stark determination. I baked bread for him, thinking that if I added certain herbs, the truth would be revealed to us somehow. Of course I was not well-versed in my baking at that time."

One of the things I adored about Olaya was her storytelling. She could weave a tale as easily as she could bake a loaf of bread; neither were particularly easy to do, but she did both with aplomb. "Did you find out what he was up to?" I asked.

"Yes and no. We found that when you want to

see something suspicious, you can make yourself believe anything. If he blinked, we thought our uncle was surely hiding something. If he sneezed, we thought he was evading a question. When he made a phone call, we knew he was talking to someone he should not be. We were very certain that he was in a relationship with someone off-limits. A married woman, we thought. Or another man, *posiblemente*. But, alas, it was not those things."

"What was it?"

"It was nothing!" she said. "He felt himself being followed, *pero* he did not know it was his nieces playing detectives. He *was* in a relationship with a woman—an eligible woman—but he thought that maybe her father did not think him good enough. He thought that perhaps the man was trying to scare him away."

"But he wasn't."

She shook her head, amusement crossing her face. "He was not. It was Consuelo, Martina, and me. We created a story where there had been none."

"Did your uncle end up with the woman?"

She laughed, waving her flour-coated hand in the air. "No, no. She was no good. She had *too* many men. We saved our uncle from that mistake, even though he did not see it at the time."

"I'm not sure what this has to do with Johnny," I said, knowing that it did in some way, shape, or form.

"We suspected our uncle. We were wrong, but if we had not followed him, he would have found out the hard way about his woman."

Her point dawned on me. "So you're saying I could be wrong about Johnny, but if there's no one else to prove or disprove my theory, then I need to follow him and he'll lead me to the truth."

"What I am saying, *mija*, is that what we think we see or know may not be the truth at all. We must break through the surface to find out what lies beneath."

Chapter 14

I put aside the notion of tailing Johnny Morales until after I'd spoken to his son Ruben and had dinner with his other son, Sergio. Part of me felt determined to build a case against Johnny, but in reality, I couldn't get Marisol's children and the very real motive of them inheriting Marisol's house off my mind. My head swam with indecision.

A conversation with Ruben was warranted. I'd texted Miguel to find out where Ruben worked, hoping it was the kind of place where I could just drop in.

He works at a solar panel company, Miguel texted. *Why?*

Paying a visit, I replied.

The three little gray dots flashed at the bottom of my phone's screen so I knew he was writing something back. It didn't take long. *Ivy,* was all it said. I could hear the warning tone in the single three-letter word.

I tapped my thumbs across my phone's keyboard. *Miguel.*

The three dots flashed, then after a minute, they disappeared. No text appeared.

"Come on, Miguel," I muttered under my breath.

And then his text appeared. *Because I know you'll track it down one way or another,* he wrote, followed by the name and address of the solar panel company Ruben Morales worked for.

I sent him a kissing-face emoji in reply, noted the address, and before long, I was walking into a solar panel showroom. A variety of panels were displayed around the perimeter of the room, but I bypassed them, heading directly to the man who'd come out of a small office to greet me. He held out his hand, welcomed me to Sun Solar, the solar panel experts of California, and offered to set me up with a free home estimate. The guy cut to the chase.

"Actually, I'm looking for Ruben Morales," I said, taking a step back to show him I wasn't actually in the market, at least not at the moment, for solar panels.

His posture changed, as did his expression. His congeniality when he thought he could sell to me evaporated. He held up a finger, and without another word, turned, poked his head into another little office, then retreated back to his own.

The guy could turn it on and off. Kind of

amazing, I thought. If I ever did decide to put in solar panels, I was pretty sure I wouldn't be seeking him out.

A figure emerged from the second office. "I'm Ruben, can I help—" He broke off when he recognized me. "Hey," he said.

"Hi. We met the other night—"

"I remember. You're Miguel's, mmm, girlfriend, right?" he asked.

It sounded juvenile to put it that way given that we were in our midthirties, but I nodded anyway. "Ivy Culpepper."

"Yeah. David said you could help figure out what happened to my mother."

I let out the breath I'd been holding. I'd been worried about broaching the subject of Ruben's mother and David, but in less than a minute, he'd brought it up. "I'm trying," I said. I looked around. No one else was in the small showroom, but it still felt too open. "Is there someplace private we can talk?"

"My office," he said, then he led me back to the room he'd come from. As I followed him, I noted the similarities between him, his brother Sergio, whom I'd met several times, and his father. Now that I'd met Johnny, I could see how closely Ruben resembled him. Marisol hadn't been tall—maybe five feet four inches, or so, and she'd been lean. Ruben had gotten his mother's green eyes, but physically, he was much more like his father. Stocky. Thick neck. Wide shoulders. Narrow hips. From appearances, I thought he might come across as gruff, but he indicated a chair for me to sit in, then pulled it out for me before taking his own seat behind his desk, wiping away that snap judgment.

He spoke before I had a chance to. "Did you figure something out? About my mom, I mean?"

"No," I said slowly, keeping my theories to myself. "But I've heard that your mom wasn't quite herself lately. That's why I'm here. I wanted to ask you about that."

"Not quite herself," he repeated. "That's an understatement. She thought she was getting dementia. Or Alzheimer's, like my grandfather. None of us—my brother and sister and me, I mean—we couldn't figure out if it was the chicken or the egg."

"What do you mean?"

"Just that she thought her mind was going, so then did it get worse, or did she make it get worse subconsciously, or was her mind actually going and it was bad enough that she started noticing?"

"Did *you* think she was losing touch with reality?" I asked.

He didn't answer immediately, instead taking a moment to really consider the question. When he answered, it was noncommittal. "After her father died, she changed."

Lisette and David had said something similar. She hadn't coped well with her father's death. "Changed how?"

"She couldn't sleep. She trained all the time. It was like she was trying to do whatever she could so she didn't have to think."

"Did she tell you about her nightmares?"

His eyes had become red-rimmed and glassy,

and from the way he held his mouth—straight and taut—I could see that his carefully buried emotions were bubbling up inside of him. "I know David was pretty worried about her. He didn't know how to help her get better."

"Are you on good terms with him?" I asked, surprised. I'd assumed Ruben and Sergio felt the same about David and Marisol as Lisette did, but maybe not.

He shrugged noncommittally. "He's a nice enough guy."

"But your sister, she doesn't like him, does she?"

"Lisette and my mom, they had their mother-daughter baggage," he said dismissively. "The guy made our mom happy. That's all I cared about."

"And your brother?"

He tapped his curved fingers against his chest. "Same as me."

Ruben was being incredibly forthcoming. And he seemed like the furthest thing from a killer. I debated how much to push my luck, but went for it. "Why doesn't Lisette like him?"

He responded with a shrug. "My sister is angry at the world. She hated that our parents got divorced. They had a sort of fairy-tale romance. High school sweethearts, and all that. But half the freaking world is divorced. It's cliché, and it's stupid because we're adults, you know, but I think she somehow thought that our parents might get back together someday. In her eyes, David ruined that."

He was right, it was a ridiculous thought for a

woman in her thirties to have. For a young child? Sure. Even for a teenager. But Lisette should have been mature enough to accept what was, and also to see her mother's happiness with David. From our last conversation, I knew she had regrets. I just hoped she could come to terms with them and move on.

"Sounds like she blamed your mom more than your father," I commented.

Ruben eyed me sharply. "What are you talking about?"

"I talked to him yesterday," I said. "He told me a little bit about what happened. That there was, um, an affair."

Ruben's demeanor changed, his shoulders straightening, his voice more stern. "My dad is a lot of things, but an unfaithful husband isn't one of them. He loved my mom. He never would have cheated on her. That is not why they got divorced."

Whatever I'd expected Ruben to say, it wasn't that. "Oh . . . I . . . um . . . maybe I misunderstood," I finally said.

Ruben leaned forward. "What do you mean? What did he say?"

How did I answer that? I replayed my conversation with Johnny. He'd started to say that he'd met someone, then that he'd made a mistake. I'd filled in the blanks, assuming the someone he'd met meant an affair. "He said he made a mistake. I guess I just assumed—"

Ruben cut me off. "Oh, he made a mistake all right. It just wasn't *that* kind of mistake."

I debated asking the next question, but went for it. "What kind was it?"

Ruben had been more open than I'd thought he'd be, but turns out he had limits on how much he was willing to say. "The kind that made it smarter—or better, I guess—for them to split up. Lisette blamed our mom for being willing to bail on their marriage."

I thought about this. "So it wasn't that they didn't love each other? Or that they really wanted to get divorced, it was . . . necessity?" I asked, wondering if I was interpreting his words correctly.

Ruben rested his forearms on his desk, interlacing his fingers, his hands flat against the black blotter. "They loved each other," was his answer.

Which, to my mind, meant that no, they didn't really want to get divorced. The idea that Johnny was involved in something illegal resurfaced. I'd learned that the best way to keep a person talking was to create space for them to do so. I kept quiet, hoping Ruben would elaborate. He didn't. Instead, he glanced over my shoulder at the clock hanging on the wall. "Ms. Culpepper—"

"Ivy," I said.

He nodded and blinked in acknowledgment. "Ivy. I appreciate your help. We all do. We want to know what happened to our mother."

I waited for the *but*.

"But I have an appointment across town I have to get to. These solar panels don't sell themselves," he said with a wan smile.

I stood. "Sure, I understand. Thanks for talking to me." The thin brown paper bag holding the bread I'd brought crackled in my arms. "Oh! This is for you," I said, holding it out to him. "Sourdough."

If he thought it was strange that I'd brought him a loaf of bread, he didn't say. "From Yeast of Eden?" he asked, breathing it in. I nodded, and he smiled. "I love that place. God, I'd be three hundred pounds if I bought bread there as much as I want to."

That was a danger of spending too much time at the bread shop, I agreed. "Too much wouldn't be good, but when you indulge, they're calories well spent," I said.

"We'll have it tonight," he said. "My wife'll love it." He thanked me and walked me out. As I watched him drive out of the parking lot in his Sun Solar truck, I thought about our conversation. The biggest takeaways were Lisette's anger with her mom, and the fact that the Ruiz divorce hadn't been because of adultery, but rather something they did in order to be "smart." What exactly, I wondered, did that actually mean?

Chapter 15

I hadn't yet been to Miguel's house, and if I was being honest, I was a little bit nervous. We'd spent countless hours at Baptista's Cantina and Grill, and our lives were busy, so when we had time together, we tended to spend it at my house, where Agatha was. I'd actually wondered what kind of place Miguel lived in, and I'd even contemplated—more than once—looking up his address and driving by to scout it out. In the end, I decided against stalking and had waited until I'd been invited.

Tonight was that night.

Within hours of talking with Ruben, I'd be spending time with Sergio. With any luck, I would be able to get his take on his sister, her anger, and the revelation that Johnny hadn't been un-faithful to Marisol. But first, I got myself ready, dressing in a white V-neck T-shirt tucked into jeans that folded up at the ankle to create a wide cuff. I slipped on a pale pink fringe-edged jacket, and black block-heeled loafers that looked like they'd been inspired by menswear and had antique hardware detailing. It was dressier than I usually was, but my first time at Miguel's house felt special. I wasn't quite sure what to do with my hair. I stood in front of the mirror, holding my curly strawberry locks up, then dropping them down. No matter what I did with it, it never looked neat. I called it disheveled; Miguel called it sexy. The truth was probably somewhere in between. The ginger color set off the emerald of my eyes, whichever way I wore it. Given the color of the pink jacket, I decided up was best. I secured it in a messy bun, ringlets softly framing my face, and headed across the street with Agatha. The poor sweet thing had been crated too much today.

"I'll be back toni—" I started to say to Mrs. Branford, who had been all too willing to dog sit, but she held up her hand to stop me.

"Maybe you will, but maybe you won't. Agatha is with me, so you have no reason to worry if you don't come back tonight."

I started to protest, but then stopped, thinking realistically. "You're right," I said. "Thanks."

She eyed me suspiciously, brushing back a floppy snowy curl from her forehead. "That was too easy. What are you up to?"

I blanched on the inside—how could she know what I was planning?—but outside I feigned innocence, pressing the flat of my hand to my chest. "Me? I'm not up to anything. I'm just going to Miguel's for dinner."

She watched me, and I could see the gears turning behind her eyes. "Oh no, you're definitely up to something. If you're going to be playing detective tonight—" And just like that, her bright blue eyes narrowed and she pointed at me. "Aha! You *are* going to be detectiving tonight—"

"I don't think *detectiving* is a word—"

She carried on. "It may not be, but you're going to be doing it tonight, aren't you?" She pushed her lips out until they resembled a duck's bill, then snapped her gnarled fingers. "You're going to do a stakeout, aren't you?" She watched me closely, then said, "Yes, that's what you're going to do. A stakeout. Who? Lisette Morales? David Ruiz? Johnny Morales? Who?"

My jaw dropped. I did want to follow Johnny, but I didn't want to do it alone, and Mrs. Branford wasn't much in terms of backup. I'd thought that once dinner was over and Laura and Sergio had gone back home to their kids, Miguel would join me in a little surveillance work. "How in the world did you know that?" I asked.

She smiled devilishly. "My dear, I've studied human nature for eight decades. I might know you better than you know yourself."

She might at that, I conceded.

"Am I right?" she asked. "Are you going to scope out Johnny?"

"If Miguel will come with me—"

"Oh, he will. That man will follow you anywhere."

I rolled my eyes. "I'm not so sure about that,

but *if* he comes with me, and *if* we can find Johnny, then yes."

"Johnny drives a late model Chevy Malibu," Mrs. Branford said. "From what I remember, he likes to frequent a brewery down the street from his apartment building."

This time I stopped my jaw from dropping. "How do you know—" I started to say, but stopped myself. I knew Penelope Branford was the Mrs. Kravitz of Maple Street, and the entire historic area of town, for that matter, but I hadn't known she was so well-informed about *everyone* in her radius. Now that I thought about it, though, I wasn't surprised. She was elderly and the reality was, she had a fair amount of time on her hands. She read. She lunched. She walked. She played bridge on her phone. She detectived with me as often as she could. And she kept abreast of all the goings-on in Santa Sofia. I waved my hands and said, "Dumb question. Forget I asked that. Where does he live?"

Her eyes twinkled. She loved having information that I didn't. "After the divorce, he got himself a place at The Inlands. Still there, as far as I know. Clear across town, about as far away from the beach as you can get and still be in town limits."

"The Inlands, and the brewery down the street from it. Got it."

"And an old Chevy Malibu. We're talking nineteen-sixties, or thereabouts. Blue. I believe it was his father's, actually. Yes, I'm sure of it. His pride and joy, from what I remember, both father and son."

Agatha had been idly standing by, her tail curled, but not entirely sure what was happening. Was she going for a walk, or staying put? I handed the leash to Mrs. Branford, set down a baggie of kibble, and bent to scratch Agatha's head. "See you later, Agatha. You be a good girl."

"See you tomorrow," Mrs. Branford said with another wink, then, before I could protest, quickly added, "I go to sleep early, so if you're back much after nine, which of course you will be, then I'll just plan on seeing you tomorrow."

"Bright and early," I said, not bothering to hide my grin. I was definitely looking forward to the night ahead.

Chapter 16

Miguel lived in Santa Sofia's Bungalow Oasis, a historic district in its own right, but different than the area I lived in. Our town, like so many of its sister cities, experienced a boom in the early 1900s when oil was discovered. Suddenly, the town, which had been settled by Spanish missionaries late in the sixteenth century and had been a haven for pioneers searching for gold in the 1800s, exploded. The first thirty years of the twentieth century brought crazy growth, although the town had always done its best to control inland sprawl. Santa Sofia had maintained its charm, in large part due to the preservation of its early history.

Bungalows dotted all of the town's older neighborhoods, but Bungalow Oasis held the highest concentration of traditional bungalow architecture, which meant single-story, low-rise houses with verandas and privacy. Bungalow Oasis was bor-

dered by Malibu Street to the east and Riviera
Street to the south, and was part of what locals
called the Upper Laguna District. Early residents
had banded together to form a homeowners association, aptly called Santa Sofia Bungalow Oasis
Neighborhood Association.

Miguel's stucco-sided house sat on a knoll with
a single-car garage at the lowest point on the
right, and a red terra-cotta tiled stairway on the
left leading up to a wrought-iron gate. Green
leafy shrubs and a railing lined either side of the
steps, and atop the pillars at the gate were massive cement pots bursting with flowers. The
Mediterranean-style house could have succumbed
to a hard-edged look, but the curved vertical
line of the wall framing the garage and creating
the base of the veranda, as well as the open
courtyard created by a retaining wall, softened
the look. The courtyard held a single tree, more
shrubbery, and a bed of flowers. The veranda
above the garage was rimmed by flower boxes
cascading with colorful blooms.

I sighed, a sense of peace settling over me. I
loved old homes: the history, the charm, the
unique elements that gave them character.
These were the things I'd fallen in love with
about the house I'd bought, and I already knew
they were the things I'd adore about Miguel's
house.

I walked up the stairway, carrying the second
crusty sourdough loaf I'd picked up from Yeast
of Eden, noting the wall of cypress trees creating
a natural barrier between Miguel's house and

the one next door. The lots were small, but they were private at the same time.

The arched wooden door opened before I could knock, and there stood Miguel in jeans and a casual cream-colored guayabera, wiping his hands on a dish towel. He took my hand as I crossed the threshold, pulling me to him. "Mmm, you smell good," he said, breathing me in, then kissing me. The feel of his hand pressed against my lower back, holding me close to him, sent a thrill through me, and Mrs. Branford's prediction that I'd need Agatha cared for all night surfaced in my brain. *That woman*, I thought with a smile.

Miguel lowered his lips to my neck, and goose bumps rose on my flesh. *This man.*

He slid the strap of my purse from my shoulder, reluctantly let me go, and hung my bag on the coatrack just inside the door. "Let me show you around," he said, taking my hand. "Laura and Sergio'll be here in a few minutes."

The small entry of the house gave way to a larger living room with sliding glass doors opened to the veranda. The honey color of the hardwood floors made the room feel warm. The seating area was grounded by a shag rug, and while the sofa and chairs looked inviting, I was drawn outside. The porch had three potted patio trees, a small bistro table with two chairs, and a rattan loveseat, two matching chairs, and a small outdoor coffee table. It was the perfect outdoor room—an extension of the house. I spread my arms wide and gripped the railing, breathing in the scent of the abundant flowers and the salty ocean air. To the south, I glimpsed downtown Santa Sofia. It was walkable from here, as was the pier where Miguel's restaurant was located. But it was the view straight ahead and to the west that was so arresting. The house had an unadulterated broad view of the Pacific Ocean. I stared. I breathed. I let the brisk air fill my lungs. "You've been holding out on me. This is beautiful."

His arms wrapped around me from behind, his hands against the flat of my stomach, the length of his body against mine. "It is," he said, but from his tone, I wasn't sure if he was talking about the view . . . or me.

He lowered his lips to the back of my neck, his feathery kisses and the roughness of his goatee against my skin making me quiver, but we pulled apart at the slam of a car door below. Laura gazed up at us, shielding her eyes from the glare of the sun, which still lit up the evening sky.

Sergio stepped out of the driver's side of the truck now parked on Miguel's driveway and grinned up at us. "Are we interrupting?"

Miguel didn't bother answering. "Come up," he said, waving them toward the stairs.

As they climbed, he put his hands on either side of my head and pulled me in for one last kiss. "To be continued," he said, and then he took my hand and led me back into the house. We walked through the living area, past a dining table already set with burlap placemats, napkins, silverware, and water glasses, and into the galley kitchen.

It was small but efficient, and from what I could tell, Miguel had gone top-of-the-line with the commercial-grade stainless steel Wolf range. It had five burners, plus a grill and two ovens. I couldn't tell what he'd cooked, but it smelled amazing.

At that moment, the front door slammed and Laura and Sergio's voices carried to us. A moment later, they came into the kitchen bearing a bottle of red wine and a square pan covered in aluminum foil. "Tiramisu from Luigi's," Laura said, skirting by us. She opened the refrigerator and slid the pan in.

Miguel nodded with approval. "Perfect."

"I know," she said, turning back to face us. She drew in a deep breath as she looked at the stove. "Sun-dried tomato pesto, right? With prawns?"

Miguel smiled, long creases like dimples carving into his face and framing his mouth. "What gave it away?"

"Garlic, for one," Laura said. She pointed to a mass of herbs on one section of the butcher-block countertop. "That pile of fresh basil, for two. And the giant pot of water, for three."

Sergio laid his hand on Laura's shoulder, giving a squeeze. "Impressive, babe," he said, nodding appreciatively, and Laura beamed.

Sergio had opened the bottle of wine and retrieved wineglasses from one of the kitchen cupboards. Clearly he and Laura spent enough time here to feel comfortable and to know where things were. He poured, handing a glass to his wife, then to me. Miguel had set to work, stirring the sauce he had simmering on the stove, then adding a light balsamic-based Italian dressing to the salad he'd prepared and tossing it until I was sure each individual lettuce leaf was coated. Using salad tongs, he filled four carved wooden bowls and took them to the table.

We sat at the rectangular table with Miguel and Laura on one side, closer to the kitchen, and Sergio and me on the other. I faced Miguel, while Laura was directly across from Sergio. From where I sat, I could see through to the sunroom in the back of the bungalow, and through the kitchen to a hallway that had to lead to the bedrooms. "Tell me about the house," I said as we sipped our wine and ate our salads.

Miguel held the stem of his wineglass between two fingers and circled, the deep purple liquid swirling inside the bowl. "It's a love-at-first-sight story," he said, and once again, I was pretty sure he was speaking in double entendres.

I felt heat rise to my cheeks as I met his gaze head-on. "That is the best kind."

"I agree," he said.

Laura rolled her eyes and took a healthy swig of her wine. "We get it. You're in love. Tell her about the house, Miguelito."

I stifled a smile at the term of endearment she'd used for her brother, a remnant of their childhood. "Please do, Miguelito," I teased.

He leaned back in his chair and stretched his legs out in front of him. They reached all the way to where I sat. His foot brushed against mine and his mouth quirked up, his eyebrows right along with it. For a moment it felt as if it were only Miguel and me at the table, but then Laura cleared her throat, bringing us both back. "It was a dump," she said, starting the story off for her brother. "Over the years, renters had torn the place apart. I thought he was crazy for wanting to buy it, but it's a good piece of property—"

"It's a great piece of property," Sergio interrupted.

"There's hardly a backyard, though," she said.

Miguel jumped in. "The yard is fine."

"It's a dirt hill."

"It's a clean palette. And I have a plan."

She rolled her eyes. "You always have a plan."

My head swiveled between them as they bickered in true sibling fashion.

Miguel ignored her sarcasm, instead talking about the terraced gardens he planned on creating on the slope in the back of the house. "It's going to blow your mind," he said.

Laura rolled her eyes. "Sounds like it's going to blow your bank account," she said, but she smiled. It was all lighthearted.

Miguel started to collect our salad plates. I stood to help him, skirting around the table and following him to the kitchen. I rinsed them at the sink while he tossed the cooked linguine with the sauce he'd made, then plated it, placing five grilled prawns around each mound of pasta. Finally, he sprinkled finely chopped flat-leaf parsley on top of each serving. I took two plates, and he took two, and we returned to the table. "There's fresh parmesan," he said, handing me the bowl of shredded cheese.

I stopped to admire the meal, thinking it couldn't possibly taste as good as it looked. But after I used my fork and the large spoon Miguel had put on each plate to twirl the linguine into a manageable bite, then placed it in my mouth, I stood corrected. The sauce was like nothing I'd ever tasted. It was creamy, rich, and flavorful. I'd never be able to eat all he'd put on the plate, but I was certainly going to give it my best shot.

We talked about the restaurant remodel, the new menu, Sergio's trucking business, the bread shop, and Laura and Sergio's kids. Eventually . . . inevitably . . . the conversation turned to the investigation. "I saw your brother today," I said to Sergio.

"You did?" Laura asked at the same time Sergio said, "He told me."

All three of them turned their full attention to me, waiting for me to elaborate. "He told me a little bit about your mom and dad," I said to Sergio.

"Yeah." He chuckled. "He said you thought my dad had an affair."

News traveled fast. "I did. I met him the other day. He said something about making a mistake. I assumed that's what he meant, but Ruben said it was something else."

"It's kind of a family secret," Sergio said, shooting a glance at Laura.

She responded by stretching her arm across the table. He did the same, their hands meeting in the middle. She nodded, which I took to be encouragement for him to keep going. "She's trying to help," Laura said to him about me.

Sergio speared a forkful of pasta, spinning it loosely around the tines before putting it in his mouth. He followed it with a bite of bread and a swig of wine. When he was ready, he cleared his throat and spoke. "My dad—he's a gambler. Poker, mostly, although if there isn't a game going, he'll go to Paso Robles."

Paso Robles is in California's Central Coast wine country. The casino over there is European in tradition—what they call boutique—meaning the games, the lounge, and the bar are all in one area, not split off in separate rooms like a bigger casino. In other words, it is small.

"When you say he's a gambler, what does that mean?" I asked, not wanting to jump to the wrong conclusions.

"He has a problem," Sergio answered. "He's gotten himself in and out of trouble with it over the years. There were a few times when it was really bad."

When I raised my eyebrows in a question, it was Laura who continued. "He lost big at a couple of games. Really big. That's what led to the divorce."

"He tried to stop a few times," Sergio said, withdrawing his hand from Laura's and clasping them in front of his plate. "He'd stay away from the games for a while, but then he'd sit in on a hand, and that was that. He was all in again. When he got involved with a loan shark to cover his debts, that's when my mom had had enough. He was in too deep. We knew my grandfather was going to leave my mom the house, and she was afraid she'd lose it because of my dad. She was afraid they'd lose everything because of his debt."

So his mistake hadn't been adultery; it had been gambling. Ruben had said that splitting up had been the smart thing for Johnny and Marisol. I was starting to understand what he'd meant by that. Also by Johnny's off-the-cuff comment that there were other ways to get money besides traditional loans. "She still loved him, but couldn't be with him," I said, appreciating now why she might still turn to him in a moment of crisis.

Sergio was quiet for a minute before saying, "The idea that love conquers all is bullshit."

I brought up Marisol's mental state, and the fact that she'd been struggling with reality. "She talked to you about that?" I asked Sergio.

"I knew she couldn't sleep," he said, pushing his now empty plate aside. "She was really messed up after my grandfather died."

We shook off the somberness in the room, clearing the table, washing up, and serving the tiramisu for dessert. An hour later, Laura gathered up their things. "The babysitter can't stay late tonight," she said, and a few minutes later, after hugs and a heartfelt thank-you, they'd gone.

Miguel and I were alone.

Chapter 17

For the time being, I'd dismissed all thoughts of Marisol's children being involved with her death. Ruben and Sergio? No way. Lisette? She was angry, but I didn't think she was a killer. Maybe my gut was misleading me, but I went with it anyway.

Which meant focusing on Johnny.

Miguel and I sat in his truck in his driveway debating our choices. "We could go knock on his door and just ask him outright," I suggested.

"I don't think that would go over too well," Miguel said. " Hey, Johnny, is your ex-wife dead because you owe money that you can't pay? Are you in deep with a loan shark?' "

"Well, when you put it that way," I said, conceding that showing up on Johnny's doorstep at ten o'clock at night probably wasn't the best idea, especially if there was a real chance that he was guilty. It seemed as if he'd had great intentions when he and Marisol had divorced; he'd wanted to protect her so she wouldn't lose everything. But what if that sentiment had changed when she'd married David? It was entirely possible that he was in such debt that he'd thought Marisol could help him somehow. That she owed him. If she'd refused, he could have gotten angry.

The downside to that theory was the fact that Marisol had asked to meet Johnny, not the other way around. If he'd been angry at her, wouldn't he have been the one to initiate a meeting? I tossed out another idea. "We can see if he's at the brewery Mrs. Branford told me about. If he's not, we can ask around about him. Maybe someone there knows something about who he plays cards with, or if he's in debt to someone."

"Maybe," Miguel said, but he didn't sound convinced.

"What?" I asked.

"I'm thinking it's not the best idea to go digging up dirt on loan sharks. If Johnny had been concerned enough about his family's safety to choose divorce, whatever he's involved in can't be good. Marisol was killed, remember."

That was a very good point, but I had an idea. Santa Sofia was a small town, after all, and as Mrs. Branford had said many times, she'd taught nearly everyone in town. I already knew that she was a gossip. If anyone would know about a loan shark in town, it would be her.

Or Emmaline. But I didn't want to call her. Not yet, anyway. We needed proof.

I dialed Mrs. Branford, knowing she was probably in bed. But I also knew that she'd be thrilled that she was my go-to person. She loved being Watson to my Holmes. Archie Goodwin to my Nero Wolf. Hastings to my Poirot. She answered, not sounding groggy at all. "It's about time," she chastised.

My first thought was Agatha. Had my little pug been a little pain? "Is Agatha okay? Do you need me to come get her?"

She responded quickly. "Agatha's just peachy. Right here by my side, aren't you, sweet girl?" she said, and I imagined her scratching the dog's little head.

But then, all at once, I registered several unfamiliar sounds. My hackles went up. Maple Street was exceptionally quiet at this time of night. Most families with small children lived in the newer homes, usually more inland where they were slightly more affordable, and where there were parks and schools more easily accessible. I shouldn't be hearing the blaring of a horn, or the chatter of people's voices, or music. "Mrs. Branford—"

"Penny, dear," she said, interrupting me with what had become a running battle of wills. She wanted me to call her Penny, or Penelope, even, but I had met her as Mrs. Branford, and there was something respectful to her age and wisdom that kept me using that instead of adopting one of the informal monikers.

"Mrs. Branford," I said, emphasizing the name by speaking it slowly, "where are you?"

She chortled. "Little Agatha and I decided we needed some fresh air."

I narrowed my eyes, my brows pinching together, because I knew she was up to something. Still, I played it off as if I weren't suspicious. "Oh, great, you went for a walk?"

"Well, no, not a walk."

"Where are you?" I asked, shooting a worried look at Miguel. My voice had dropped an octave and my heart suddenly pounded in my chest. Mrs. Branford's night vision wasn't great—she saw halos—and I knew by the way she'd responded that the fresh air she and Agatha had wanted had been achieved by them taking a drive. Mrs. Branford was a self-proclaimed non-driver at this point in her life. She preferred the volunteers who came and took her to the library or market or movies, or she waited for me to do those things with her. She had a beautiful old Volvo coupe, sage green, in her garage, but I'd been the last person to drive it. Mrs. Branford's only daughter—Katherine, whom she'd named after the character in Shakespeare's *The Taming of the Shrew*—and who she said I reminded her of, had lost her battle with cancer years ago. She had two sons who would inherit the majority of her estate, but her car, which she and her husband had loved, she was bequeathing to me. I didn't think she'd be out tooling around in it, and certainly not at this time of night.

She exhaled, loudly, but didn't answer my question. I mouthed to Miguel to start driving as I posed it again, more insistently this time. "Mrs. Branford, where are you?"

"Ivy, dear, Agatha and I decided to get a jump on things—"

Oh my God. "Tell me you're not staking out Johnny Morales's apartment."

Miguel snapped his head in my direction. "What the hell?"

I dropped the phone to my lap and pressed the speaker button. "I am not staking out Johnny Morales's apartment," she said.

I sighed with relief—until I thought about the way she'd phrased her denial. She was playing semantics with me, answering the question literally, which still left her whereabouts in a gray area. "Mrs. Branford," I said, a tone of warning in my voice.

This time she sighed. "We *were* staking out Johnny's apartment, but when he left, we did, too."

"You followed him," I said. It was a statement, not a question. I knew Mrs. Branford well enough to know that she would have stuck to Johnny like glue. I also knew enough about Johnny and what he was involved in that worry filled me. Mrs. Branford, with her snowy hair, distinctive velour tracksuits, and pristine white orthopedic shoes, didn't exactly blend in, especially not in the gambling circles Johnny was likely to frequent.

Miguel stopped at a traffic light, waiting to hear where she was so he'd know which way to drive.

Mrs. Branford didn't hear my chastisement, or she chose to ignore it. She couldn't keep the excitement out of her voice. "He's at the bar down the street from his apartment, just like I said he might be."

Chalk one up for Mrs. Branford's armchair detective skills. "Stay in the car," I directed. "We're on our way."

I'd written down the address of the Inlands apartment complex. I showed the paper to Miguel. He took off the moment the light turned green and just as Mrs. Branford said, "What car?"

My brows knitted together. So she hadn't driven the Volvo. "You didn't drive," I stated matter-of-factly.

"Ivy, dear, you know me better than that. Driving, especially at night, is not something I do anymore."

"Then how did you—oh, Uber," I said.

"Lyft, actually," she corrected. "Very nice driver, I might add. He's a young man saving money for college. He offered to wait for me, but I sent him on his way because I knew, of course, that you'd be along at some point."

"Mrs. Branford, where are you right now?" I asked, hoping she wasn't actually inside the bar.

"Sitting in the bar," she answered glibly, as if she could read my mind and loved being contrary, "but don't worry, Johnny isn't here."

Miguel and I looked at each other. "If *he's* not there, why are *you* there?"

She chuckled. "Let me rephrase, my dear. He is *here*, he's just not *here*."

Miguel turned onto Broadway, following it east. I rubbed my head, puzzled and a tiny bit frustrated at her word games. "What?"

She lowered her voice and spoke, but her words were lost amidst the din of the background noise.

"I didn't hear you. What did you say?" I asked, raising the volume of my own voice.

"There's a gam—oom—" she said, but again, her words faded away as an electric guitar blared. She started to speak again, but the connection crackled. "I'm lo—sing y—ou," she said, her voice breaking, and then, before she could say anything more, the line went dead.

"Mrs. Branford?" I stared at the phone, watching as the screen turned dark. I immediately called her back, but it went straight to voicemail. I looked at Miguel. "How could she lose service in a bar?"

His expression was grim. "I think she was saying that there's a gaming room."

"Gaming, as in poker?"

He nodded. "Most likely. And if it's downstairs, which it probably would be given that gaming's illegal, reception wouldn't be as good."

Oh no. "You think she was going downstairs to spy on Johnny?"

His frown gave me the answer to that question.

We were silent for a few minutes as he drove, leaving the palm trees and beachy feeling of downtown behind the farther east we traveled. He made a left turn, followed by a quick right, then another left. We headed north for another mile before he turned onto Pelican Street.

"There," I said, spotting Inland Apartments a half mile down.

Miguel slowed. He scanned the left side of the street while I searched the right, looking for the bar/brewery Mrs. Branford had followed Johnny to. "That's gotta be it," I said, pointing to the sign that said THE LIBRARY, sporting not books but a frothy mug of beer.

"Clever," Miguel said. "Where were you tonight, babe?"

I put my flattened palm against my chest and feigned innocence. "Who, me? I was at the library."

Miguel smiled crookedly. "No lie there."

I spotted an old blue car parallel parked across from the bar. A Chevy Malibu. "That's probably his."

Miguel pulled the truck into a spot on the next block. We doubled back to the bar, stopping just inside the entrance. For a Wednesday night, the place was hopping. I'd thought the guitar I'd heard over the phone had been from a juke box, but a live band was set up on a stage in the back of the room. They were in the midst of playing a Paramore song that I'd heard a million times on the radio. The bar itself was on the right side of the room with tables set up in an orderly manner. Along the wall were shelves with books lined up, lending a bit of corroboration to the name of the bar.

I scanned the perimeter, looking for a stairwell or any other clue or sign that a poker game might be going on somewhere on the premises. Nothing jumped out at me, and there was no sign of Mrs. Branford or Agatha. I didn't want to ask at the bar to alert the people here that an elderly woman with a little dog was lurking around, so I headed toward the back hallway where the restroom sign hung, Miguel right by my side.

The hallway was dark and narrow. On one side were two scuffed dark wood doorways clearly marked GUYS and DOLLS. The restrooms. On the opposite side of the hall were two more doors, one marked with a placard that read OFFICE—PRIVATE. The other was unadorned.

"I'm going to check in here first," I said, wanting to make sure Mrs. Branford hadn't just hidden herself away in in the women's bathroom before Miguel and I ventured into an illegal gambling den.

It took all of ten seconds to crouch down and see that one of the stalls was empty and the other was occupied by someone wearing flip-flops. Someone who was not Mrs. Branford. I returned to Miguel in the hallway. He notched his thumb to the men's room. "She's not in there, either."

My heart had been pounding since I'd found out Mrs. Branford was out detecting on her own, but now it was practically hammering out of my chest. Who knew what was behind door number four and what she might have gotten herself into. If Johnny was mixed up with the wrong sort of people and they were sitting at a table with him playing illegal cards, then they wouldn't be too happy having an old lady snooping around—or Miguel and me, for that matter.

We looked at each other, nodded simultaneously, and before I could talk myself out of it, I turned the handle of the door, slowly pulling it open. An old sconce hung on the wall with a low-wattage lightbulb screwed into it. The illumination was dim, but it was enough to see the

stairway leading down. I couldn't hear anything—no voices, no interrogation of Mrs. Branford, no barking—so I stepped into the depths.
Miguel followed, quickly closing the door behind him. It was an old building, with what looked
like creaky wooden stairs. We tiptoed down,
making as little noise as possible, managing to
get to the bottom without alerting anyone who
might be down here to our presence.

I didn't move forward, but instead held my
right arm up in a silent gesture, feeling like a
SWAT team officer noiselessly communicating
with the rest of her team before doing a coordi-
nated attack. The room was filled with cases of
liquor. From where I stood, I could see boxes of
bottled Michelob, Budweiser, Corona, Coors,
and a handful of other brands, all in both regular and lite. Along another wall were boxes of
the well liquor the bar used, as well as a variety
of the top-shelf varieties like Tanqueray and
Bombay gin, Glenfiddich, Patrón, and so many
more. This was a drinker's paradise. With this
much alcohol, I couldn't believe they didn't
keep the door locked. Unless—

"Do you think Mrs. Branford knows how to
pick a lock?" I whispered.

Miguel looked over his shoulder to the top of
the stairs as if the answer would be there, then
turned back to me. "Does she have a secret
sketchy life we don't know about?"

Neither one of us could answer either question so we left it and walked stealthily around
the room. There was a built-in refrigerator where

I assumed more beer was stored, as well as the kegs for the beer on tap. Shelving lined one section of wall housing bulk packages of napkins, stir sticks, massive cans of maraschino cherries, green olives, and other bar paraphernalia. I rounded a stack of boxes and stopped suddenly. Miguel's hand landed on my hip as he came up short behind me. "There," I said, pointing to a closed door. It could be another office or storage room, but it could be the secret gambling den Johnny played in.

He nodded at me, and we both crept closer. I put my ear to the door and held my breath, my heart skittering when I heard faint voices. I couldn't make out any of them, though.

Miguel's hand clasped my arm at the sound of a door opening at the top of the stairs. "What the hell?" someone said, then footsteps pounded quickly down the steps.

Miguel yanked me behind the stacks of rum and whiskey boxes, ducking out of the way and crouching down on our haunches just as a figure approached the door. An arm jetted out, grabbing the handle and flinging it open. From where I hid, I could only see the man's back, but the anger in his voice was unmistakable. "Why the hell is that door up there unlocked?" he demanded, followed quickly by a flabbergasted, "Who the hell are you?"

"It's cool, man," a voice I recognized said. It was Johnny. "She used to be my teacher."

Mrs. Branford!

Miguel squeezed my hand. My feisty friend was safe, and in the poker room.

"I don't care who she is. How the hell did she get down here?"

"I ran into her outside the john," Johnny said. I thought I detected a hint of contrition in his voice, but wasn't sure.

"It's my fault," Mrs. Branford said. Her voice was strong and confident. "When Johnny came out of the unmarked door in the hallway, I was curious. I know places like this have poker rooms, so I took a chance and asked him."

"She's not the cops, if that's what you're worried about," Johnny said, stating what had to be obvious to anyone who met Penelope Branford. "I can vouch for her."

What a guy. I suspected he wouldn't feel that way if he knew why she was really here.

"Is that a dog?" the man at the door asked, incredulous, then again, "Is that a goddamned dog?"

Mrs. Branford's elderly voice piped up. "Have you heard of the poverty-of-vocabulary hypothesis?" After the man at the door responded with a negative grunt, she continued. "The theory is that swearing shows the weakness in your vocabulary, which is a direct result of poor education, laziness, or simply lack of impulse control. People will tend to judge you, perhaps unfairly, based on your use of vulgarity. They may, for example, see you as less friendly than your non-swearing counterparts."

The man stiffened and started to speak, but Mrs. Branford cut him off. "That is not to say

that I believe this is all true, although I am not
sensing the friendliness of your nature," she said
as an aside. "There are those who believe, conversely, that people who have a particularly strong
vulgarity index may, in fact, be extraordinarily
intelligent. Imagine, if you will, the difficulty
that exists when one tries to translate untranslat-
able words from one language to another. There
isn't a way to express some things because the
word only has meaning in one language. Like-
wise, certain so-called taboo words communicate an idea or emotion more effectively or
succinctly than any other words might be able
to. It is a linguistic strength, then, to effectively
communicate using these words."

Someone in the room with Mrs. Branford
sniggered. "Are you saying Brent is some sort of
genius? Because I don't know if that's true."

"It is a possibility," Mrs. Branford said. "He
first asked if this was a dog, then he inserted the
invective into the sentence, effectively changing
the tone of the question. His intent was quite
clear. The first question simply checked for understanding. Yes, in fact, this is a dog. But the
second question conveyed his extreme displea-
sure in having said dog on the premises, all by
adding a single word." She paused, and I imagined her surveying her audience around the
poker table. "Language is fascinating. An individual's personal lexicon says so much about them.
You, sir, run a business, suspected me of wrong-
doing of some sort because I'm down here in
this room with your regulars, yet you haven't

dragged me out of here because you know that I am not a threat. You're curious. I probably remind you of your grandmother."

The man at the door laughed. From where Miguel and I hid, I could see his body visibly relax. His shoulders dropped and he shifted the weight from both of his legs to one, looking more at ease. "You do. She's a feisty mama, too, just like you."

"Your use of the endearment 'mama' is quite telling," Mrs. Branford said. "I'd be willing to bet that she raised you. You're closer to her than one might normally be to their grandmother."

"Who are you, lady?" the man at the door, Brent, asked with a bit of reverence in his voice.

"As Johnny said, I was his teacher. English, but I'm sure you figured that out."

"I bet you're one hell of a poker player," Brent said. "An observer of human nature."

"I can hold my own," she said modestly. I could picture her in my mind's eye looking a trifle sheepish at the compliment, blooms of pink coloring her cheeks. I'd said it before, and I'd say it again: The woman had missed her calling. More than one. She could have run therapy groups, and, truly, she should have been on the stage.

Brent held the door handle, turning to go back the way he'd come. "Make sure the door's locked next time," he said, speaking, I was sure, not to Mrs. Branford, but to the men in the room. A command, not a request.

It was Johnny who responded. "Will do. Sorry about that."

"Don't let it happen again," Brent said. He nodded to the room—or maybe just to Mrs. Branford—closed the door, and headed back up the stairs, leaving Miguel and me in awe of Penelope Branford. "She's good," I whispered, my esteem for her clear in my voice.

"She certainly is," Miguel agreed.

We crept back up the steps, listening at the door until we were sure the coast was clear, and left Mrs. Branford to her poker game. We sat at a table, knowing we'd get a full report when she finally finished playing, both poker and the detective game she was smack in the middle of. I crossed my jean-clad legs, my chunky-heeled black loafer dangling from my foot. I figured we were in for a little bit of a wait.

Miguel flagged down a twenty-something cocktail waitress wearing belted high-waisted jean shorts that crept up her booty and a crop top that just barely revealed her bellybutton piercing. She sauntered over and took our drink order, then sashayed away again as my phone jingled from my purse. I dug it out, noting that the number displayed on the screen wasn't familiar, but was local. I'd scarcely said hello when David Ruiz, clearly agitated, interrupted. "You're still trying to figure out what happened to my wife, right?"

"Absolutely," I said. "Why? What's wrong?"

"I found something." His voice cracked with emotion. "I-I can't believe—Christ, she didn't tell me."

I uncrossed my legs and sat up straighter. "Tell you what, David?"

"I can't—I don't know—Where are you?" he finally said. "I'll come meet you."

"I'm at The Library," I said, hearing in real time how misleading that sounded. I gave him the address. "It's a bar on the east side of town."

"I'm on my way," he said, and after we hung up, I wondered what he'd found and why he felt it was so urgent to share it with me.

David arrived at The Library in less than twenty minutes. He had to have been halfway out the door when he called. He came in, spotted me right away, then did a double take when he saw Miguel sitting with me. His expression clouded for a split second, but then it cleared and he headed our way. Miguel rose, holding his hand out to David. They shook, and Miguel placed his left hand on David's shoulder, giving it a bolstering squeeze.

He was looking worse for wear, which, given the state he'd been in when Miguel and I had visited him at his house, was saying something. The salt-and-pepper stubble on his face was scruffy and uneven, emphasizing the dark circles under his eyes and the ashen tone of his skin. It had only been a few days since the discovery of Marisol's body, but he looked as if he'd lost ten pounds, which was weight he couldn't afford to be without. His cheeks and eyes were sunken, and his clothes hung loose on his body. Any thought I'd entertained about him being behind his wife's death dissipated slightly. This was clearly a grieving man.

David refused the drink Miguel offered to buy for him. He pulled out one of the two empty chairs at our table and sank onto it, his body slouching against the hard back. He folded one arm over his chest, propping the opposite elbow on it and pressing his fingertips against his forehead. He looked like he was barely holding it together, so I cut to the chase. "What did you find, David?"

He exhaled loudly, straightened up, and stuck his hand into the pocket of the lightweight windbreaker he had on over a worn Jupiter Farms T-shirt. When he withdrew it, he held an envelope that had been folded in half once, then again. He placed it in the center of the table.

"What is it?" I asked staring at it as if it might be a bomb. A bombshell was more like it, from the way he was acting.

He laid his hands flat on the hard surface of the table, his breathing heavy and labored. "It's a letter Mari wrote."

He wasn't being overly forthcoming, so I kept prodding. "A letter she wrote to you?"

At this, he shrugged. "Not to me. I think it's to—" He stopped. Regrouped. "I don't know. Maybe I'm wrong. You tell me."

I nodded toward it. "May I?"

He lifted his hand in a permission-granting gesture. "That's why I brought it. To see if you could make sense of it, because I sure as hell can't."

I restrained myself from speculating as I unfolded the envelope and pressed it flat, taking a moment to note any markings. It was wrinkled and looked as if it had been handled a lot, but there was no writing of any sort on it. The paper inside was equally worn, looking as if it had been folded and unfolded over and over and over again. I placed it on the table between Miguel and me so we could read it together.

> *I know what you did. What you're doing, I should say, and I'm disgusted. But I don't know what to do. What do I do?! Do I tell? We've been grieving for my father. You know how much I miss him. How lost I am. And you do this? We've known each other since . . . since forever. I should have been able to trust you. I can't get my head around the idea that you betrayed me like this. My father . . . oh God, my father. And my kids . . . what do I tell them?*

Several things hit me at once. The first was that it seemed so clear that the letter was written to Johnny. He'd betrayed her with his gambling and debt, which had led to their divorce. She referenced her father's death here, though, so this letter was recent. Which led to the second thing, namely that Johnny had betrayed her again somehow, and not only her, but her father and children.

I wondered at the value of Marisol's house and if that had anything to do with what happened to her, but Johnny had no stake in the house. I couldn't get two and two to add up to four in this case.

I remembered the change in the will. Marisol had made David the beneficiary, but had put in stipulations that prevented him from actually benefiting from it financially, and prevented her kids from taking legal possession for at least ten years. Could she have done that to protect the house that had belonged to her father? Maybe she feared that if her kids inherited it, Johnny would somehow end up with it.

"David, who would have inherited your house if Marisol hadn't changed her will?" I asked.

He sat with his elbows propped on the table, his head in his hands. "Johnny. It all would have gone to Johnny."

I gulped. "Not to the kids?"

He shook his head. "That's why she wanted to change it. If something happened to her, she wanted it to go to the kids, but she wanted to protect it, too. To give them time to accept things before they decided what to do with it."

If Johnny didn't know about the change in the will, whether or not he was in serious debt, his motive for murdering Marisol just grew exponentially.

I put that aside for the time being, coming back to the details of the note. "It's definitely her writing?"

"Oh yeah. One hundred percent. She does—did—this combination of printing and cursive. She usually wrote neater than this, but it's definitely hers."

With that verified, I moved on. "Do you think this is a draft?"

"What do you mean?"

"A draft, meaning that she wrote this, but then rewrote it and maybe sent it or gave it to someone?" Whenever I wrote a letter, which, granted, wasn't often, I started with a salutation. This wasn't a happy letter, so maybe Marisol didn't want to begin that way, but still. There was no closure to it, either. It felt more like an excerpt than an entire letter. "It doesn't feel complete, does it?"

Miguel had nodded along as I'd tried to explain what I meant. "I see what you mean. It's missing the opening and the closing."

David stared at us. "Does that matter?"

"Maybe," I said. "If this is it, the only thing she wrote, and it stayed in her possession, then it's more like she was venting or capturing her own emotions, right? Kind of like a journal, only without the book. Whoever she was writing it to never saw it. But if this was, say, a practice version, and she rewrote it or sent something similar, then that's different. She's calling someone out for a betrayal. That could be a motive."

What color David had left drained from his face. "You're saying that if she sent this—well, not this, but a copy of this—that *whoever* the recipient was might have killed her over it?"

We sat in silence. I knew David thought, like I did, that Marisol had written the letter to Johnny.

A flurry of voices intermixed with a dog's bark—a bark I instantly recognized as Agatha's—came from the back hallway of the bar. Mrs. Branford appeared, holding the dog's leash loosely in her hand. Agatha trotted alongside her. Next to her was a man I didn't recognize, and next to him was Johnny.

The man next to Mrs. Branford stopped, turned to her, and said something that made her smile and laugh. "I will, indeed," she said.

"Good," the man said, and then he wandered off, passing us by without a glance, leaving The Library for the dark of the night outside.

Mrs. Branford scanned the room, her gaze alighting on our little table. Her sly grin told me everything I needed to know—at least for the moment: She had had a successful poker game. She headed over to us, Johnny still in tow, a wad of cash visible in her hand. Recognition crossed his face, but it was only when he registered David that he stopped. The smile he'd worn vanished. Clearly he and his ex-wife's husband did not have a convivial relationship.

I sensed his desire to turn tail and scurry away. Before he could do that, I jumped up and hurried toward them. "Mrs. Branford! And Mr. Morales! What a surprise to see you both here." I spun, gesturing to the table I'd just left. Miguel was just where I'd left him, but David was gone. My gaze darted to the table. No letter, either. I stumbled on my words, trying to hide my surprise. "We—we're out having a—a drink." I turned back to them. "Care to join us?"

Johnny forced a tight smile. "Was that David Ruiz?"

"Yes. Right, of course you know him."

"No, not really," Johnny corrected. "I mean, we're not soc—We don't—He married my ex-wife, that's it."

I moved back toward the table, hoping he'd simply follow me. He did. I scooped up Agatha as Miguel stood to help Mrs. Branford into the chair vacated by David. Johnny, however, stayed standing. "He's broken up about Marisol," I said to explain David's presence . . . and then disappearance.

Johnny didn't respond, so I kept going. "He, uh, found part of a letter she wrote."

Johnny's eyes narrowed, tension lines crinkling on either side of his eyes. "What kind of letter?"

I weighed my words carefully, not wanting to spook him, but wanting to read his reaction. "Something about a betrayal. There weren't any details."

Johnny was visibly uncomfortable. His nostrils flared and he folded his arms over his chest like a barrier. "Who was it to?"

I stroked Agatha's flat little head, pretending to focus on her rather than Johnny. I was fishing, following the most likely lead I had at the moment, which was that Johnny's gambling troubles had caught up with him, and that somehow, it had led to a betrayal. What it had to do with Marisol's father, I didn't know yet. One thing at a time. "It didn't have a name. I thought that maybe it was about your affair, though," I said, surreptitiously watching him.

"My what—?"

"Your affair. I mean, you said you made a mistake and that's why you and Marisol got divorced. Maybe it was an old letter when she was working through dealing with the end of her marriage."

I knew that couldn't be possible, given the reference to her father's death, but Johnny didn't know that. He also hadn't had an affair, but he'd been so ambiguous about his so-called mistake that it was an obvious assumption on my part. He didn't know Sergio had told us the truth.

He jumped at the explanation, visibly relieved. "That must be it. She always did hang on to old letters and journals. Rough for David to find it."

"The whole thing's been rough on him," Miguel said.

"Quite understandably," Mrs. Branford said, piping up for the first time since she'd sat down. "Having the funeral tomorrow will help everyone. A chance to say goodbye gives closure, cliché as it might sound."

"I don't know if I'll go," Johnny said.

My head snapped to look at him. "Why wouldn't you?"

Johnny's dark eyes turned glassy. "I put myself in David's shoes. If I was him, I wouldn't want me there. The ex-husband? Come on."

I couldn't help but glance at Miguel. Luke showing up unexpectedly had put us in a similar situation. Since the encounter at my house, I hadn't seen hide nor hair of Luke, and I still didn't know why he'd come. I hadn't had time to give it much thought, and I still didn't. I pushed the visit to the back of my mind where Luke had resided for so long, refocusing on Johnny Morales.

"Your children would want you there," Mrs. Branford was saying.

If I assumed he hadn't had anything to do with Marisol's death, I'd agree with her, but at this point, he was the lead suspect in my mind. If he proved to be Marisol's killer, how would his kids feel about him having been at the funeral? "See how you feel tomorrow," I suggested as Agatha grunted contentedly in my arms.

Johnny looked at me for a beat too long, then abruptly changed the subject. "You still thinking about that yard remodel?"

"What yard remodel?" Miguel asked.

Mrs. Branford jumped in, patting Miguel's hand with her own arthritic one. "A hot tub. A new deck. Ivy has a lot of grand plans."

I hemmed and hawed. "I don't know. I don't think I want to take out a loan against my mortgage."

Johnny wrapped his hands around the top of the chair he stood behind and leaned in. "I get that. I know a guy, though. He isn't with *my* bank—"

Was he with any bank? I wondered.

"—so there's no impact on your credit or your mortgage. Easy to borrow, no credit check. Something to think about."

Miguel shifted in his seat, clearly not liking the implication of borrowing money from "some guy." I shot him a look that said *I got this*, before he could jump in and interrogate Johnny about it.

"I'll think about it," I said with a smile.

He nodded amiably, the worry over Marisol's note diffused. "I have to get back to the game. Gotta win some of my money back." His laugh held an undercurrent of dismay. "Let me know if you want to play again, Mrs. B. I'll set a place for you."

Mrs. Branford wiggled her fingers at him. "I'll do that, Johnny."

"Keep in mind, beginner's luck only works once," he added, giving her an indulgent smile.

Based on the pile of money sitting on the table in front of her, her beginner's luck had taken her a long way. I expected a retort of some kind, but from her devilish grin, I knew this had not been Mrs. Branford's first poker rodeo.

The second Johnny was out of sight, Miguel and I both turned to Mrs. Branford. "Did you have a secret life as a card shark?" I asked, looking pointedly at the stack of bills.

"Bridge and poker are not dissimilar," she said. "I prefer bridge, but Jimmy always favored poker. I was a quick study." She tapped the stack of greenbacks in front of her. "I am severely out of practice, I admit, but I did okay against the likes of Johnny Morales and the other men at the table."

"I guess you did. Did Johnny say anything about . . . anything?" I asked. He'd been as overt as I thought he would be by mentioning his "connection," who could loan me money. I didn't imagine he'd be more forthcoming at the poker table—they had to be discreet, after all—but anything was possible.

"I did well, so no need for anyone to extend me credit," she said. "I came away with zilch—in terms of information."

That was disappointing, but the night hadn't

been a complete bust. Thanks to David, we'd gotten a better glimpse into Marisol's state of mind before her death, and thanks to Mrs. Branford, Johnny was on high alert. I was more convinced than ever that we were on the right track.

Chapter 18

The next day was completely dedicated to helping Olaya prepare for the funeral, and then to the funeral itself. I started with a walk around the neighborhood, then took Agatha over to my brother's. He hadn't known Marisol like I did, which meant he didn't mind missing the funeral to do a little Agatha-sitting. He lived about five miles from the house we'd grown up in, was a contractor, and usually had enough flexibility to help out our dad—or me—if either of us needed it. I could have crated Agatha, or even taken her to Mrs. Branford's again, but it was going to be a long day. Plus, Mrs. Branford would be coming to the funeral, so her dog-sitting hours would be limited.

I hadn't seen Billy since before Emmaline had planned to propose to him. He'd been available for Agatha, so I'd jumped at the chance to see him, even if only for a few minutes.

His house was a small single-story fixer-upper with a one-car garage. He'd bought it as a foreclosure, without seeing the inside. Emmaline and I had gone with him to see it for the first time after the sale was finalized. Whoever had owned it—and lost it—had taken a bat to the walls, spilled cans of paint over the flooring, ripped out the bathroom faucets, broken most of the light fixtures, and left the place uninhabitable. Billy had gotten it for a steal, though, and since he was a contractor, he had access to resources at wholesale and the know-how to bring the place back to its mid-century glory. It was a work in progress, and he loved every minute of it.

I pulled up to the house, parking alongside the curb. Billy's truck was in the driveway. The garage door was open and he was hunched over a rectangular table that sat in the middle of the space, electric sander roaring in his hand. He flipped the switch, turning it off when he saw me, sliding the clear safety goggles up to his forehead.

"This is beautiful," I said, running my fingers along the smooth surface of the table. The base was made from what looked like reclaimed wood beams from a barn, the joints connected with industrial-looking metal. It looked, and felt, like Billy was doing the final sanding of the reclaimed wood top.

"Yeah, I think so," he said, putting the sander down and scratching Agatha's head affectionately.

She looked up at him with her bulging eyes and blinked.

"Good to see you, too, Ags," he said.

Billy's hobby was woodworking and carpentry, which usually took the form of handmade furniture. Any jobs he got were strictly through word-of-mouth and he was very selective about the projects he took on. He was a perfectionist and did everything at 110 percent. People were willing to pay the price. I set Agatha down, holding on to her leash. She sniffed around at the sawdust, turning in a circle, her paws leaving footprints in the powdery particles of wood. "Who's it for?" I asked.

"It's for me." He smiled mischievously, his hazel eyes twinkling. "And Em."

I felt my eyebrows lift. "You *and* Em?" They didn't currently live together, and as far as I knew, he wasn't aware of the imminent marriage proposal.

He laid the goggles down next to the sander and headed into the house, crooking his finger at me so I'd follow. He headed straight for the kitchen, grabbing a glass and filling it with water. He gulped it down before facing me. "Can you keep a secret?"

I laughed. Could I ever. I wanted so badly to tell him about Emmaline's romantic plan, the cool ring she'd found for him, and the marital bliss in his future, but I'd been sworn to secrecy, and that was a promise I'd never break. "Um, yeah," I said smugly. "I can."

He hesitated for just a second before sliding open one of the kitchen drawers. He withdrew a little gray box tied with a pink ribbon. He opened it and took out a small black velvet jewelry box.

My breath caught in my throat. Delicately perched inside was a stunning white-gold engagement ring with a marquis-cut center diamond. Small round diamonds were in a pavé setting like a halo in the band. "Oh my God," I breathed, cupping my hands around his and the velvet box. "It's beautiful."

He grinned, looking goofy and thrilled and excited, like a little boy on Christmas morning with a stocking chock-full of trinkets and goodies. "You really think so?"

"Billy, yes. God, it's gorgeous."

"You think she'll like it?"

He sounded nervous, which was absurd. Emmaline was my oldest friend. I knew her as well as I knew myself. Better, maybe. If Emmaline were to pick out her own ring, this would be exactly what she'd choose. "She's going to love it," I said, and then giddiness overcame me and I jumped up and down, rubbing my hands together. "You're going to propose?"

He nodded, his expression turning sheepish.

"You're going to propose!" I exclaimed. There couldn't be two people more perfect for one another than Billy and Emmaline, right down to the fact that they'd both planned to propose to one another . . .

"When?" I asked, wondering who'd beat who to the punch. "How?"

He tucked the ring box back into the drawer. "I was going to do it the other night at the beach, but then, well, you know. The dead body kinda spoiled the moment."

I blinked. He'd been intending to propose at the same time she had? Talk about simpatico. "Yeah. So what now?"

He ran his hand through the waves of his dark hair. Billy looked like my dad, with his brown hair, blue-green eyes, and lean stature. I, on the other hand, had taken after our mom with her fairer skin and curly, ginger, untamed hair. "Not till this case is solved. She's pretty consumed by it."

"I know the feeling." Death, no matter whose it was, had a way of creeping in and staying put.

"Funeral's today, eh?"

I nodded. "Thanks for taking Agatha."

He looked down and winked at the pug. "No prob, right, Ags? We're going to clean up the garage so I can do the finish work on the table."

"She can play in the backyard, too," I said, not wanting him to feel as if he had to have her by his side the entire day. Dog-sitting was a responsibility, but it wasn't as all-consuming as babysitting, and Agatha was relatively independent as dogs went. She liked to be my shadow, but she was perfectly capable of entertaining herself or taking a good long nap in the sun.

"I got it, Ivy. Me and Agatha, we'll be just fine."

I crouched down and looked her in the eyes. "See you later, alligator."

She sniffed at me, then pressed her cold nose to mine. It was her version of a kiss. I unsnapped her harness, slipped it over her head, and with one last look at me, she trotted off to explore Billy's house.

*   *   *

I arrived at Yeast of Eden fifteen minutes later, where I found Olaya already elbow-deep in bread dough. Whatever she was making, it was not part of the menu we'd planned for the funeral. "Italian sfogliatelle," I repeated after she'd told me what she was working on. "What is that?"

"*Mija,* you are in for a treat. It is a delight." She turned the wood-grip hand crank of a chrome-plated steel pasta machine that was clamped to the counter at her workstation. The sheet of pasta dough she fed through the plates of the machine emerged as a long, thin, six-inch-wide rectangle.

"Pasta?" I asked, puzzled. I'd never seen her use a pasta machine in the bread shop's kitchen, or anywhere else for that matter.

She tapped the pads of her fingers on the top of the appliance as if it were a beloved house cat. "This machine, it is good for more than simply pasta. Sfogliatelle comes from the Campania region of Italy. They are sweet delicacies, a bit like the French croissant."

I watched, fascinated, as she finished pressing the dough through the machine. Next, she cut the rectangle of dough into roughly twenty-inch-long sections, brushing each one with melted butter, layering them as she went. Finally, she tightly rolled the stack into itself like a jelly roll, wrapped it in plastic, and moved on to the next one. In all, she made six rolls, taking them to the walk-in refrigerator when she had them all buttered, layered, rolled, and wrapped.

"These will be for the shop tomorrow," she said. "A special treat."

Yeast of Eden was not a traditional bakery. Olaya's focus was always on bread, specifically long-rise yeast breads. Once in a while, however, she baked other unexpected things. Usually these specialty items were related to an event she was catering or some special request someone had made. I'd seen her bake things like Russian babka, British clangers, and Scandinavian kringlers, but I'd never seen the likes of these Italian sfogliatelle. She took some already prepared rolls of dough from the refrigerator and unwrapped the first one. Using a sharp knife, she cut the roll into one-inch slices, then repeated with the others until she had sixty pinwheel-like rounds lined up on the counter.

"This is the difficult part," she said as she took a dough round in one hand and began pressing the thumb of her other hand into the center.

"It all looks difficult," I said. I'd put my things down and washed my hands, and now picked up one of the pinwheel rounds, following her lead.

She started to stretch the dough, warning me not to push into it yet. "You do not want to make a cavity too soon. First it must be bigger and flatter."

I did as she said, stopping when the dough was several inches in diameter.

"Now you must start to smooth it out. Push down in the center. Yes, that is right. You are creating a hollow in the dough, like a cone."

"It looks like a clamshell," I said, holding up the finished cone. The large opening was about three inches, tapering down to the smaller end, which was just about an inch wide.

Olaya nodded approvingly. I took mental notes as she brushed a bit of butter on the dough and then deftly turned it inside out, cupping the now inside-out cone in the palm of her hand. She quickly walked to the stove, returning with a large frying pan filled with a sautéed onion, colorful finely chopped bell peppers, and crab. She carefully deposited two large spoonfuls of the filling into the hollow of dough, filling it to the top. Finally, she closed the mouth of the cone by carefully folding the dough over onto itself as if she were closing two halves of a clamshell together.

She laid it carefully on a baking sheet and then moved on to another.

I stood by her side, stretching, shaping, filling, and closing the sfogliatelle pastries until all sixty were finished. We brushed each one with an egg wash before baking them.

"Those for tomorrow, here at the bread shop, they will be sweet with a ricotta and lemon filling." She pointed to the rolling bakery rack off to one side of the kitchen. "But for the funeral today, we have the savory filling."

I walked to the rack to get a look at the finished sfogliatelle, my lips parting in awe as I saw them all lined up, row after row after row. There had to be at least sixty here already. They had puffed up during the baking process, and looking closely at them now, I saw what the rolled pinwheels had created. The process of rolling the thin layers of dough into rounds, then pressing them out into cones, had created layer upon layer upon layer of flaky pastry. They looked like stacks of leaves, I thought. Each one was a work of art. I took my camera from its bag and snapped a few pictures. The pastries were delicate and beautiful, and I wanted to capture them on film.

Olaya always arrived at the bread shop in the wee hours of the morning, but she must have come practically in the middle of the night to get these made, I thought.

"Marisol was a friend," she said, as if she'd read my mind and wanted to explain why she'd made so much of something so complicated. "In America, these are filled with cream and called lobster tails. See how they are similar? Marisol, she loved the water. These crab-stuffed sfogliatelle are not traditional, *pero* they reflect her passion."

I felt my eyes prick. No one else might recognize the symbolism of Olaya's pastry, but it was a beautiful sentiment.

She waved her hand in a gesture telling me to go ahead and try one. I carefully picked one up, cupped my free hand under my chin, and took a bite. The thin layers of dough were similar to a croissant, yet different at the same time. Crispier. More delicate. The crab filling was still warm and mixed with the fine pastry leaves to create an explosion of texture and flavors in my mouth. I didn't think I'd ever had anything this good.

"They're brilliant, Olaya," I said when I'd swallowed the first bite. "Better than brilliant."

With the back of one hand, she brushed a

strand of her charcoal hair from her face. "You are easy to please," she said, but her eyes gleamed. She knew they were good, and she knew that, in her own way, she was honoring Marisol with them.

We worked through the morning, baking the bread for the sliders and meatballs, rolling flour tortillas, smearing three rounds of brie with fig compote, covering them with puff pastry, and readying them to bake. The list went on and on, but we stayed on task and by one o'clock, we had loaded up the bread shop's van and headed to Vista Ridge Funeral Home.

We drove around to the back of the building. I always had my camera handy, taking pictures of interesting things in my day-to-day life. In the back of the funeral home parking lot, a brick wall was in progress along one side, a pallet of bricks carefully wrapped in plastic sitting against the already completed portion of the wall, piles of yet-to-be-used bricks from a partially used pallet, and bags of mortar stacked alongside it. It looked like it would create an enclosed courtyard when it was done. An extension of the memorial garden, perhaps? I loved the look of the worn bricks the Alcotts had chosen for the enclosure, and the unfinished state leant itself to interesting composition. Olaya stopped for me so I could frame the shot from a few different angles, then she found a parking spot close to the double doors leading into the building.

A row of windows ran under the roofline, and a driveway led down to a basement-level loading bay. I shaded my eyes and peered down the mild incline. A hearse was parked at the bottom. A woman appeared at the back corner, hose in one hand, a scrub brush on an extended pole in the other. She pressed the finger trigger on the hose. A stream of water shot out like pressurized water from a fire hose. The jet hit the back of the black car, spraying out on all sides. The woman leapt out of the way, turning her head, and I recognized her. Suzanne Alcott. I took a few more pictures, capturing the stream of water. When I looked at it later, I hoped to see droplets in midair falling around the woman.

Suzanne Alcott directed the hose to the ground, zigzagging it back and forth, steering it clear of herself. "Hello!" I called, waving to her.

She jumped, releasing the trigger, and the stream of water stopped suddenly. She dropped the brush, whipping her head around. "Oh, Christ, you scared me."

"Sorry," I called. "I didn't meant to startle you. We're here for Marisol's service."

She peered up at me. "Of course. It's Ivy, right?"

"That's right. Good memory. We're going to set up."

"Sure. Okay. Her husband was here earlier. I'm just finishing up. Benjamin ran an errand, but he'll be back soon. Do you need help?"

I looked over my shoulder at Olaya, who was already hauling a tray of baked goods from the Yeast of Eden van into the funeral home. "I think we've got it," I said, "but thanks."

"I'll see you inside, then," she said, before depressing the trigger of the hose nozzle. Once again, the water shot out. She directed it to the hearse and got back to her task at hand.

"The sfogliatelle first, *por favor,*" Olaya called to me. She'd propped open the door with a partial bag of cement from the brick wall construction and was on her second trip. "The crab cannot sit here in the van."

I lifted my hand in acknowledgment, headed to the back of the van, and took out one of the several trays filled with the lobster-tail pastries. Olaya had waited for me at the door, directing me to the reception room. Inside, I placed the tray on one of the tables that had been set up for us and took in the surroundings. A blown-up framed photograph of Marisol sat on an easel at the front of the room, as well as a small bouquet of flowers in a green vase. They looked like they'd come from a grocery store florist. David, I thought, my heart going out to him.

"We will need more tables," Olaya said, bringing me back to the food. "Miguel, he is on his way soon. There will not be enough room."

"I'll go ask," I said, as we walked back outside together. Olaya went back to the van to get another tray while I made a sharp turn at the end of the railing, skirted around a spilled bag of fine gray cement, and walked down the sloped driveway. Suzanne had finished her task. The hose was wound neatly around the wall-mounted reel. The car-wash brush with the extended handle still attached, along with a looped-end commercial string mop, sat in a large yellow bucket with casters and a wringing basket.

I walked around the black hearse and stood on the threshold of the open doorway. My lungs constricted as I took in the utilitarian room before me. Laminate cabinets lined two of the four walls. Stainless steel tables on wheels looked as if they raised and lowered with a pneumatic system. Sinks, tubing, and other equipment I couldn't begin to understand sat on the countertops and were connected to machines. The reception and visitation rooms upstairs, the memorial garden, the casket room—all of that represented the polished side of the mortuary business; this space, with the body drawers and the worktables and the drains in the floor, showed the other end of the spectrum. The room was purely functional and not something that anyone wanted to think about.

"Suzanne?" I called.

Silence.

I tried again, thinking maybe I was being too familiar. "Ms. Alcott?"

The beige door at the end of the room flung open. Suzanne Alcott burst through, clutching her cell phone to her ear. "That's fine," she was saying, then she listened, responding a minute later. "Twelve o'clock. Great, see him then." She paused, then spotted me, surprise sliding onto her face. She tilted the phone up. "Hey. You really shouldn't be down here. Can I help you?"

I pointed up toward the ceiling. "We need more tables."

She raised her eyebrows in a question. I started to say it again, but she held up a finger, turning her back on me and going back to her phone conversation. "Got it," she said. "Yep. Yep. Okay."

She hung up, slipped the phone into her back pocket, then turned back to me. "Sorry about that. What do you need?"

"We need a few more tables in the reception room upstairs. For the food."

"Oh, right. Marisol's service." She looked around the room as if a few tables might magically appear. "I'll get some for you. Is two enough?"

"Perfect," I said. I took another moment to look around while she hung up the waterproof apron she'd been wearing and straightened her hair. The space was clean, but it looked like Suzanne had either been about to work on something, or had just finished and was cleaning up. Given that she'd just been outside hosing down the hearse, it seemed more likely she was going to move on to her next chore. I noticed several jars sitting on one of the counters, although from where I stood, I couldn't tell what was in them. Something shiny. Gold. Or maybe yellow. A section of one wall held several rows of large rectangular drawers. Television and movies had given me enough context to believe that they housed the bodies that came in. I knew that embalming was optional, but I'd also read that some funeral homes didn't have coolers for bodies, so embalming became essential. *You don't need to embalm if you have the viewing within a few days,* Billy and I had been told after our mother died.

I checked my watch. We only had an hour and

Olaya had no place to put the rest of the baked goods from the bread shop, but Suzanne Alcott didn't seem to be in a hurry. "I'm sure you're busy. Can I help you get them?" I offered, wanting to light a fire under her.

She checked her watch again, then glanced at the round analog clock hanging on the wall above the door. "Today is a little crazy. Yours is the third service, so a lot of coordinating, and one of our part-time helpers called in sick, so we're short-staffed."

Death waits for no one, I thought. "You can just tell me where they are and I'll get them."

"No, I'll show you."

I smiled, just wanting to get out of this particular room in the funeral parlor and up to reception, where we could all ignore the harsher realities of the business and just deal with the grief.

I'd come in through the driveway entrance, but Suzanne led me through the interior door, closing it behind me after I passed through. We went up one flight of stairs to the main floor, but instead of pushing through the door at the landing, she turned and continued up the next flight. "Do the police know any more about what happened to Marisol?" she asked as she opened the door at the top of the stairs.

"I'm not really sure," I answered truthfully. I didn't know where Emmaline was with the investigation, I had yet to fill her in on my suspicions about Johnny, and I didn't know if David had handed over the note he'd found, which supported that theory.

"They released the body to us, but I didn't hear anything about the autopsy findings." The row of windows visible from the back of the building outside were right in front of me. Light streamed into the attic space, eliminating the need for us to turn on the lights. The glow of the sunlight illuminated a fine layer of dust over the surfaces in the room. I spotted several portable tables. The legs were collapsed and they leaned up against one of the walls next to a stack of folded chairs. Two plain wooden caskets sat side by side under the windows. White shipping boxes were stacked in the back right corner, and other containers marked *hazardous* were piled up next to them, and in front of them was a wardrobe rack. Several dresses, one maxi length, the other two shorter, a beach cover up, a few men's shirts, three or four men's suit jackets, and a pewter-colored puffer jacket hung on it.

I grimaced. Clothing for corpses?

A stack of towels was neatly folded next to the wardrobe rack.

From the window, I could see the plastic-covered pallets of bricks outside. "When will your retaining wall be done?" I asked.

She followed my gaze. "It's a work in progress. We decided to make it bigger, so we've had to start again. Or revamp it, anyway. No idea when it will be done."

"Are those the tables?" I asked, pointing to them.

"Mmm-hmm. They're pretty light. You can get one and I'll get the other."

She pulled one out, lifting it by the lip. She

was right; it was lightweight, with a white plastic top and aluminum legs. I maneuvered it through the door and down the stairs, throwing open the door to the main floor and hauling it into the reception room. Suzanne followed with the other table. We set them up next to the one already laden with Yeast of Eden delectables.

"I have a few things to finish up. Need anything else at the moment?" Suzanne asked.

"I don't think so. I'll let you know if we do."

"Text me if you do," she said. She rattled off her number, which I entered into my phone and tucked it back into my pocket. She wandered out of the room as Olaya came in with another tray of sfogliatelle—the last one, from what I could tell. She set it down on the table and pointed to a clear plastic storage container. "The tablecloths. Please spread them on the tables, *mija*."

I did as she said, spreading out the ivory cloths and flattening the wrinkles with my hands. I'd worked with Olaya long enough to know how she liked to set up her food displays. Adding interest to the table by adding height was key. I pulled a set of nested boxes and tins from the second storage container she'd hauled in, then artfully draped several other burlap cloths over them, adding long sprigs of white silk flowers and berries to soften the look.

"*Perfecto,*" Olaya proclaimed as she came back in carrying another tray of food. "Miguel entered right behind her, his arms wrapped around a large cardboard box. He set his load down, took Olaya's from her and placed it on one of the tables, then wrapped his arms around me, pulling me into a hug.

"Ready for today?" he asked after brushing his lips against my cheeks.

"As much as we can be," I said.

He stepped back and started unloading the box he'd brought in, looking around. "We're going to need another table. I have more food in the car."

"There are more tables upstairs. I'll ask if we can go get more." I took my phone from my pocket and quickly composed a message to Suzanne, then got back to unloading.

"Okay?" Miguel asked ten minutes later as he came back in with his third box and Olaya and I had made two more trips to the van.

I checked my phone. The status remained *delivered*, rather than *read*. That could be because she had her phone set up that way, or because she hadn't seen it. I shook my head, but followed that with a little shrug. "I know where the attic is. We can just go get them."

He followed me back to the hallway, through the closed door, and up the hidden stairs to the storage room. "How many more?" I asked him, pointing to the five tables left leaning against the wall.

"At least three. Maybe four." He lifted the first easily, handing it to me. "This one is smaller. It can be for beverages."

I'd been so wrapped up in the details surrounding Marisol's death that I hadn't even thought about that detail. I let the table lean against my legs. "Do we have drinks?"

"Coffee, iced tea, and water," he said, lifting another table.

I led the way back down the stairs and through to the reception room. We popped open the legs of the tables, setting them up. "Let's get two more, just in case," he said, and we retreated back to the attic.

This time, once inside the dusty room, he stopped to look around the space. "This is where we brought my dad," he said, his voice subdued. Then he smiled wryly. "Not the attic, I mean, but Vista Ridge. Seems so long ago."

"Are you glad you came back home?" I asked. His father's death is what brought him back to Santa Sofia. He'd taken over the family business, leaving behind his military career, but he'd never said how he felt about that.

"Not glad he died, obviously, but happy that you and I found each other again." His gaze settled on the wardrobe rack and one eyebrow arched. "Clothing for the deceased?"

"That's my best guess," I said.

He strode to it, sliding the hangers over as he looked at each piece. He stopped at one of the men's suit jackets. It was dark gray with pinstripes. I was no expert, but it looked to me to be nice, falling somewhere in the mid-range area of a suit-quality distribution scale. He looked at the front, then slid the hanger over to peer at the back. As he slid it off, I noticed the coordinating slacks hanging over the base of the hanger. Miguel's brows knitted together.

"What is it?" I asked, stepping next to him to look more closely.

He flipped open the lapel to look at the label. It read Van Heusen, 42 regular. "This is just like the one we buried my dad in," he said.

"Black pinstriped suits all look the same," I said, wanting to dismiss the similarity. I didn't want painful memories to be dredged up for him.

"Yeah, and forty-two regular is a pretty common size. It just reminds me of him."

I didn't know if it was a common size or not, but something about the seriousness of Miguel's expression gave me pause. "Are you thinking this was his?" I asked.

He didn't answer right away, instead draping the suit over his arm so he could slide his hand into the interior pocket. He froze for a second before withdrawing his hand. He took what he'd found with his other hand, gripping it between his fingers and closing his eyes for a beat.

I touched his arm, squeezing lightly. "Miguel, what is it?"

He responded by unfolding the paper and holding the sheets out to me. "They're pictures Laura's kids drew for him before he died. He wanted to take them with him so I put them in his coat pocket before I brought the suit here."

One of the drawings was more sophisticated than the other, but both were sweet and filled with love. They each featured an older man, who had to be Miguel's father, holding the hand of a child. One of them had a rainbow framing the two figures, while the other said: *I love you, Abuelo.*

I looked from the drawings to Miguel. "But if these are here, then—"

"This is my dad's jacket," he finished.

I absorbed that sentence. "So he wasn't buried in it?" I said slowly.

"Apparently not." He was silent for a beat before adding, "But we had an open casket and he *was* wearing it, I'm sure of it."

There had to be a logical explanation. "Maybe Laura or your mom wanted him buried in a different suit," I suggested. "Did they know about the drawings? If they didn't, then they wouldn't have known—"

"Laura knew."

There went that theory. "Call her," I said.

He looked at me for barely a second before taking his cell phone from his pocket, pressing his thumb against the home button to unlock it, and swiping to dial his sister. Thirty seconds later, he pulled the phone away from his ear. I could hear her voicemail greeting. He didn't leave a message, instead pressing the off button.

He pocketed the drawings before putting the coat back in place on the wardrobe rack. He scanned the rest of the attic, but came back to the clothing. His jaw tensed, evidence that he was clearly bothered by the revelation, but he moved across the room and picked up one of the remaining folded tables. He handed it to me, taking another and stepping back so I could leave first. We walked back to the reception room silently, careful not to bang the walls of the stairwell as we went.

We each went about our work, lost in our own thoughts. In my estimation, there were only two logical explanations for Mr. Baptista's suit to be upstairs at Vista Ridge: One, someone had brought a different suit for him to be buried in; or two, someone else had removed that suit for some unknown reason. What I couldn't figure out was why anyone would do that, only to leave it hanging up on the rack. Option one seemed much more likely.

The next fifteen minutes were spent finishing setting up the tables with the food. I took my Canon from my camera bag again and walked around the buffet tables, taking a series of pictures. Afterward, I moved to the front of the room. While we'd been setting up, Sergio and Ruben, as well as Ruben's wife, had brought in more flowers and photographs of Marisol, displaying them at the front. So far, there'd been no sign of David, Lisette, or Laura, but I knew they'd be here.

Benjamin Alcott popped his head into the reception room to check on us, back from wherever he'd been. "Is there anything else you need?" he asked. He was very accommodating, I thought again. The perfect mortician.

Miguel's face was tense and he turned away. His father's suit hanging upstairs weighed on his mind, but until he spoke to Laura and his mother, I knew he wouldn't say a word about it.

I answered for all of us. "I think we're good for now, thanks."

"Don't hesitate to let me know if I can help in any way. I'll be greeting guests as they arrive," he said, bowing out of the room.

By the time we were done, the service was minutes from starting and people were starting to gather in the funeral home's lobby with its muted mauve walls and neutral chairs and side-boards. The somberness of the occasion perme-ated every muffled comment and subdued voice. I grabbed the outfit I'd brought in with me in a small duffel bag on one of the trips to and from the van, and slipped into the bathroom to change. The cap-sleeved black dress hit at my knees. I slipped into the nude suede booties I'd brought, added a simple necklace, and after combing my fingers through my hair, I pinned it up in a messy bun on the back of my head.

With my jeans, top, and sneakers tucked back into the small duffel, I headed back to the van, set it on the floor of the passenger side, checked to be sure we hadn't left anything behind, and went back into the funeral home. I flung open the door, wanting to hurry back and help with any last-minute details—and ran smack into Suzanne Alcott.

She jumped back, centimeters shy of being hit by the door. She caught it with her hand as she uttered a surprised, "Oh!"

I stopped short. "I'm so sorry! I didn't know you were—"

She held up her hand and my apology died on my lips. "It's fine. No harm, no foul. I just saw your text. Sorry I missed it."

This time I waved away her apology. "No prob-lem. We got what we needed."

She didn't ask how we managed, and I didn't offer.

"Everything looks great," she said. "I'll be down-stairs, but Benjamin is here if you need any-thing."

I thanked her and then she disappeared through to the stairwell and headed downstairs while I wove through the growing crowd of mourners. The double doors to the reception room were now open and people were milling about. They comforted each other, offered quiet theories about what led to Marisol's death, and slowly made their way to the chairs.

Benjamin Alcott had moved from the entry hall into the room. He greeted people, looking appropriately solemn, his hands folded together in front of him. He led people to their seats, which were slowly filling up.

I saw Mrs. Branford amble toward the front, cane in hand. She used it to get down the center aisle of the room without difficulty. One of my eyebrows lifted in surprise. Gone was her usual velour lounge suit and orthopedic shoes. She'd pulled out all the stops for her former student, wearing navy pants and a matching cardigan, a button-up blouse underneath, and a narrow hand-knitted scarf she'd decorated with a funky clay pendant. She walked right up to Mr. Alcott, who stood by Marisol's photograph, and shook his hand. She leaned one arm on the podium for support, her cane in front of her as they spoke. The funeral director never broke character, maintaining his ceremonious persona, giving her his attention, yet keeping an eye on what was going on around the room at the same time.

I started toward the front to help her find a place to sit, but Mr. Alcott beat me to it. He gently led her by the elbow to the end chair in the second row. I changed direction, going instead to where Miguel stood next to Olaya at one of the food tables. They spoke quietly, both looking pensive. "No David yet," he said as I approached them. "My mother saw him at the restaurant this morning, but no sign of him since."

I scanned the room, although not for any particularly good reason. If Miguel said he wasn't here, then he wasn't. "You've called him," I said, more statement than question, because I knew that he would have done that first thing.

"Straight to voicemail."

Olaya had started busily adjusting some of the breads on the table next to her. She looked up at us. Since I'd spent the morning with her I'd filled her in on Mrs. Branford's poker game the night before, as well as David's visit with us at The Library. "Did he go to the sheriff with the letter?" she asked now.

That was a good question. I hadn't talked to Emmaline, so I didn't know.

"I haven't seen Lisette, either." Miguel checked his watch, which prompted me to do the same. We had five minutes. "I'll go check out front," he said. "You check out back, okay?"

I nodded, squeezed his hand, and walked toward the now very familiar back entrance while Miguel went in the opposite direction. From the doorway, I scanned the parking lot. I didn't see Lisette.

The lot was full of cars, so I left the building to walk up and down the rows in case she was sitting in her car, lost in her guilt and grief. I walked past the partially completed brick wall and driveway leading down, turning to look just in case

Lisette had made her way down there for some privacy or to escape. The hearse that had been there earlier was gone, a white van, a lot like the one Olaya drove for the bread shop, in its place.

Suzanne and a tall, lanky man stood talking by the open doors, but no Lisette. "Hello!" I called, raising my arm.

They turned, shading their eyes as they looked up the driveway at me. Suzanne responded. "Do you need something?"

"I'm looking for Lisette Morales," I said, then added, "and David Ruiz. The service is about to start."

"Haven't seen anyone come this way," she said as the man got into the van and started it up.

He rolled down the window. "Me, neither," he said as Suzanne closed the back doors. He looked back at her. "See you bright and early—or should I say dark and early?" he said, and laughed at his own mystifying joke.

She waved at him as he drove up the driveway. I followed the van with my eyes as it drove through the parking lot. A silver sedan passed it coming into the lot. Finally, Lisette!

"There she is!" I called to Suzanne, but she had picked up a discarded Styrofoam container and disappeared back into the workroom of the funeral home. She was an odd duck, I thought, but then again, maybe that came with the job of mortician. As the door at the base of the driveway closed on its pneumatic hinges, I hurried toward the car.

Lisette drove erratically, crisscrossing between the aisles. Given how late she was, I guessed she was trying to get as close to the door as she could. I couldn't dodge between cars as fast as she was driving, so I finally stopped, flapping my arms over my head like an air traffic controller. She whipped around a parked Jeep and suddenly caught sight of me. Her jaw dropped and she slammed on the brakes, the tires skidding slightly on the pavement as she jerked to a stop next to a white van marked with a Vista Ridge Funeral Home decal. She pressed a button in the car and the driver's-side window slid down. "Jesus Christ, Ivy. You scared me."

"I was looking for you," I said, considering her. Her voice was off and her eyes looked glazed, as if she'd been drinking. "The service is about to start."

She gave a short nod, rolled the window back up, and turned off the ignition. A moment later, she was out of the car, her feet tangling under her as she walked, despite the flats she wore. She lost her balance and her knees buckled. I grabbed her elbow, holding her upright. "Are you okay?" I asked, relieved that she'd managed to make it here in one piece. Now that I was next to her, I could smell the alcohol on her breath. She clearly should not have been driving.

"I hate this place," she said, her words slurring. "But David said I had to get Mama from here. That I had to get her and then it would be okay." She looked at me, tears pooling in her eyes. "I don't ever wanna to come back here."

I guided her toward the door, glancing surreptitiously at my watch. We were just barely going to make it on time. "You don't have to come back. You'll all have your mom's ashes. You don't have to come back here," I said, thinking of all the time I'd spent at my mother's graveside in the months following her death. Marisol had had her father's ashes, but the memorial garden had been the place that had given her comfort. For Lisette, this place was going to be a sad reminder, not a place of serenity. Sprinkling her mother's ashes in the vastness of the Pacific meant that the beach, the boardwalk, or whatever part of the sea she associated with her mother would be her source of comfort.

Lisette didn't respond. She just plowed ahead, reaching for the door handle as we approached. It opened before she made contact with it, though, and she jumped back, startled. Miguel appeared, opening it for us as if he'd seen us coming. The smile of thanks I started to offer froze on my face when I saw his expression. His face was grim, his eyes dark with worry, but he spoke to Lisette as he took her arm and escorted her to the reception room. "Just in time."

I noticed Johnny sitting in the back row by himself. So he'd decided to come. Was that what had Miguel so tense? Johnny's spine was straight, his feet planted firmly on the ground. He didn't have a tissue, and from my vantage point it didn't look like he'd shed any tears, but he was here. If he had killed his ex-wife, that was twisted and sadistic. If he hadn't, it was the right thing to do for his children.

Miguel shot me a look that made me stop at

the door instead of following him in. Something was definitely wrong.

I watched from the threshold as he led Lisette down the aisle to her seat next to Ruben in the front row. Sergio was already at the podium, welcoming the mourners. Benjamin Alcott stood in the back corner of the room, very still, hands clasped in front of him. Up and down each row, people clutched wads of tissues, sniffled, and sat stoically still.

Miguel walked back up the aisle toward me, turning briefly to catch Olaya's eye. They acknowledged each other and she nodded in a way that indicated she had everything under control. The service itself would consist of various mourners telling anecdotes and offering reflections about Marisol in a celebration of her life. The question of who had stripped that life from her would be left unspoken, like an elephant in the room.

Miguel rejoined me in the hallway, gently closing the door to the reception room behind him before taking my hand and leading me into the room across the way. The casket room. "Uh-uh, not here," I said. There was something disconcerting about being surrounded by caskets. It made my chest tighten and my breath grow shallow. Death was inevitable. I knew that. But being overtly surrounded by it, as we were in this room, left me feeling uncomfortable.

This time I led the way, leaving the caskets behind and following the hallway to the right, past the door to the stairwell leading both up and down, and through yet another nondescript door. This one, however, had a placard on the wall next to it that read MEMORIAL GARDEN.

We exited the building to find ourselves in a courtyard. A trickling fountain sat up against the wall about seven feet from the door we'd entered through. A brick pathway wound through the space, which was interspersed with planted areas filled with blooming flowers, benches, trees, and two additional fountains. Along the back of the brick wall that enclosed the garden, placards were engraved with the names of the deceased who'd been scattered here. The memorial garden was bigger than I'd expected, and from what Suzanne had said, it would be even more so when they were done with their remodel.

The second we sat down, a decorative tree creating a canopy above us, Miguel turned to me, his arm draped across the back of the bench. "David's dead."

I just stared at him, trying to absorb those two little words. David's dead. David's dead? We'd just seen him last night. He'd looked worse for wear, but I hadn't sensed a level of distress that would lead to, what, to suicide? Had he been so unable to cope with losing Marisol that he'd taken his own life? "Dead?" I said at last, not comprehending.

"Emmaline tried calling you, but you didn't pick up. She called me—"

"When?"

"When we were looking for Lisette," he said. "Check your phone."

I reached for it in my back pocket, only to realize that I'd changed into my dress. "I must have put it in the bag with my other clothes."

"He's dead," Miguel repeated, and then, after a moment's pause, he added, "Murdered."

My heart thudded in my chest. Instantly, an unbidden image of Lisette jumped into my mind. She'd been so upset about the will. Had she learned that there were stipulations in it about her and her brothers inheriting Marisol's house? Had it pushed her over the edge? "When?" I asked.

"Sometime between this morning, when my mom saw him at the restaurant, and about one o'clock today when his body was discovered. The coroner will know more after an autopsy."

I thought back to David's phone call to me the night before, to the letter he'd brought to The Library, and to his sudden departure when Johnny came out of the back room.

Miguel was still talking. "Apparently David called the station sometime this morning. He told the deputy who answered that he had information about his wife's death and that he wanted to come down and talk to whoever was in charge. But he never showed up. Emmaline sent a car to David's house. That's where they found him."

I raised my eyebrows in an unspoken question.

"Suffocated," he said, closing his eyes for a beat. "Apparently he fought. Claw marks on his face from his own fingernails, most likely."

"He had to have realized something last night with the letter, right?"

"Right," he agreed.

Something Johnny said floated to the front of my thoughts. *She always did hang on to old letters and journals. Rough for David to find it.* "Could he have found another letter? Or a journal?"

"If he did, and he had it in his possession, whoever killed him would have taken it."

True. "So what do we do now? How do we figure out what he knew?"

Miguel leaned forward, resting his forearms on his thighs. "Whatever it was, he was killed because of it. Someone is getting desperate."

Someone, I thought. David left the bar last night as soon as Johnny showed up. Marisol went to meet her ex-husband the day she died. I looked at Miguel. "I hate to even think it, but—"

"Johnny," he finished.

"Johnny," I agreed.

Chapter 19

Miguel's phone rang—a call from the restaurant. He took it, walking to the far side of the memorial garden so he could deal with whatever crisis had arisen in his absence. I stayed put on the bench, letting the temperate air in the courtyard fill my lungs. Flowers filled every available bit of the planter beds. It was easy to forget the reason for this space, and to see it just as a lovely garden, but through the flora, I caught sight of little mounds of ash, light against the dark soil and bark. This reminder—that this place was for remembrance and memorialization of loved ones—made me antsy for some reason.

Finally, I couldn't sit still anymore. I stood and started pacing up and back on the brick path. Had Marisol known she was in danger? And if so, had she known just how far someone was willing to go in order to stop her? My mind stayed focused on Johnny. She'd reached out to him, so she clearly wasn't fearful of him. Had she misjudged her ex-husband, or was I barking up the wrong tree? She and Johnny had been high school sweethearts. They'd been married for years and years before ending things. She knew him, so much so that they'd gone through, in the words of Gwyneth Paltrow, a conscious uncoupling. As much as it made sense that Marisol had discovered Johnny's extreme debt, there wasn't a clear path for Johnny to get money from Marisol. Inheritance of the house, were it to have gone to their kids, was not a quick payoff. Given the fact that it went to David for ten years meant there was no way he could get anything from it. If he'd known about her change to the will, then his motive to kill her evaporated into thin air.

Aside from Johnny, who had a motive to kill Marisol? And, as collateral damage, David?

Sergio, Ruben, and Lisette were obvious suspects. Any one of them could have killed for the house, not knowing about the change in the will, or out of anger because they'd found out about the change and couldn't forgive their mother's cutting them out. Any one of them knew enough about their mother and her routine to track her down, or to find her at the beach. The one puzzle piece that didn't fit was that they'd have known about Marisol's swimsuit and her superstition about color.

For that matter, so would Johnny.

Thinking about Lisette brought a different

thought to the surface. The arguments for and against her killing her mother were the same as they were for her brothers, but Lisette was filled with anger in a way Sergio and Ruben weren't. From what I'd observed, she seemed to have the propensity to act out of passion. She'd been angry at her mother for marrying David. She claimed not to have known about the change in the will, but what if she was lying about that? What if she'd known, had confronted her mother, and ended up killing her in a moment of passion?

Lisette's disdain for David made the idea of her killing him seem possible. Even plausible. She blamed him. In her mind, it might have been easy to get rid of him, too. I thought of her demeanor just a few minutes ago. She'd driven erratically in the parking lot and had been scattered when I walked with her into the funeral home. I'd smelled the liquor on her breath, but could she have turned to drink to bolster her courage for the murder she'd been about to commit, or did she drink to calm herself down after the fact?

The letter David found didn't fit, though. Was it related to her death, or was it connected to something else entirely? Why had he left The Library so suddenly the night before, and what had he wanted to share with Emmaline? Something about the letter?

Once again, everything circled back to Johnny. He'd betrayed Marisol. They'd known each other since they were kids. But what did any of

Johnny's problems have to do with Marisol's father? Something didn't fit; I just couldn't figure out what it was.

I sank back onto the bench just as Miguel hung up and slipped his phone back into his pocket. "Everything okay?" I asked.

He scrubbed his hand over his face. "The staff just heard about David."

"Oh God. I didn't think about that." They'd both been long-standing employees at Baptista's Cantina and Grill, and now they'd both been murdered. I couldn't imagine what Miguel's employees had to be feeling. "Do you need to go? Olaya and I can handle things here."

"Maybe a little early, but not yet," he said.

The door to the memorial garden jerked, as if someone was trying to open it, but nothing happened. The knob turned and then it did open with a sudden whoosh and Laura poked her head through. "There you are," she said when she saw us. "The service is almost over."

Which meant the mourners would be making their way to the buffet tables. Miguel and I both stood. I ran my hands down my sides, straightening my dress, and then started for the door. Miguel put his hand on my lower back, walking close beside me. It was going to be a long afternoon.

Grieving did not stop people from eating . . . or from gossiping. Olaya, Miguel, and I manned the buffet tables as the mourners filled and refilled their plates. We reorganized the displays, filling in the gaps with extras from the trays we had placed on one of the tables behind us, nodding sympathetically at the people who wore their raw emotions on their sleeves, and observing and listening—just in case.

News of David's death had spread, but it seemed that the details—suffocation and presumed murder—hadn't been released. "Poor soul, died of a broken heart," was a sentiment I heard over and over. It was true, in a way. He'd been distraught and had sought to understand what had happened. His broken heart had led him to some truth that someone had killed to protect.

I looked around for Lisette, hoping the alcohol she'd consumed earlier had worn off. There was no sign of her anywhere.

After an hour and a half, the mourners had decreased by half, our food offerings by more than that. I took stock. Only a few crumbs were left where the mini tostadas and quesadillas had been. A dollop of fig preserves and a bit of puff pastry were left on the plate that had featured the baked brie en croûte with spicy fig compote. It wasn't enough to keep on display, so I removed the serving tray. The rest I consolidated, removing trays and combining things to fewer tables.

I put away the boxes I'd used to create height on the table and folded up the burlap and tablecloths. Miguel flipped the first table to its side, collapsing the legs and folding them into place before leaning the table against the wall and moving on to the next.

"I'll take them back up," he said.

Benjamin Alcott had circulated in the room, quietly talking to mourners the entire time. He played his part well and I knew he'd be here until the bitter end. "I'm sure Mr. Alcott can do it," I said. Being understaffed had meant we'd had to step up in the beginning, but they would be able to clean up once we'd all gone.

"I'll do it," Miguel said, then added, "Laura can help me."

The subtext was clear. Returning the tables to the attic provided Miguel the perfect opportunity to show his sister their father's suit and try to clarify why it was there. He carried the tables to the hallway before crooking his finger at her. A moment later, they disappeared into the hallway.

Olaya had started to take empty trays back to the van, so I was left manning the buffet tables on my own. I kept myself busy, cleaning up as much as I could. I didn't want it to appear as if we were trying to subliminally push people out.

Five minutes passed. I'd stacked up another three bakery trays for Olaya to take to the van, but when she returned, she looked spooked. Once she was back behind the tables, I placed my hands on her arms. "Are you okay?"

"Go," she ordered.

I drew back. "What? Go where?"

She pointed a finger to the ceiling. "To Miguel."

"Why?" My voice rose. "Olaya, what's going on?"

"Laura, she is in the hallway. Crying. Something has happened. Go, *mija*."

My heart hammered in my chest. Without another word, I hurried out of the reception room. I glanced up and down the hallway, spotting Laura heading out the door to the back parking lot. There was no sign of Miguel. Was he still upstairs in the attic? I started toward the stairwell door, but stopped at the last minute, changing directions. Between the two of them, my gut told me to check on Laura.

I pushed through the door, letting it slam behind me. She was quick, despite the high wedge heels she wore. My hesitation had given her a good head start. By the time I got to the asphalt of the parking lot, she was already to the brick wall past the driveway leading to the depths of the funeral home. I called to her. "Laura, wait."

She slowed when she heard me, stopping at the wall and turning. Even from where I was, a good hundred feet from her, I could see the red rims around her eyes and the sadness radiating from her. She didn't respond but waited where she was.

"Are you okay?" I asked as I caught up with her.

From the expression on her face, she didn't know how to answer. She threw up her hands helplessly. "I don't know."

I led her to an unfinished section of the brick wall, heaving up an unopened bag of mortar mix that sat on it and dropping it to the ground to make room for us to sit. "It's your dad's suit," I said—a statement, not a question. The drawings in the pocket proved that.

She nodded. "You never get over it, do you?"

I knew she was referring to losing someone close to you, especially a parent. "Never," I said. "But you adjust and find a new normal."

"Right, but then you see or hear something and you're right back to where you were, like it just happened. Seeing my dad's suit took me back to church on Sundays—and my wedding. It all just flashed in my mind and now I can't shake it."

"You don't have to," I said. "Those are good memories. You want to keep them."

She dragged her fingers under her eyes, smearing her mascara and eyeliner as she swept away her tears. She cradled her head in her hands. "God, I have a headache."

Crying messed with my head, too. "We should go back inside. Get you some water."

She nodded, but didn't move. She gripped the edge of the wall with the heels of her hands, her fingers curling over the edge. "He was supposed to be wearing that suit," she said. "I don't understand. My dad is buried, but not even in his own clothes. It's like, one job, right? How can they make a mistake like that? Tomorrow morning we're supposed to go to the pier to scatter my mother-in-law's ashes." She looked at me questioningly. "Should we have done that with our father?"

"I think it's a personal choice, Laura. Whatever happened with your dad's suit was probably just a mix-up. You said your goodbyes. You have to let it go."

We sat in silence for a minute, then she drew her lips in, pressing them against each other, and nodded.

I stood, holding out my hand. "Come on. Let's go back inside."

She took my proffered hand, hauling herself upright, teetering a moment on her wobbling ankles. She found her balance and we walked back to the building. During the time I'd been gone, the reception room had cleared out. Olaya had finished stacking the trays and packing up the boxes. Sergio and Ruben had put the photographs of Marisol in a box, and had moved them, along with the flowers and the urn with their mother's ashes, to one of the sideboards in the entry. Now they were gathered around, dry-eyed and weary—and focused, not on their grief, but on Miguel and Benjamin Alcott.

The two men stood facing one another in what I could only describe as a standoff. Miguel's hands were fisted by sides. The tendons in his neck strained. The funeral director, on the other hand, looked conciliatory with his hands up, palms facing Miguel. We'd walked in mid-conversation, but Alcott was clearly trying to calm Miguel down.

Miguel, however, didn't want to be placated. He wanted answers. "How did this happen?" he demanded.

"I apologize, sir. It must have been mixed up

with someone else's," he said, but Miguel shook his head, not buying it.

"That makes no sense. If it was mixed up, that other person would be wearing my father's suit. That's not the case. Is someone buried naked, then?"

"Mr. Baptista, please," Alcott said, patting the air with his open hands. "Give me a little time. I'll get to the bottom of this."

Miguel's nostrils flared as he drew in a stabilizing breath. "You do that, and fast. I'm this close to filing a complaint against this place. This is unconscionable."

Alcott's Adam's apple slid down his throat as he swallowed. "I agree, it should not have happened. Rest assured, I will get to the bottom of it."

With his scowl, and piercing eyes staring Alcott down, Miguel looked menacing, but he relaxed his hands, blinked to break the tension, and nodded.

Benjamin Alcott made himself busy and tried to be invisible in the front of the room while Miguel grabbed one of his boxes, told me he'd be right back, and strode out with it. I think every one of us wanted to get out of there and go back to something familiar. For Miguel, that probably meant Baptista's. He had the dinner service starting, David's chef position to fill, and probably myriad other tasks to do that could distract him from the day. For Olaya, it was Yeast of Eden. The bread shop was closed for the day, but she had to be there bright and early, before the crack of dawn the next morning, so I knew she'd go check on the state of the kitchen, make sure the closing procedures were followed, and would possibly go home from there. Or she might find Martina so they could comfort each other.

My familiar place was my house. I'd pick up Agatha, then go home, where I would bake a loaf of bread and immerse myself in sorting through the photographs I'd taken over the last few days. I didn't know what Marisol's children would do now that the funeral was over. Would they stay together, or go to their own homes? Who would keep their mother's ashes until they gathered tomorrow to scatter them? And finally, what was their plan?

Sergio answered that last question a moment later. "We're meeting at the pier by Baptista's tomorrow morning at ten."

Miguel had come back into the room in time to hear the plan for the morning. "I'll have a table ready for lunch afterward," he said. He believed in breaking bread together, in this case to celebrate Marisol—and David—one last time at his restaurant.

"Where's Lisette?" Ruben asked.

They all looked at each other. Looked around the room. The brothers gave each other knowing looks. They'd seen the state their sister had been in when she'd arrived—barely on time, words slurring, unsteady on her feet. Their expressions, almost identical to one another, seemed to indicate that they knew she'd gone to drown her sorrows on her own.

We all walked out of Vista Ridge Funeral Home

together, each of us carrying something—a piece of the day—but there was no closure. With Marisol's killer still out there, and none of us closer to knowing why she died, there was no sense of peace as we left.

All there was were questions.

Chapter 20

After I'd helped Olaya unload the Yeast of Eden van and clean up, I picked up Agatha from Billy's, went home to change, and took an evening walk with her around the neighborhood. Mrs. Branford must have seen me coming because by the time I got to her house, she was outside on the porch sitting on her worn wooden rocker, creaking back and forth, back and forth, back and forth. She waved me up the walkway, gesturing so I'd sit in the other rocking chair.

"Such a sad turn of events," she said, shaking her head sadly.

I hadn't had time to sit and really think about the fact that David was dead, too. It was beyond tragic. "Did everyone hear?"

"I'm sure they did. Benjamin Alcott—you know he was a student of mine back in the day—"

"Everyone was a student of yours back in the day," I remarked.

"How right you are. That is the byproduct of living a long, long life in one place. You see a lot of people come and go, but it's the ones who stay that you never forget. Anyway, I spoke with him earlier and he told me, and then, of course, it was discussed quite a bit throughout the service. Lots of speculation." She lowered her voice ominously. "Was it murder?"

"Looks that way," I said.

"As I feared. So much gossip. People love to be the first to tell a story, you know. Being early in the know makes people think they have power or authority. It's akin to being an early adopter of the newest technology. It elevates one's status, even if only in one's own eyes."

My cell phone rang. It was Emmaline. I'd called her back from the bread shop, but, not surprisingly, she hadn't answered. Instead of leaving a message, I'd texted just three words: *Tag, you're it.* Six months ago, I would have said it was rare for her not to answer my call, but since she'd moved from deputy sheriff to the head honcho, it was more fifty-fifty. She was busy leading Santa Sofia's entire law enforcement community within the sheriff's office, so she couldn't always drop whatever she was doing to talk to me.

"Hey," I said. "I heard about David." Cut to the chase. With Em, there was no need for preamble. "Miguel said it was suffocation?"

"Right. He said he had information about his wife's death, but we have no idea what that information was."

"We saw him last night," I said, bracing myself for her chagrined reaction, but she was calm.

"Miguel told me about your Mrs. Branford's poker playing and the letter David showed you."

"Did you find it? The letter, I mean."

"No sign of it. If that was what he wanted to share with us, then I assume that's why he was killed. Someone at the bar may have overheard him sharing it with you, or maybe he told someone else. Whatever happened, it's gone."

My heart dropped. I'd told Johnny. "That may have been what he wanted to show you," I said, "but I'm not sure. He left really suddenly, like he'd thought of something." I thought back to his reaction after he'd shown us the letter. He'd said *Oh my God,* Johnny had appeared with Mrs. Branford, and then he'd vanished, letter in hand.

"We've searched the house again. Nothing." She sounded exhausted. Two murders in her Santa Sofia jurisdiction meant she was burning the candle at both ends.

"He figured something out," Mrs. Branford said from her rocking chair, jumping into my side of the phone conversation.

I put Em on speaker and held the phone out between us. "He had to have. He figured something out, left the bar to pursue it, somehow alerted whoever is behind Marisol's death, and that's why he's now dead."

"That's the thing I don't understand," Em said from wherever she was. I never called her at her office and she rarely called me from her office phone, instead opting for her cell. I had no way of knowing where she was. Her office? Back at Billy's house? At her own apartment? "Why would he have alerted the killer that he was wise to him?"

I rattled off the reasons I could think of. "Blackmail is the obvious one. But what if he wanted revenge and decided to go all vigilante? He could have figured out who the killer was and gone to confront him—"

"Mmm, but we found him in his house," she countered.

I wasn't ready to give up on my theory. "There's no doubt about that? He couldn't have been killed somewhere else and taken back to his house to make it look like he died there? It happened with Marisol. She was dead when she went into the water. This could be the same."

"Sure, it's possible," Em said, but she sounded skeptical.

"No letters or journals?" I asked. Johnny had said Marisol had journals, so where were they?

"Nothing. I'll let you know if we find something, though," she said before signing off.

Agatha hopped up when I tugged on her leash. I stood, too, ready to go home and crawl into bed. After a good night's sleep, maybe I'd see things more clearly. I wished Mrs. Branford a good night and headed down the walkway. She called after me just as I reached the sidewalk. "People hide their diaries, you know."

I turned to look at her, Agatha stopping alongside me. "What?"

"Diaries are, by nature, private. One doesn't leave them out for the world to find, wouldn't you agree?"

"Yesss," I said slowly. It was true. As a child, I'd tucked mine under the mattress of my bed. My mother, perhaps an anomaly, had kept hers at her bedside, faithfully writing in it each morning, but I'd been afraid of my parents' discovering my girlhood secrets. If Marisol had written in a journal about whatever it was she'd discovered, she wouldn't have kept it in the open for anyone to find. She would have hidden it away in a safe place.

But where? Her house had been searched. She didn't seem to have confided in her children. My mind skidded to a sudden stop. I thought back to the funeral when Miguel and I talked about the fact that David wasn't there yet. Miguel had said that his mother had seen David at the restaurant this morning, but there'd been no sign of him since. "Oh my God," I said.

Mrs. Branford perked up from her rocking chair. "You figured something out?" she asked.

"Maybe." I ran my fingers through my tangled curls and spoke aloud, processing through my thoughts. "If Marisol was keeping notes or a journal, where are they? We've checked everywhere logical. No journals or notes or letters at her house. Or with her kids. Or in her locker at Baptista's. We checked there," I said. My heart thudded, because the one place we hadn't checked was David's locker at the restaurant.

Chapter 21

"Go, my dear," Mrs. Branford said. She stretched out her hand, wiggling her fingers. "Give me Agatha."

I took the porch steps in a single leap, Agatha scurrying up them on her short little legs. "Thank you," I said breathlessly, handing her the leash. "I'll keep you posted."

Both sets of eyes were on me, I knew, as I raced across the street. I grabbed my purse from where I'd left it on the kitchen counter.

A minute later I tore down the street in my pearl-white Fiat crossover.

Twelve minutes later I barreled through the door of Baptista's Cantina and Grill.

Miguel's mother perched on her stool at the entrance. She kept one eye on the portion of the dining room she could see, asking questions of the hostess who was seating people so she stayed informed about what was happening in the rest of the restaurant. She kept her hair dyed chestnut brown. I remembered the days back in high school when I'd spent a lot of time at the Baptista household. She'd walked around the house with sections of her hair haphazardly wound around hot rollers and stuck to her head with metal butterfly clips. I couldn't help but smile. Her hairstyle hadn't changed in twenty years.

Her gaze fell on me the moment I was through the door. She started to smile, but stopped when she saw the grim urgency on my face. "*¿Qué pasó?*" she asked. "What has happened? Are you okay?"

I put my hands on the counter, calming my breath. "*Hola, señora,*" I said. "I'm okay. Um, Miguel—is he here?"

"*Sí, sí. En la cocina.*"

I started through the dining room, but thought better of it. I turned back to her. "Is it okay? Can I—?"

She gave one succinct nod and waved her hand, signaling me to keep going.

"Thank you!" I said, then hurried on through the busy dining room and pushed through the right swinging door to the kitchen. The restaurant's cooks operated on the line with their steaming pots and pans on the commercial stoves. They also manned the ovens, while the other kitchen workers handled the salad, soup, and sauce stations. The waitstaff snatched freshly garnished plates, carefully balanced in one hand, and backed out of the kitchen to deliver to their tables. They were a team performing a dance, and executing it expertly.

I'd observed the kitchen before, reveling in how different it was from Yeast of Eden's. Olaya's space was calm and serene by comparison. Her traditional bread-making took time—the long rise, the shaping of dough, the bake. The frenetic energy of Baptista's kitchen was absent from the bread shop's, yet both produced such fine food.

My preference tended toward the relative calm of Olaya's kitchen, while Miguel thrived in the exhilarating activity of his restaurant's kitchen. He'd taken what his father had created and had expanded it, making it truly his own.

I searched for Miguel amidst the steaming pots, spotting him at last in front of the comal, a large griddle sizzling with what looked like corn cakes. Once they were crispy on the outside, he transferred them to a baking dish and slid them into the oven. I didn't want to interrupt him or the flow of the kitchen, so I waited, tapping my foot impatiently, looking over my shoulder at the stairs leading up to the staff room. Should I go up without him? Search all the lockers? But no, Emmaline could do that, but only with a search warrant. Other than that, only Miguel, as the owner of Baptista's, could decide to open David's locker.

At long last, he looked my way and I caught his eye. He immediately sensed that I needed him—that something big was happening. He held up his finger, telling me to wait. He took the corn cakes from the oven, deftly slicing them in half. He slathered guacamole on one side, spooned on black beans, layered roasted plantains, and topped it with chopped purple cabbage and cilantro. He plated them, slid them onto the center table for the waitstaff to take, then whispered something to the woman manning the fryer. She said something back to him, tore a piece from one of the corn cakes, and tasted it. Then, almost dismissively, she lifted her arm as she turned her back and returned to the fryer.

Miguel rolled his eyes. "She's a diva in the kitchen, but she's good," he said as he came up to me, but then he took my hand and pulled me to a small section of the kitchen that was isolated from the rest and out of earshot. "What's going on?"

I took a deep breath and spilled out my theory. "I've been trying to make sense of what happened to David since we saw him last night. Something Johnny said stuck with me."

"What's that?" he asked.

"He said it was rough that David had to be the one to find Marisol's letters and journals. David found that partial letter, but when he realized that we thought it was a first draft or only part of something more, I think he went to find the rest of it."

"Or," Miguel said, "he may have realized that Marisol had to have notes or letters or journals somewhere else."

I pointed at him, the idea developing even as we spoke. "Right. What if he realized that whatever had turned up in the house wasn't all there was?" I let this idea sink in before continuing. "What if the rest of it was here?"

"But—"

"Think about it. Where was Marisol's life? At her home, training . . . and here. Her house has been searched. Nothing. We found her training bag. Nothing. But Johnny said she wrote and journaled and had letters. So where are they?"

"David was here this morning," he said slowly. "My mother saw him come in."

My skin pricked. "Did he find something?"

"She didn't see him leave," Miguel said.

I slowed my brain down, thinking only about what I knew. "He was here. He went to the funeral home after that."

"Right," Miguel said. "He brought the picture of Marisol for the easel."

"Did he plan on coming back for the service? Maybe not. Maybe he came early to say his good-bye." I couldn't answer that question, so I back-tracked. "He came here to get Marisol's journal or notes. Did he find them? And if he did, did he take them with him, or leave them?"

Without another word, Miguel grabbed my hand and pulled me up the staircase, down the narrow hall to the break room with its lockers and couch and table. I stood in the doorway, trying to see it with fresh eyes. The round table and five chairs; the kitchenette; the brown couch; the six-foot-tall lockers.

When we'd come with Emmaline, only two of the lockers had been secured with locks. She'd cut the combination lock off of Marisol's, but the other we'd left alone. Now, however, none of the lockers were secure. How had we not thought to ask if the other belonged to David?

"This was David's," Miguel said, opening a locker at the end of the row. A baseball cap hung from a hook at the top right, a lightweight windbreaker from the hook on the left, and a rolled-up newspaper sat on the shelf at the top. That was it. No journals, notebooks, letters, or anything else that looked like it might have belonged to Marisol.

My eyes skimmed the other lockers. "Can we take a quick peek—?"

Miguel grimaced. "I'm going to check on things in the kitchen," he said pointedly. I took that to mean that he wanted no part in searching his employees' lockers, and he was leaving me to my own devices in his absence.

He left, and I was alone. Searching the lockers was an invasion of privacy. I knew that. But I also knew we were on the right track. This is where David had come. I'd lay down money that he'd found what he'd been looking for, and he'd ended up dead.

I worked quickly, opening each locker, searching only with my eyes—unless I had to move something aside, in which case I did that, albeit with lightning speed—then closing it again. Purses hung from hooks, spare shoes sat at the bottom, extra changes of clothes swung from hangers, but there was nothing that looked like it might have belonged to Marisol. No journals, letters, notes, dollar-store composition books. "Nothing," I muttered.

I sat down facing the little kitchenette, elbows propped on the table, head in hands, and racked my brain. Marisol had discovered something. If she'd written letters or notes, as Johnny indicated was her habit, she had to have kept them somewhere. If not her house, then where? The restaurant—this break room—*this* was the only logical answer. "I'm not wrong," I said under my breath, thinking that David must have taken them. If he did, then the killer now had them. That was obvious. And yet . . .

Something Miguel said niggled at the back of my brain. When we'd met Emmaline here and she'd searched Marisol's locker, Em had asked if everyone used the break room. Yes, he'd said, but Marisol more than anyone. She'd come up here, make a cup of tea, and relax until her shift started. I tried to put myself in her place. She was spooked about whatever it was she'd discovered. She'd wanted to talk to Johnny—whether because he was part of it or because she needed someone to confide in, I wasn't sure. If I assumed that she had written down some notes about the situation, or had written a letter, or had journaled, I could also assume that she'd hidden those notes somewhere. She hadn't kept anything like that at her house, presumably for fear of discovery. Was David involved, then? Had she been hiding it from him? Is that why she'd called Johnny instead of her own husband?

If she didn't want David to discover her notes or letters, then she certainly wouldn't have hidden them in his locker. But Baptista's still made the most sense. If not in the lockers, where else might she have hidden something? I stood abruptly, dragged my chair across the room and climbed onto it. I peered at the top of the row of lockers, thinking maybe she'd stuck something there, then I sighed. Nothing but a thick layer of dust.

I turned and faced the room, still on my perch. My gaze fell on the sofa. Could she have stuck something underneath it? Or in the cushions? I climbed down, dropped to my knees in front of the couch, and peered into the darkness. There was no way I was blindly sticking my hand into the narrow space. I quickly inspected the cushions, but they were not the removable type, so there was no way Marisol could have hidden anything between them.

I stood all the way up, grabbed hold of the sofa's armrest, and pulled it away from the wall. Dust bunnies danced around in the revealed space, but nothing else. I put my hands on my hips and spun around, looking at other possibilities in the room. All that was left was the kitchenette area. One by one, I flung open the cupboards. Miguel had outfitted the break room space with a matching set of dinner plates, small plates, bowls, and mugs. In the next cupboard were both large and small glasses. Next to that was a bag of coffee grounds, boxes of crackers, granola bars, teas, containers of salt and pepper, and a few other snacks designed to tide over a hungry server or hostess. The second shelf held several more larger boxes: cereal, more crackers, a bag of granola, and two bags of chips. With all the good food the restaurant made, I couldn't imagine stuffing myself with the processed foods up here, but when you're hungry, you're hungry, I reasoned, and black bean *arepas* were not always at the ready.

There was a small sink in the middle of the counter with an equally small drying rack positioned next to it. A single plate and mug lay haphazardly on the rubber-coated slats. I crouched to my haunches, opening the bottom cupboards. A mini-fridge was built in. Inside it were colorful cans of sparkling water, two bottles of kombucha, a container of hummus, a carton of almond milk, a quart of whole milk, and a baggie of baby carrots mixed with celery slices.

The space directly under the sink held a roll of paper towels, a spray bottle of cleaner for the countertop, an unopened package of sponges, as well as a single shriveled sponge that had seen better days, a cylindrical container of abrasive cleanser, and a drain stopper. All the things you'd expect to find underneath a sink and nothing out of the ordinary. There was no "what doesn't belong" item. No stationery or metal lock box. No bag tucked away in the back corner.

I hauled myself to standing again just as the door opened and Miguel reappeared. He took in the altered state of the room—the chair next to the lockers, the couch pulled away from the wall, and the cupboard doors open—and frowned. "Nothing?"

"Not even an illicit pack of cigarettes. Your employees are squeaky clean."

He strode across the room, replaced the chair and the table and moved the sofa back against the wall. "I really thought you might find something," he said as he moved to the kitchenette and began closing the cupboards I'd opened.

"Lots of cereal and crackers," I said, "but no letters or journals."

Miguel froze, one hand on the knob of the cupboard door he'd been about to close. "Unless . . ." He took out a box of crackers and turned it this way and that, looking at the front and back. He replaced it and took out another box. "Some of these are communal, but sometimes people bring in their own stuff and label it."

My skin pricked again as I watched him finish the bottom shelf then move on to the contents of the upper shelf. One by one, he removed the boxes, checking for names, popping open the lids and peering inside, and one by one, he slid them back into the cupboard. One bag of all-natural organic granola was labeled DAVID. The bag was half full. A box of Wheat Thins had RUBY scrawled across it. It was unopened. A box of Pop-Tarts was empty save the crumbled remains of half a pastry. JULIAN was written in faint pencil.

The last few items in the cupboards were cereal boxes. Miguel took the first two out, handing them to me to inspect, then reached for the last one. "This one is Julian's," I said. His name was scratched into the cardboard with a pencil. The sugary cereal was nearly gone. "He has a bit of a sweet tooth."

"He does. He's a good guy, but I have to watch the flan and churros when he's on shift."

I handed him the box to put away and looked at the last one. It was a whole-grain organic concoction filled with nuts, dried berries, and ancient grains. Not the type of cereal Julian would go for, but it was the type a health-conscious athlete might eat. I searched for a name, drawing in a sharp breath when I saw Marisol's name written in block letters across the top in bold black Sharpie. "This is hers," I said, setting down the box and reaching to look inside, but my heart sank. It was brand-new, so she couldn't have hidden anything inside.

"So much for that theory," Miguel said, but as I lifted the box to slide it back into the cupboard, the bottom flaps loosened.

"Look," I said, breathless after I'd flipped it over. It had been opened from the bottom.

Miguel and I looked at each other for a moment. Could my hunch really have paid off? I held my breath, opened the flaps, and looked inside. The thick plastic of the interior bag crackled as I pulled it out. It was unopened. I could see something else inside the box. I set the cereal bag aside, then turned the box right side up, holding the flaps open. A sheaf of folded papers fell to the counter, scattering as they hit the beige Corian.

"That's Marisol's writing," Miguel said.

"You're sure?"

"I've worked with her and seen her order tickets come through the kitchen since I was a kid. I'm sure."

I held my breath as I picked them up, moved to the table, and spread them out.

Chapter 22

Miguel and I spent more than forty minutes reading and rereading, deciphering and discussing the notes we'd found in the cereal box. With each passing minute, the weight pressing down on me grew exponentially. The first sheet was an apology letter she'd started, but not finished, to her father. One line stuck out to me: *I don't know where you are, but you will always be in my heart. In my soul.*

"What does that mean, she doesn't know where he is?" I mused aloud. It was like her father had disappeared, not died, but Miguel couldn't answer that question any more than I could. I set aside the letter and moved on to another sheet of paper. It was a list of items and questions, but with no specific rhyme or reason.

Betrayal
Donors

Legal?
Regulations?
Cement
Bricks
Garden
CFB
How many?
Records
The van

I read it to myself, then aloud. "What's CFB?"
I wondered as I took out my cell phone. I saw a
missed call and message from Lisette. I listened
to it, squinting my eyes closed as if that would
heighten my ability to hear and decipher the
slurred words. I couldn't make it all out, however, so I put it on speaker and pressed play
again.

The connection was bad, broken up with sta-
tic to the point where there were big gaps in her
speech. "It's Lis—can't leave her—David tried—
getting my mom—still there—"

"I can't make sense of that," I said after playing it a third time.

"Neither can I," Miguel said.

I tried to call back, but the phone went
straight to voicemail. I left her a message telling
her that we had some new information and to
call me back ASAP. Then I went back to the Internet browser on my phone and looked up
CFB.

Listing after listing came up for financial ad-
visers and banks. None of it seemed to connect
in any way to Marisol. I tried one more page—

the sixth—and scanned it. And then, just like that, the room seemed to turn upside down. "Oh no."

Miguel had been studying one of the bits of information, but his head snapped up at my voice. "What is it?"

I handed him my phone, pointing to the link partway down the page. He read aloud. "CFB.CA.gov. The Department of Consumer Affairs, Cemetery and Funeral Bureau." And then he looked up at me. "Oh. My. God."

I'd been so off-base, but now I felt as if the fog was lifting. "Does this mean what I think it does?" I finally asked him after we'd gone over Marisol's list with a new focus in mind. It was a rhetorical question, because I knew that we'd stumbled upon the truth. A truth full of holes and questions, but still the truth. My voice was quiet. Shocked. Horrified.

Miguel had his elbows on the table, his hands clasped, his index fingers steepled in front of his mouth. He met my gaze, his lips drawn into a grim line, accentuated by his closely trimmed goatee. I took his silence as confirmation.

"Do you think David found this stuff?" I'd gathered up the papers, queued up a scanning app on my phone, and was now laying them down, one by one, taking pictures so they'd be compiled into a PDF.

"If not these, then something else that led to his murder."

I looked up suddenly. "We thought he went to

the funeral home to provide a picture of Marisol for the service, but what if he'd arranged to meet the killer there? To force a confrontation?"

Miguel's cell phone vibrated against the table. "Damn." He stood abruptly. "I'll be right back. Don't go anywhere."

I scoffed at the very idea. I had a plan, but it was not something I wanted to do alone.

After he left, I finished scanning the last of Marisol's papers, generated a PDF, and emailed it to myself and to Emmaline with the subject line: *Marisol Ruiz.* Inside the email, I wrote a brief explanation:

> *Em, Miguel and I found these notes written by Marisol. We think David might have found them, too. We are going to Vista Ridge to find out the truth once and for all. ~Ivy*

Next, I called her, but the call went straight to voicemail. After I hung up, the time reappeared on the screen of my phone: 9:36. How had it gotten to be so late? I tried the actual sheriff's office on the off chance that she'd be there burning the midnight oil, but the call was answered by a recording stating it was after hours and directing me to 911 if it was an emergency. I dialed the cell phone again, this time leaving a message telling Emmaline that Miguel and I had discovered something big and to check her email. Finally, I sent a text saying the same thing as my voicemail message had. I was zero for three in successful communication, but she wouldn't be off the grid for long.

I put Marisol's notes in my purse, replaced the cereal box in the cupboard for the time being, turned off the light, and went downstairs to wait for Miguel.

Miguel and I headed to Vista Ridge, new thoughts spinning through my mind. The Alcotts. Suzanne and Benjamin. Sister and brother. Morticians. Long time Santa Sofia residents.

My skin turned cold. The way I interpreted Marisol's list led me to believe there was a very dark and sordid side to the funeral home. I summoned up an image of the sign in front of the building, remembering the backlit rectangle with the stark white background and VISTA RIDGE FUNERAL HOME in bold navy blue letters. But it was the services offered that I conjured up in my mind.

*Burial * Donor * Pre-Need * Monuments * Cremation*

Marisol had written the word *Donor* on the list we'd found. A quick Internet search had shown me that there were, in fact, strict regulations in place for donor services. I'd also found that it was rare for a donor business to be aligned with a funeral home. "Could they be donating body parts without signed consent?" I asked aloud, speculating. I'd read enough to understand that organs and body parts were used for research and education. This wasn't about organ transplants, but about selling organs and body parts for profit. I reorganized my thinking about the letter David had shown us. Could it have been written to Benjamin Alcott instead? I repeated it in my mind, redesigning the recipient:

> *I know what you did. What you're doing, and I'm disgusted. But I don't know what to do. What do I do? Do I tell? We've been grieving for my father, and you do this? We've known each other since we were kids. I should have been able to trust you. I can't get my head around the idea that you betrayed me like this. My father . . . oh God, my father. And my kids . . . what do I tell them?*

It made sense. More sense than if she'd written it to her ex-husband, in fact. I broke the letter down by line. Marisol knew what the Alcotts had done. Selling organs from the dead, presumably. But she was overwrought and betrayed because she'd trusted her old friend, and it had happened to her own father. Marisol had known them a long time, I realized. Mrs. Branford said Benjamin Alcott had been her student. That would have been around the same time as Marisol and Johnny had been.

Miguel's lips were drawn into a tight, grim line. He didn't have to say anything for me to know what he was thinking. He hadn't forgotten the fact that his father hadn't been buried in his suit. If Vista Ridge was operating their donation services without family consent, it was possible that had happened to his own father.

"Miguel," I said, but he shook his head and

gripped the steering wheel. He didn't want to think about the possibilities relating to his father at the moment. I didn't blame him.

Instead, he asked, "So why'd she call to meet Johnny? Was she going to confide in him? Tell him what she suspected? Ask for his help?"

I'd given this some thought and had a theory. "I think she wasn't sure if she was on the right track and needed some validation."

"Why not go to David?"

I'd also given this consideration. "Here's what I think. The letter David found was written to someone Marisol had known for a long time. I thought it was to Johnny—that this was all about his gambling debt and the house. But it wasn't. It's not. Santa Sofia is a small town. There are still a lot of people here who never left. Look at us."

"We left," he said. "We just came back."

"True. But my point is that she might have been questioning her own thought process, because she's known the Alcotts for a long time. They both said they knew Marisol in school. I think she wanted to run her theory by someone else with a long history here. Johnny. I mean, without proof, saying a funeral home sold some organ of your loved one is hard to believe, isn't it? Johnny could have helped her get perspective. He could have told her if she was way off-base or supported her if he thought she was on to something."

As "on track" as I felt we were in discovering what had led to Marisol's death, it also felt as if there was a gaping hole that still needed filling.

It had to do with some of the other things Marisol had noted. What van was she talking about?

And what about the garden, the bricks, and cement? Was Marisol just noting that the funeral home was expanding the memorial garden? But again, why? What made that important?

Miguel pulled around the back of the mortuary. A Jeep and two sedans were parked in the lot, but our attention immediately went to the white Vista Ridge Funeral Home van. Miguel rolled up next to it and threw his truck in park. Less than thirty seconds later, we were peering into the windows of the dark van, but to no avail. The parking lot had no overhead lights, and our own smartphone flashlights simply reflected light back to us. We couldn't see a thing.

We gave up, walking quickly toward the back entrance of the building instead. "It's not going to be unlocked," Miguel said. I knew he was right, but we had to give it a try. I grabbed hold of the handle and gave a yank. It didn't budge. Three more tries didn't make it suddenly become unlocked, either.

We decided to walk around to the front of the building, but I got sidetracked by the partially constructed brick wall on the other side of the driveway leading down to the mortuary's workroom. I shined my flashlight along the pavement as I walked, picking my way around to the opposite side of the wall. It was more complete than I'd originally thought. There was still an opening, but the newly defined space was blocked on one side by a cinderblock wall that stood a good eight feet tall. That, I remembered, was in the memorial garden, covered with climbing plants and a wall fountain. Were they planning to rip out that wall to expand the entire garden? The expanded space didn't make sense otherwise.

Miguel and I started to head back, dodging the stacks of bricks, cinderblocks, and bags of cement when an idea struck. I stopped short, spinning around, looking at the options.

"What are you doing?" Miguel asked me in a low whisper.

"The front door isn't going to be open," I said. We were fooling ourselves to think otherwise. I gestured with my hands as I suggested, "But there's a door inside that leads to the memorial garden. We could go up and over, then into the building through the door."

He stared at me. "That would be breaking and entering, Ivy."

"Is it, though?" I asked, feigning innocence. "I mean, if you're visiting your loved ones in the memorial garden, then surely you have a right to be there."

"Except my loved ones aren't in the garden, and neither are yours." He grabbed my hand to pull me away from my ludicrous idea, but I wasn't willing to give up just yet.

"Wait, Miguel, let's think about this."

"Okay, let's. If Marisol was right about the funeral home directors, then we're saying he—or she—or both—are murderers."

"Right . . ." I said slowly.

"And someone who's murdered once—and maybe twice, if we think they were behind

David's death, too—isn't going to have a problem killing again."

"True, but—"

"What do you think we're going to find in there, Ivy?"

"I don't know, but Marisol is pointing us here. David asked me to figure out what happened to his wife and now he's dead. I can't just drop it."

"You can wait for Em—"

"She's going to need a search warrant and that'll just give the Alcotts time to hide whatever it is they might need to hide—"

"Illegally obtained organs to be donated?"

I thought about the phone call Suzanne had been on when I went into the stainless steel workroom earlier, and then about the man she'd been talking to out on the loading bay. My heart skittered. The man in the van. The van from Marisol's list.

"I think Marisol thought they were using the donor service part of their business to harvest and sell without family consent. If she sent them the full version of her letter, there's their motive for killing her. So that's what we need to find."

My thinking had won him over. "So if David went to accuse them—"

"He did! Remember, he went to the restaurant first this morning. Let's assume he found something incriminating. After he left there, he came here under the pretense of bringing the picture of Marisol, but if he confronted them, he would have spooked them. Maybe he left and they followed him—"

It felt like a lot of supposition, when what we needed was evidence. That proof might be inside the funeral home.

I bent to shove a pile of bricks, but of course they didn't budge. My foot caught on something. I bent to untangle it from a piece of plastic that wrapped around the pallet, hitting my shoe against an already torn bag of cement in the process. The gray powder spilled out over the ground. I tried to maneuver it back into a pile, but just made it worse so I left it.

I gripped the torn-off piece of plastic my shoe had caught. I stared at it. Could it be the murder weapon? Or, well, not this piece specifically, but the plastic from the brick pallets. David had been here. I held up the piece of plastic and suddenly realized what might have happened. "They might have killed him here and then taken him to his house to make it look like he'd been killed there. He was suffocated," I said, holding the plastic out to show Miguel.

He stood stationary for a minute, and then, making up his mind, Miguel started moving the loose cinderblocks next to the wall, laying several next to each other before stacking the blocks on top of one another. I helped, heaving up one of the cement blocks and handing it to him. "Use your legs, not your back," he reminded me.

I squatted and picked up another, exhaling as I stood. I didn't think using my legs made it easier to lift, but I did as I was told. If he said it would protect my back, then I believed him. As I lifted the next block, the lights from a passing car reflected off the mirror of one of the cars in the parking lot.

A sedan.

A silver sedan.

Lisette.

Miguel came to get the cinderblock from me since I hadn't come to him. "What is it?" he asked, seeing my face.

I pointed to the four-door car. "That could be Lisette's."

He stacked the block on top of the others, and then came back to stand next to me. "Maybe she left it here earlier."

It was possible, but we'd all noticed her absence at the end of the memorial service after we'd cleaned up, and I remembered scanning the parking lot looking for her and her car when we left. There had been no sign of either. "Maybe, but I don't think so."

I pulled my phone from my back pocket, scrolled to my voicemail messages, and pressed play on Lisette's. *It's Lis—can't leave her—David tried— getting my mom—still there—*

I listened to it again. Had she been telling us she was coming here? David had tried . . . Tried what? To confront Benjamin Alcott? What did she mean, getting her mom, except that's what David had told her. What had she said this afternoon when she'd driven up, drunk and a mess? *David said I had to get Mama from here. That I had to get her and then it would be okay.*

Still there, she'd said in her message. What

was still there? Marisol? Did she think her mother was still here at Vista Ridge? My first thought was that that didn't make sense, but it did, actually. Lisette had vanished after the service ended. She didn't know that her brother had taken her mother's ashes and that they were to meet at the pier in the morning.

"I think she's here," I said, my voice lowering with a newfound urgency. If David had told her that she had to get her mother, it meant Lisette had actually spoken to David. Which meant, in turn, that David could have told her his theory. Which meant . . . "And if she is, then she's in danger."

By stacking the cinderblocks, Miguel had already agreed to go along with the plan to sneak into the funeral home, but now his expression changed and he moved with purpose. "Let's go," he said, taking my hand to steady me as I climbed onto the platform he'd created. He'd made it big enough that he could fit, too. He stood next to me, lacing his fingers together so I could step one foot into the crevice. My hands skimmed the sides of the wall as he lifted me. I grabbed hold of the top as he kept pushing me upward. I was able to crook my elbows and heave myself up and over.

I hadn't thought this all the way through because there was no platform and no foothold on the other side. We hadn't tried to position our daring climb so we'd wind up at the fountain on the other side. I'd managed to position my forearms on the top of the wall as I catalogued my options. That took all of two seconds, because there were no options. I could only drop and hope for the best. A flowerbed lay beneath me. I carefully lowered myself down, clinging onto the top with my fingers, trying to stretch as far as I could to minimize the distance I'd be dropping.

"You can do it," Miguel said, trying to encourage me from the other side.

I could. I knew I could. It's not even that far down, I reasoned. The way I was stretched, it was a two-foot drop, max. I pushed off with my feet so I wouldn't scrape the front of my body and I let go. And then my feet hit the ground with a thud and it was over. Anticlimactic, but at least I was down and uninjured.

Miguel didn't have the help of a boost like he'd given me, but he made it up and over the wall as if it were part of a military obstacle course. Easy peasy. I lifted one eyebrow at him as he deftly dropped next to me.

He grinned sheepishly. "We had a lot worse in basic training."

I stepped out of the flora, brushing my hands down the fronts of my thighs and stomping my feet to get the powdered cement I'd landed in off my shoes. Except . . .

"Why is there cement in the flower beds?" I asked quietly, crouching down to take a closer look.

As I dipped my fingers into one of the little piles, he said, "It isn't cement. It's ashes."

I leapt up, scrubbing my hands against my pant legs, but then I stopped. It looked just like the spilled cement on the other side of the wall.

It was the same color of gray, and it had the same texture. "It's not," I told him. "It's cement."

He bent down, touching his fingers to it, then bringing them to his nose to smell. And then he touched his fingers to his tongue and I cringed. What if I was wrong?

But then he stood, looking baffled. "You're right. That's definitely cement."

"Someone must have spilled a bag," I said, but even as the words left my mouth, I wasn't sure I believed them. They weren't building a wall on this side of the memorial garden. There was no reason for there to be cement. It would kill the flowers eventually, wouldn't it?

Miguel took my hand and led me down the garden path, pushing the anomaly of cement in the flowerbed to the back of my mind where it needed to be. If Lisette was here, we needed to find her. As we approached the doorway leading into the hallway of the funeral home, I doubted the wisdom of my plan. It was after hours, so it was likely that that door would be locked, too. I didn't know what we'd do if it was. I didn't have a plan B, other than trying to figure out how to get back over the wall without the benefit of a cinderblock platform.

Miguel grabbed the doorknob like he was going to yank the door open, but he didn't. He twisted his hand on it slowly, sending me a raised-eyebrow look when it turned. Then he pulled, very slowly.

It didn't open.

His brows knitted together and he tried again, but it still didn't move.

"It sticks," I said suddenly, remembering how it had jerked twice before Laura had been able to get through it earlier.

He turned the handle a little more, cocking his head like he was listening for the click in the mechanism. He must have heard it—or felt it—because this time when he pulled, the door opened. He'd tugged gently, so it opened just a crack, but we both froze, and I held my breath, praying no one was on the other side or walking down the hallway.

The coast was clear. There was not a single sign of life in the funeral home. All was eerily quiet. I wondered if I'd been wrong about Lisette. Maybe that wasn't her car outside, and maybe I'd misinterpreted her garbled phone message. But we were here now and there was no turning back, at least to my way of thinking. Miguel left the door slightly ajar—for a quick getaway, I imagined—and we tiptoed down the hallway. The first question I'd asked myself was where Marisol's letter might be, assuming Benjamin Alcott had it—or anything else incriminating. The obvious answer was Benjamin Alcott's office.

I put my ear to the door, listening for any sort of activity or sound inside. When it was apparent that no one was inside, I turned the knob and pushed, just slightly. The lights were out and the office was empty. I slipped inside, Miguel right behind me, the door quietly clicking closed behind him.

Once we were in the office, the next question that came to my mind was lights or no lights?

The low light from my cell phone flashlight wasn't sufficient to effectively search the office. The blinds were drawn, but that didn't mean that turning on the lights wouldn't be noticed from the outside, it just meant that we wouldn't be seen. It was possible a sliver of light would be visible from beneath the door, as well. It was a risk we were going to have to take. I used my flashlight beam to locate the light switch, then held my breath as I flipped it on.

No sirens blared and no one came rushing in, of course, so I exhaled and we set to work. I looked at the office with fresh eyes. The high-backed black office chair was pushed in. The blotter pad was perfectly aligned to the edge of the desk. A desk tray cradled a stack of papers. A computer monitor sat at an angle on the right side of the desk, the CPU right behind it. The man was tidy to a fault, which, in my experience, meant that his files would be organized—all the easier to rifle through.

Miguel sat in the chair and pulled open the drawers while I looked at the brochures I'd noticed last time I'd been in here. I realized, upon closer inspection, that they sat not on a table, but a small wooden horizontal filing cabinet. What I'd taken in at cursory glance the first time I'd been here, I now looked at more carefully, zeroing in on Vista Ridge's crematorium and donor services. The brochure started with facts: 114,000 people were on the waiting list for an organ donation; viable organ donors are rare because organ donations can only happen when there is brain death, or sometimes after cardiac death; however, tissue donations of eyes, bone, skin, veins, heart valves, and tendons can be made even after the heart has stopped. Vista Ridge donor services specializes in tissue donation; most people, upon death, are potential donors.

The funeral home, then, couldn't be selling organs. Those, it seemed, would have to come from a hospital setting where a person was brain dead, but on life support. But the tissue donations—that could be happening here, without consent. If it was, there had to be records of some sort. Companies Vista Ridge sold to. Order forms. Something.

I pulled open the top drawer of the filing cabinet. The colorful tabs reminded me of the wall of files in a doctor's or dentist's office. I quickly realized the two primary colors—blue and red— were code for the type of service Vista Ridge had provided: burial, with or without embalming, or cremation. Those labels marked with an additional black band meant that client had been a donor.

Miguel had come up with nothing at the desk and pulled up a chair next to me. After I explained the filing system, he pointed to a red labeled folder with a black band and an additional white strip. "What's that mean?"

I hadn't figured that out yet. I handed him one with the white strip and I took out one without. We compared. Each had an intake form attached to the left side of the folder, which included the date, the deceased's name, address, date of birth, gender, and the family member or person responsible for setting up the contract for burial or cremation services. The contract itself was attached to the right side of the folder. It read like a menu, with specific services checked off, followed by disclaimers requiring the initials of the person in contract with Vista Ridge, and a final signature page.

Following that, the donor services contract, tissue donation options, and acknowledgment page. It also required a signature and initials, whether or not the deceased's tissue was to be harvested and donated. Miguel's folder had one more set of pages. "This one has two donor contracts, but . . ." He paused, looking at each one, then flipping back to the original. "It's a duplicate, but with consent given."

I didn't understand. The folders with the black labels had contracts that gave consent. I asked what he meant.

"Look." He held the folder open so I could see. "On the first contract, they declined to be a donor."

He was right. The decline box was selected and initialed, and the final signature also refused donation services.

"But the second contract is the opposite. They opt to be tissue donors. This one is for 'eyes only.' "

"Is it the same signature?" I asked, trying to figure out what this meant.

He shrugged noncommittally. "It looks the same, but it can't be, can it? Unless they just changed their mind."

I pulled out another white-striped folder. It was the same: two donor contracts, one declined, one approved. We checked folder after folder after folder. Those with just a black-banded label had only one donor contract, and usually it was initialed and signed with acceptance. Those with the white stripe had two contracts, one where donor services were declined, and one where they were accepted.

"Look at this one," Miguel said, handing me the open folder he held.

It had three contracts. It took me a minute to see what was different about them, but then I spotted it. The first had donor services declined. The second accepted them, specifically for eyes and bone. The third, however, had all spaces ticked off.

"They're forged," I said, pointing to the signatures. They were done with different pens, so clearly had been signed at different times, but it was the signature itself that struck me as off. "Look at the loops of the letters M and L on this one." I flipped to the first, and presumably original, contract. No loops.

"So they forge contracts depending upon what might be needed at any given time," Miguel said. He bent over the open drawer, his fingers dancing over the tabs of the folders.

"What are you looking—" I started to ask, but then realized. The file on his father.

He sat up. "It's not here."

"They go back six months," I said. "They must keep the older ones somewhere else."

I replaced the folders I still held and slid the top drawer closed. I tugged to open the bottom drawer, but it stayed closed. "Locked."

Before I'd even finished saying the word, Miguel was up out of his seat and back at the desk, rifling through one of the desk drawers. He stood a second later, holding out a ring jangling with about ten keys. "Maybe we'll get lucky."

The lock was small and built into the cabinet, so he eliminated the few keys on the larger end of the spectrum, trying the smaller keys instead, one by one. Finally, the second to last one slid in and turned. The interior mechanism clicked, releasing the lock. He depressed the button on the handle and the drawer opened.

More files filled the drawer, but not documenting the burial or cremation of the deceased. "There must be another filing cabinet somewhere," I said. In the back of my mind, I knew that Emmaline was going to kill me, because Miguel was right. We were breaking and entering. But whether or not the forged donor contracts were what Marisol had discovered, what Benjamin Alcott was doing was definitely not legal and needed to be stopped.

The folders in this drawer didn't have a color-coding system. Instead of the blue and red labels in the upper drawer, these were all yellow. Inside the folder I'd withdrawn was a single sheet. It had an eight-digit number written in a designated box in the upper right corner. The paper itself was another checklist of menu items. Given the fact that these folders were under lock and key, the items on the list felt, if not sinister, then at least more questionable.

Miguel read aloud. "Head. Right leg. Left leg.

Right arm. Left arm. Torso with arms. Torso without arms." He stopped reading, drawing in an audible breath before exhaling heavily. "What the hell is this?"

Marisol's list came back to me, specifically the words legal and regulations. Could this be what she'd been talking about? Regular donor services were legitimate, although not typically associated with a funeral home. But this . . . this was not your regular donor services, was it? This . . . this would have explained Marisol's distress.

"There's no name," I said, looking again at the number in the corner. The eight numbers were written with periods rather than hyphens, but they reminded me, nonetheless, of birthdates. And then it hit me. "It's backwards," I said. "Look—3319.0715. It could be July fifteenth, 1933."

He nodded, his jaw pulsing. "So a code. Which means there has to be a list somewhere linking the number to the donor."

We both swiveled to look back at the desk. "Probably on the computer," I said.

Miguel pulled out a thick stack of folders, looking at the codes in the upper corner. We didn't know Marisol's father's birthday, so he wasn't looking for that. Searching for his father, I realized. I didn't need to look at any more folders. I focused my attention instead on Marisol. How had she come to realize the truth about what Benjamin Alcott was doing? Her father had been cremated. My gaze fell to my shoes, still lightly coated with the powdered cement from the memorial garden and from the spilled bag. And then a chill ran up my spine. I grabbed Miguel's leg, my fingers clawing into it. At the very same moment, he uttered a sharp, "Holy shit."

We stared at each other, the rest of the truth settling into place.

Chapter 23

The sound of the door flinging open and hitting the wall was like a shotgun going off, ricocheting in my head. I swiveled around, moving in what felt like slow motion. I'd expected to see Benjamin, but it was Lisette. Her face was pale, her eyes wide and frantic. She wore the same black slacks and black-and-white striped shirt she'd had on at the funeral. She'd looked disheveled then. Now she looked completely undone. "Did you find her?" she asked frantically, as if we'd been in the middle of a desperate conversation and she had just picked up where we'd left off.

My brain kicked in and I jumped up, yanking her into the room and quickly closing the door behind her. "Find . . . her?"

"My mom," she said, her voice shrill and nearing hysteria. "Did you find her?"

I hesitated, not sure what was going on inside

her head. At last, I said, "Ruben took your mother's ashes with him after the funeral. You're all supposed to meet up in the morning on the pier—"

She began shaking her head, the ordinary movement turning almost violent. "No. No, no, no. Don't you see? I saw David. He told me what happened to my grandfather." Her lower lip trembled and her chin quivered. She jabbed her finger at me as if I were the culprit. "I am *not* going to let that happen to my mother."

"Not going to let what happen to her?" I asked.

She waved her hands around wildly, her gaze darting around. "We don't have my grandfather at home. They cut him up." She sobbed, her breath shallow. "They shipped him off to God knows where."

I put my hands on her shoulders and guided her to the chair I'd been sitting in. She buried her face in her hands, her shoulders shaking with her heaving sobs. Miguel crouched in front of her. "Lis," he said softly, shortening her name affectionately. Marisol had worked at Baptista's for as long as I could remember, which meant Miguel had grown up seeing Lisette, Sergio, and Ruben. They had history, but would he be able to talk her off the ledge she was teetering on?

He continued to speak to her in a low, calming timbre. She dropped her hands and he took them in his. His touch relaxed her. Bolstered her. Her breathing deepened, and her tears ebbed. She pulled her hands free and dragged the backs of her fingers under her eyes, wiping away what was left of her tears and smearing the remnants of her mascara. "Thank you," she said after another minute.

"Are you okay?" he asked, his voice calm, but concerned.

She closed her eyes, but nodded slightly. "I think so."

I wasn't sure about broaching the subject of David and her mother after she'd just regained control of herself, but she did it for me. "I t-talked to D-David."

Her voice broke with emotion, but she held herself together.

"Today?" I asked, wanting to understand the timeline of events.

"B-before the funeral. N-Not long before . . . before h-he died."

Miguel had stood and now leaned against Benjamin Alcott's desk, his arms folded over his chest. I knew he still had his father in the back of his mind. The fact that we'd found his suit was all the more concerning in light of the illicit donor services. Was his father buried in the casket they'd put him in? Was his body whole?

"What did he say, Lisette?" I asked.

She looked at me, her eyes still glassy, but she was under control now. She sat up straighter, placing her palms on her thighs. "He told me about part of a letter he found. He said at first he thought it was written to my dad, and that my dad had done something to betray her. And he thought my mama was going crazy with all her talk about my grandfather's ashes and something not being right. But then he realized that the letter wasn't to my dad, and that she wasn't crazy at all."

"Did he find proof?" Miguel asked.

Lisette retrained her gaze on him and continued. "He said he came here to find out the truth, but they just showed him the c-consent forms my mother had s-signed." She stopped, her voice starting to crack again with emotion.

"Giving permission for tissue donations?" I asked.

Her gaze snapped back to me. "You know?"

I notched my head toward the filing cabinet she sat next to. "We found a lot of files with consent."

She swallowed hard as she steadied her breath. "My mother's?"

My skin pricked with cold. We hadn't looked for Marisol's file, but surely it would be here. I yanked open the top filing cabinet drawer. My fingers danced over the top edges of the folders, slowing as I came to the Rs. I skipped to the end of the section, slowing to read the names. Rodriguez. Rogers. Rowells. Ruggins. There is was. Ruiz, Marisol.

I pulled it out, noticing right away that the label was red, which meant cremation. It had a black label with a white stripe, so Marisol had been a donor, but based on what Miguel and I had figured out, there would be at least two consent forms in here, one probably legitimately signed, the other forged. A quick flip through the papers confirmed it. Lisette, I remembered, had been the one to sign the contract with Vista Ridge. I had to remind myself that the first meeting with Benjamin Alcott had only been a few days ago. It seemed like a blip in my memory, but I closed my eyes for a minute to bring it to the surface.

Alcott had gone over the contract. Lisette had initialed and signed. David's signature and initials were there, as well. Was that signature authentic, or had it been forged? Alcott hadn't given Lisette a copy, I realized, remembering how he'd steered us out of his office the second the contract was signed. Lisette, for her part, had scarcely read what she'd signed, trusting that Benjamin Alcott had accurately explained what was represented on paper. I hadn't thought anything of it at the time, but in hindsight, Alcott had orchestrated the encounter well. And why not, he was well versed at it. How many unwitting bereaved families had he gotten to sign and initial without even a second thought? He used people's grief to his advantage.

Now, however, Lisette looked carefully at the contract she'd signed. Cremation had been selected, without tissue donation. When she flipped to the next page, however, her expression changed. "I didn't sign this," she said, looking at the second tissue donation form. She pointed at the bottom line. "That is not my signature. And that's not David's," she said, pointing to the scribbled name.

Now I understood why Vista Ridge stuck with pen-and-paper contracts, and nothing in duplicate or triplicate. It was easy to simply create a new page and forge the bereaved's signature. The Alcotts relied on people being too sad to pay close attention, and if a problem ever arose, they would no doubt blame the poor memory of the bereaved, in their grief.

Manny knelt down in front of the filing cabinet again, pulling out the bottom drawer. He looked at me, his mouth grim, before asking Lisette, "What's your mom's birthday?"

"October twenty-first," she said.

"Year?"

She rattled it off and Miguel set to work converting the set of eight numbers into the code the Alcotts used in their underground donor business. He made short work of it, pulling out the yellow-tabbed folder. Without the master list, there was no way to confirm for certain that this was Marisol's file, but the identifiers—fifty-seven-year-old Hispanic female—fit. Three checklist boxes were marked, each with a heavy X.

Lisette glanced at the list and let out a pained wail. "We have to stop this!"

My own stomach had grown uneasy. The dead deserved to be treated with dignity. It should be a given, I thought, not something hit or miss. My mind went back to Marisol's list. She'd written *Regulations?* Regulations demand adherence to protocols that safeguard those who can no longer protect their own interests—namely, the dead.

"She's here," Lisette said, and I thought of what she'd said when she'd first come into the office. *Did you find her?* she'd asked. I understood now. She was assuming that the ashes we thought were Marisol's were not, and that her body was still here awaiting—

"Oh my God," I said. "What time is it?"

I fished for my cell phone in my pocket, but Miguel wore a watch. "Ten forty-three," he said.

We'd spent all of this time in Benjamin Alcott's office looking at the contractual side of the illicit business the funeral home was running, but we'd given no thought to the practical side of it. Someone had to prepare the tissue and the body parts. Blood and bones. Marisol had been haunted by that phrase in her nightmares because that's what it all came down to. Blood and bones.

"Suzanne." She wasn't an innocent in all this. Her brother ran the business side of things, and her domain was downstairs—in the sterile surgical room off the loading bay. The one with the stainless steel tables, and the equipment I hadn't wanted to think about . . . and the body drawers, just like those in a morgue. "I heard her on the phone earlier. She planned to see someone at twelve o'clock. I'd thought that meant tomorrow, as in during the day, but I also saw her talking to a man with a van outside the morgue room downstairs. He told her he'd see her bright and early, but then he corrected himself to dark and early."

"As in midnight?" Miguel said, piecing together what I was saying.

"What if he's coming to pick up—" I broke off, not knowing how to finish the sentence.

"My mother," Lisette said, doing it for me.

An hour and fifteen minutes before midnight. If Marisol's body was here—and still intact—we had to hurry.

*   *   *

Lisette clutched the file folder in her fist as we ran down the hallway. At the door leading downstairs, we regrouped, catching our breath and stilling our racing hearts. I held my finger to my lips. We didn't know what we'd find downstairs, but we needed to approach with stealth, not the thundering footsteps of a herd of elephants.

I opened the door and led the way, creeping down the stairs with the lightest tread I could manage. Lisette was on my heels, close enough that I felt her breath on the back of my neck. Miguel, with his years in the marines, had stealth down to a T. I couldn't hear him, but I knew he was there behind us somewhere.

The door at the bottom of the steps that led to Suzanne's workroom was slightly ajar. I held up my right arm, crooked at the elbow, hand fisted, signaling Lisette and Miguel to stop. We pressed our backs against the wall, once again calming ourselves. The familiar strains of a Taylor Swift song suddenly drifted out to us. I pinched my thumb and forefinger against the bridge of my nose, trying to merge the idea of a pop princess as the soundtrack to the gruesome practices that took place in that room.

Something whirred, drowning out the sound of the music. Lisette grabbed hold of my arm, her fingers clawing into me. "Ivy," she said, her voice a hoarse whisper.

My heart was in my throat, but we had no more time to wait. I glanced back at them, then wrapped my fingers around the edge of the door, slowly opened it, and then, without another conscious thought in my head about what we would find, I charged into the room, Lisette and Miguel hot on my heels.

Suzanne jumped, dropping the small hand tool she'd been holding. It hit the floor with a loud crash. Her sudden release of it cut off the power and the whirring sound we'd heard, leaving only Taylor Swift's voice belting through the speaker system. "What the hell are you doing here?" Suzanne yelled, disconcerted anger in her voice.

She sidestepped, bending to retrieve the electric hand tool she'd dropped, but Miguel had skirted around me, had ahold of the cord, and yanked it out of her reach. "I'll just take that," he said, picking it up.

I gave the room a cursory glance. The door to the outside delivery bay was propped open with a bag of cement. Suzanne was the only person in the room. No bodies on the stainless gurney-like tables. No blood. No bones. Unless Suzanne had done it already, maybe we'd gotten here in time to stop her from doing to Marisol what had been done to so many others right here in this very room.

"What do you want?" Suzanne asked, but with the three of us surrounding her, she'd lost some of the bravado from a moment ago.

"Where's my mother?" Lisette's voice had waffled between broken and barely controlled since she'd ambushed us in Benjamin Alcott's office, but now it was brittle with accusation.

Suzanne's jaw gaped. "She was cremated."

"Uh-uh." Lisette shook her head, taking a step closer to Suzanne.

Miguel was now behind Suzanne, his back to the body drawers. I directed my gaze at them, dipping my chin and lifting my eyebrows to communicate to him.

He got the message. He turned, grabbing hold of one of the chrome handles. I could see him brace himself for what he might find. He took a breath and pulled. The drawer opened just enough for him to see inside. He threw me a glance over his shoulder, gave a little shake of his head, and shut the drawer again.

"We know what you're doing," Lisette was saying to Suzanne. "Cutting up the dead and selling them for your own profit. You're sick."

Miguel moved on to the next drawer, gripping the handle, inhaling, and pulling it open. Once again, he shook his head and closed the empty drawer.

"I don't know what you're talking about," Suzanne ground out. With Miguel behind her, Lisette smack in front of her and moving closer, and me on her right blocking the door to the stairs, she was like a trapped animal. Her eyes had grown wide and feral. She searched for a way out, but there was none.

"Recognize this?" Lisette thrust the file folder with the coded number and Marisol's identifying characteristics at her. "That's my mother's file, isn't it? This is what you've sold of her. She wasn't cremated. You're going to sell her for parts."

"You're crazy," Suzanne said, but at the same moment, Miguel yanked open the third drawer, and this time there was no shake of his head. He didn't close it again. He closed his eyes for a beat, his nostrils flaring, his lips pressing hard together, and then he pulled it open enough for us to see the body lying there. It was covered with a thin sheet, but there was no doubt in my mind that it was Marisol.

"Is she?" Miguel asked.

Suzanne spun around. When she saw the open drawer, her face collapsed in defeat. She had nowhere to run, and nothing more to say.

Chapter 24

Music had the power to affect the entire mood of a place, but the song playing on the speaker system changing from Taylor Swift to OneRepublic did nothing to lighten the air in the room. Lisette stared at the body in the drawer, her tears flowing freely. "Do we—" She paused, gathering herself together. "If my mom is there, whose ashes do we have?"

The answer hit me like a brick to the head. I glanced at the heavy black-and-yellow bag propping open the outside door, then at my dust-covered shoes. The truth was hiding in plain sight. "It's not ashes. It's cement."

Lisette let out a pained cry and stumbled toward her mother's body. Miguel caught her with his arm around her waist. "No, Lis. Don't."

With the two of them distracted, Suzanne seized the opportunity to make a run for it. She headed straight for me. I spread my legs and bent my knees, bracing myself. I'd do whatever it took. She was not getting by me.

She faked left, trying to juke me. My body instinctively followed, but then I corrected, lunging right. She barreled into me. I channeled every linebacker move I'd ever seen during my UT college-football-watching years, wrapped my arms around her, and tackled her. We fell to the ground in a huddled mass, with me on top.

At that moment, heavy footsteps pounded down the stairwell just beyond the door. A voice bellowed, "Suzanne, what the hell were you doing in my office?"

The door banged open, hitting the wall, and Benjamin Alcott appeared above me, something cradled in his arms. He tried to stop himself from careening into us but he'd been going too fast, hadn't anticipated an obstacle, and tripped over us. Whatever he'd been holding flew from his arms and crashed to the floor, shattering.

He scrambled up, but his shoes lost their grip against the shards of ceramic and gray powder spilled across the floor. He stumbled, careening against the counter, his arm splaying across it, knocking a jar over. It crashed to the ground, spilling its contents. Gold nuggets scattered across the floor, mixing with the shards of ceramic.

Something skittered on the ground until it lay right in front of me. My stomach turned over as I recognized what had been in the jar. Gold fillings. Not only had they been selling off parts of dead bodies, they'd been collecting whatever treasures they held, right down to the teeth fillings.

Miguel had managed to keep Lisette away from Marisol's body. He'd shut the door and now he leapfrogged over her, landing squarely on Benjamin Alcott, pinning him back to the floor. "Not so fast, partner," he said, channeling Clint Eastwood. He pinned the mortician's arms behind his back and hauled him upright. "We have some questions for you."

I heaved myself up and off Suzanne. It wasn't graceful, but I managed to stand up, dragging her alongside me. "And for you," I said. I fished my phone from my pocket to dial 911, but a text flashed across the screen. Emmaline had sent a message fifteen minutes ago. *I'm on my way.*

The next two hours were a blur of activity. Miguel and I had managed to restrain a defeated Suzanne and a volatile Benjamin for the remaining ten minutes it took for Emmaline and her law enforcement team to arrive on the scene. Emmaline, gun drawn, one hand braced on top of the other, along with another officer, came through the delivery bay door. They split up, checking the back room and ensuring that no one else was lurking nearby. Seconds later, they had handcuffed Suzanne and Benjamin.

As she read them their rights, another pair came down the stairwell and through the door. "All clear upstairs," one of them announced.

She held up a tri-folded paper. "I would have

been here sooner, but I had to wait on Judge
Abernathy for the search warrant. Took a while
due to exigent circumstances."

"Layman's terms," I said, still working to calm
my jackhammering heart.

"We had to show good cause for a nighttime
intrusion and probable cause for felonious activity," she explained. "Turns out David didn't
leave things to chance. He found a legal pad of
notes and a few letters Marisol had kept. She out-
lined her suspicions and what she'd discovered
about what was going on here at Vista Ridge."

I knew it! I only wished Marisol had gone to
the authorities with her suspicions from the beginning. "Where did you find it?"

"David put it in an envelope and dropped it
off at the station sometime this morning. Being
as small as we are, you'd think it would have gotten to the right person quickly, but . . ." She let
the sentence fade away, the implication clearly
being that Santa Sofia's size didn't mean incom-
petence or apathy didn't exist. It was something
she'd have to work on. I knew it would weigh on
her because making the discovery earlier might
have saved David's life.

She turned to Benjamin and Suzanne. "So,
which one of you is the brains behind the business?"

Suzanne stayed silent, all the color drained
from her face. She knew the jig was up, but her
brother was indignant, his face red with fury,
drool dripping from the corner of his mouth.
"We have all the licenses we need," he said, spit-
tle flying from his mouth alongside his words.

"I looked up your licenses, actually. You don't have current funeral establishment or tissue bank licenses on file with the State of California."

"What?" Suzanne screeched, swinging her head to face her brother.

Emmaline gave her a sad, resigned look. "It's true. Your brother ran the business side of things, I take it?"

Suzanne gave a slow nod. "He's got the degree in mortuary science. I went to medical school, but didn't finish—"

"See, that's another interesting bit of information," Emmaline said, interrupting her.

"Shut up!" Benjamin pulled against the restraints of his handcuffs, but the officer next to him gave a hard yank, jerking Benjamin back into submission.

"What's interesting?" Suzanne asked. Her lower lip quivered. "We did everything we needed to do to open this place."

"If by everything you mean forgery, then yes, I agree," Em said, her voice sweet and encouraging, when in reality, the words themselves were problematic.

"No, no, there's no forgery. Tell them, Ben," Suzanne pleaded with her brother.

"Shut. Your. Mouth," he said through gritted teeth. The quiet and reserved mortician was gone. In his place was an angry, cornered animal.

Emmaline moved closer to Suzanne. "See, what he doesn't want you to know is that you both have a little trouble with the follow-through. He never graduated, either."

Suzanne's jaw dropped. "No degree in mortuary science?"

Emmaline shook her head.

"No funeral establishment license?" she asked.

Again, Emmaline shook her head. "Nope."

"N-No tissue bank license?"

"That's the trifecta," Emmaline said, holding up the warrant as if Suzanne had just won a prize. "But here's the pièce de résistance. This stuff you do down here? The body parts?"

Suzanne nodded, gulping, her eyes wide.

She dropped her voice to a confidential whisper. "It's not actually legal."

"But we sell to labs. For research. I don't understand."

"Saying you've cremated someone, then turning around and harvesting their body parts without family consent? Not legal no matter who you're selling to."

From her reaction when we barged in, I suspected that she knew that deep down. She just chose to ignore it and trust her brother.

She looked at Benjamin, her eyes wide with fear. "Ben, what's going on?"

"Dammit, Suzanne, shut the hell up." He looked at Emmaline. "We want a lawyer."

Emmaline was calm. "Sure thing," she said. "You're going to need it. We're charging you with two first degree murders. You better hope your lawyer's a good one."

"Murders?" Suzanne shrieked. "What are you talking about?"

Emmaline cocked her head, trying to get a read on Suzanne. "Marisol Ruiz. Murdered because she figured out what she had were not, in fact, her father's ashes, but powdered cement. All that time she spent in the memorial garden, even though she had what she thought were her father's remains? She figured out what was going on behind closed doors in here. And David, her husband, because he figured out what had happened to his wife."

Suzanne shook her head violently. "Uh-uh, no, no, no. I did not murder anyone." She turned to her brother again, horror on her face. "Did you . . . Ben, oh my God, did you kill them?"

Benjamin lunged, taking everyone by surprise. "I'm going to kill you if you don't shut your mouth," he snapped. He closed the distance between himself and his sister before the deputy who'd been charged with detaining him managed to grab his handcuffed hands and yank him backward.

Suzanne spun her body around to face Emmaline. "I want my own lawyer," she said.

"I'll make a note of that," Emmaline said. She took Suzanne by the arm and led her outside, handing her off to a female deputy. "Take her in, and keep her separate from her brother."

"Sure thing, Sheriff," the deputy said.

Em went back to the deputy whom she'd charged with watching Benjamin. "You have him under control now?"

"Completely, Sheriff," he said, jerking Benjamin's handcuffs to illustrate the point.

"Good. Take him in, book him, and put him in a cell. No interaction with his sister. Got it?"

"Got it," he said, and he dragged Benjamin Alcott out of the surgical room.

"Black market body parts?" Emmaline asked me as the rest of her team donned gloves and started to execute the search warrant.

All I could do was grimace. Blood and bones. Marisol's nightmares made sense. I looked at Miguel, reading his expression. He still didn't know what had happened to his father. Was he in the casket they'd buried, or had he been a victim of Suzanne's tools and Benjamin's black market business? Was that why he hadn't been buried in his suit? We wouldn't know immediately, but Emmaline would find out the truth for the Baptistas, and for so many other families.

It was over.

Chapter 25

The invitation to Billy's house came as a welcome distraction from all that had gone on over the past week. "We could all use some friends-and-family time," he'd said to me, and I couldn't have agreed more.

Miguel picked me up. I scooped up Agatha, we climbed into his truck, and fifteen short minutes later, we were at my brother's house. Cars lined the street on both sides. Miguel found a place to park a block away. I put Agatha in her harness and we walked back. "This is more than a few friends and family," I said.

"Is that . . . ? It is, that's the bread shop van," he said, pointing to a white vehicle beyond Billy's house.

"What is going . . . Ohhh. Oh wow. I know what's happening." I hadn't spoken to Emmaline since she'd arrested Benjamin Alcott and officially charged him and Suzanne with the murders of David and Marisol, but enough time had passed for things to settle down for her again.

The door opened and she stood there beaming. She notched her chin up, acknowledging Miguel, but grinned at me.

"You did it!" I squealed.

"Did what?" Miguel asked, looking from me to her and back.

Emmaline ignored the question, instead just waggling her head. "Mmm, not exactly."

I tilted my head, puzzled. "Okay, you got me. I'm confused."

"What's going on?" Miguel asked again.

Emmaline looked over her shoulder before stepping out onto the front porch and pulling the door shut. And then, with dramatic flair, she held up her left hand, fingers splayed. The white-gold ring with the marquis diamond that Billy had shown me sparkled on her ring finger.

I cupped my hand over my mouth, feeling my smile spreading beneath it. "Oh my God, *he* proposed?"

A smile spread on Miguel's face. "Billy popped the question?"

Emmaline had left her sheriff persona behind and was, at the moment, a giddy bride-to-be. She nodded, the tight curls of her black hair bouncing with the movement, a tinge of pink coloring her dark burnished skin. "And," she said, pausing dramatically, "he made me a table. A table! The first piece of furniture for our house together."

"Did you give him your ring?" I asked.

"Wait," Miguel interrupted. "You got him a ring?"

Her eyes widened and her grin grew. She nodded. "And he loves it."

Billy's house was bursting at the seams with his friends, her friends, and their friends. Even my friends had come. Mrs. Branford held her cane in one hand and had woven her other arm around a jaunty-looking older man who I immediately recognized as one of her old teaching friends, one Mason Caldwell. She said something to him, he threw his head back and howled, and together, they sauntered off toward the backyard.

I scanned the room and spotted Olaya. Neither Billy or Emmaline had gotten to know her well yet, but they knew she had become a huge part of my life. Her back was to me and her head was down. She didn't know anyone, I realized, with the exception of Mrs. Branford. And Mrs. Branford was otherwise occupied. I started to head over to Olaya, Miguel's hand in mine, but stopped when she turned. Her face was bright and happy. She laughed, moving slightly, and I saw that she was talking to someone tall. Lean. With dark hair. I recognized that cotton plaid shirt and those khaki pants. I recognized that smile.

Olaya was talking with my father.

It was the first time I'd seen my father relaxed

and just having a good time in, well, I didn't even know how long. He was celebrating his son's engagement. He looked happy.

I wondered if Olaya had brought him bread infused with lavender or some other herb. If she had, she needed to keep it coming. My heart felt as if it swelled inside my chest. My family—those I was born to, and those I'd chosen—including Miguel, who was right by my side.

Behind us, the tinkling of a utensil lightly tapped against a wineglass drew our attention. Miguel and I turned to see Billy and Emmaline, arm in arm. He cleared his throat and raised his wineglass. "Thanks for coming, everyone. My fiancée—"

"It's about time!" someone—one of Billy's friends—hollered.

Billy was unfazed. "Good things are worth waiting for. To the bride-to-be," he said, lowering his head to kiss her.

The room erupted in a collective cheer. "To the bride and groom," Miguel said, raising his glass.

I smiled, wrapping my arm around Miguel, but his body suddenly tensed, his arm around my shoulder tightening. "What's wrong?" I asked, but then I saw. Coming in the door just behind Billy and Emmaline was a familiar blond-haired man. My ex-husband, Luke Holden. He spotted me, threw up his hand, and headed straight for me.

"Luke," I said, barely holding back the disbelieving anger that instantly flooded me. "What are you doing here?"

"I need you, Ivy." He didn't smile, and his voice was dead serious.

Miguel unwound his arm from my shoulder and stepped forward, blocking me slightly. He'd gone into protective mode, affronted by the appearance of my former husband. "You're not invited here, man," he said, his jaw pulsing.

"Maybe not," Luke said, folding his arms over his chest, "but I need to talk to Ivy. She needs to know—"

"Know what?" Miguel demanded.

I put a calming hand on Miguel's shoulder. "What's going on, Luke?" I asked. Bees with honey, I wanted to tell Miguel. Bees with honey.

"It's Heather." He swallowed hard, his Adam's apple slipping up and down in his throat. "I told her how I feel about you and—"

Miguel took a menacing step toward him. The entire room had gone silent, every pair of eyes focused on us. "What the hell?"

"I get it," Luke said, throwing up his hands. "You're together. I'm not here to break you up. Well, I mean, I would if I could, but I get it." He looked at me. "I blew it. I know that now, but Heather—"

Miguel used his body to force Luke back toward the door. "You need to leave."

Luke nodded, but there was something unsettling in his eyes. "Yeah, sure. No problem." He craned his head, looking back at me. "But she's here, Ivy. And I need you to know. She said she's going to kill you."

Connect with Us

Visit us online at
KensingtonBooks.com
to read more from your favorite authors, see books
by series, view reading group guides, and more.

Join us on social media

for sneak peeks, chances to win books and prize packs,
and to share your thoughts with other readers.

facebook.com/kensingtonpublishing
twitter.com/kensingtonbooks

Tell us what you think!

To share your thoughts, submit a review,
or sign up for our eNewsletters, please visit:
KensingtonBooks.com/TellUs.

Books by Bestselling Author
Fern Michaels

___The Jury	0-8217-7878-1	$6.99US/$9.99CAN
___Sweet Revenge	0-8217-7879-X	$6.99US/$9.99CAN
___Lethal Justice	0-8217-7880-3	$6.99US/$9.99CAN
___Free Fall	0-8217-7881-1	$6.99US/$9.99CAN
___Fool Me Once	0-8217-8071-9	$7.99US/$10.99CAN
___Vegas Rich	0-8217-8112-X	$7.99US/$10.99CAN
___Hide and Seek	1-4201-0184-6	$6.99US/$9.99CAN
___Hokus Pokus	1-4201-0185-4	$6.99US/$9.99CAN
___Fast Track	1-4201-0186-2	$6.99US/$9.99CAN
___Collateral Damage	1-4201-0187-0	$6.99US/$9.99CAN
___Final Justice	1-4201-0188-9	$6.99US/$9.99CAN
___Up Close and Personal	0-8217-7956-7	$7.99US/$9.99CAN
___Under the Radar	1-4201-0683-X	$6.99US/$9.99CAN
___Razor Sharp	1-4201-0684-8	$7.99US/$10.99CAN
___Yesterday	1-4201-1494-8	$5.99US/$6.99CAN
___Vanishing Act	1-4201-0685-6	$7.99US/$10.99CAN
___Sara's Song	1-4201-1493-X	$5.99US/$6.99CAN
___Deadly Deals	1-4201-0686-4	$7.99US/$10.99CAN
___Game Over	1-4201-0687-2	$7.99US/$10.99CAN
___Sins of Omission	1-4201-1153-1	$7.99US/$10.99CAN
___Sins of the Flesh	1-4201-1154-X	$7.99US/$10.99CAN
___Cross Roads	1-4201-1192-2	$7.99US/$10.99CAN

Available Wherever Books Are Sold!
Check out our website at **www.kensingtonbooks.com**

Romantic Suspense from
Lisa Jackson

Available Wherever Books Are Sold!
Visit our website at **www.kensingtonbooks.com**